ACCLAIM FOR *JEREMY BATES*

"Will remind readers what chattering teeth sound like."
—*Kirkus Reviews*

"Voracious readers of horror will delightfully consume the contents of Bates's World's Scariest Places books."
—*Publishers Weekly*

"Creatively creepy and sure to scare." —*The Japan Times*

"Jeremy Bates writes like a deviant angel I'm glad doesn't live on my shoulder."
—Christian Galacar, author of GILCHRIST

"Thriller fans and readers of Stephen King, Joe Lansdale, and other masters of the art will find much to love."
—*Midwest Book Review*

"An ice-cold thriller full of mystery, suspense, fear."
—David Moody, author of HATER and AUTUMN

"A page-turner in the true sense of the word."
—*HorrorAddicts*

"Will make your skin crawl." —*Scream Magazine*

"Told with an authoritative voice full of heart and insight."
—Richard Thomas, Bram Stoker nominated author

"Grabs and doesn't let go until the end." —*Writer's Digest*

FREE BOOK

Mosquito Man

World's Scariest Legends 1

Jeremy Bates

Mosquito Man

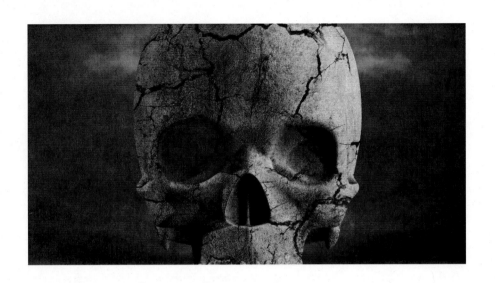

PROLOGUE

1981

You would think a missing person case would be a pretty straightforward affair.

The person goes missing. They either turn up alive, or they turn up dead.

If it's the former (which is usually the case), you can get all the answers you want straight from their mouth. If it's the latter, you can piece together what happened to them with a combination of investigative work and forensic evidence. The woman who embarked on an evening run and ends up half naked and dead in some park bushes: rape. The kid who didn't come home for dinner and whose body parts are discovered beneath cement in the neighbor's dingy basement: pedophilia.

The gambler or drug addict whose wasted body is found decomposing in an alleyway Dumpster: bad debts. The hiker whose skeleton is uncovered in the spring thaw at the bottom of a gorge: misadventure.

Yet it's when the missing person never turns up that things get tricky.

Because now you're not only dealing with the relatively straightforward questions of why they ran away, who took them, or what happened to them. Now you have to start exploring a plethora of other possibilities. Were they being held against their will? Were they alive? Were they going to be alive for much longer? Were they in an accident? Were they suicidal? And so forth and so on. The questions chain ad infinitum, and until you have a body, be it warm or cold, they are unanswerable.

These were the thoughts going through Chief of Police Paul Harris' mind on a wet August night in 1981, as he sat inside his beat-up Crown Victoria out in front of the Chapman's log cabin that overlooked Pavilion Lake, British Columbia.

Two hours earlier, Troy and Sally Chapman's seven-year-old boy, Rex, had been picked up on Highway 99 by the local pest and rodent expert, Shorty Williams. Shorty had been coming back from an extermination job in Cache Creek. Rex had been walking barefoot along the shoulder of the highway, fifteen kilometers from Pavilion Lake and forty from the town of Lillooet, to which it appeared he'd been heading. He was white as a ghost and mute as a fish. When Shorty dropped off the boy at the police station, Paul's wife, Nancy, fixed him a bowl of chicken noodle soup and a glass of warm milk, but he wouldn't do anything but stare hauntingly at his hands in his lap. Wouldn't say a word to Nancy either, who was about as threatening as a permed Cockapoo, or to Paul himself, who had a friendly Good Cop way with kids. So Paul got in the Crown Vic and cruised down Main Street until he spotted Ed Montgomery, his volunteer and sometimes sober deputy, eating dinner at the picnic table at the Esso gas station, and together they drove out to the Chapman's place to see what was up.

Given the spooked state of young Rex Chapman, Paul had expected to find Troy and Sally in some nuclear domestic dispute, cussing and shouting and slamming doors, perhaps Sally bloodied and beaten. Or the worst case scenario: both of them, along with Rex's older brother, Logan, dead in a double murder-suicide.

Yet what he and Ed found was...nothing. Not a thing. The cabin was in perfect order. No toppled furniture, no broken tableware, no blood, nothing to indicate anything sinister had taken place.

So what had driven Rex to flee barefoot to the highway?

Where had Troy and Sally and Logan gone?

Was an outside party involved? Had he kidnapped the family, with only Rex escaping? But who would do this? And why? And where would he take them? And were they still alive? And were they going to be alive for much longer?

All those damn missing person questions.

Paul shot a Marlboro from his pack and lit up, winding down his window a few inches to let the stuffy air out of the cab.

Ed wound down his window too and said, "Car doesn't stink enough of cigars? You gotta add cigarette smoke to it?"

Paul's father and the previous Chief of Police of Lillooet had smoked three cigars a day for most of his life. One after lunch, one after dinner, and one before he went to bed. He was a man of habit and seldom varied from this routine. Paul's mother had forbidden him from smoking the stogies inside the police station or the constable quarters above it, where they lived, so he smoked them in the patrol car, where he could relax while listening to whatever baseball game he could pull in on the radio.

Paul had believed from a young age that it was his birthright duty to follow in the footsteps of his father. So when he turned nineteen earlier that year, he "applied" to become a deputy. Getting the job had been as easy as it had been during the days of the American frontier when all you had to do was show up at the sheriff's office with a revolver and an impressive mustache. Paul had neither the facial hair nor the six-shooter, but with the chief being his dad, he had only to fill out the required paperwork and that was that. He received a uniform, boots, handcuffs, a portable radio, a weapon, and ammo—along with the sage advice to try not to shoot anyone.

When his father died unexpectedly two months ago at the age of fifty-two due to a stroke, Paul also got the beat-up Crown Vic with 250,000 kilometers on the odometer.

"I don't mind the smell," Paul said, staring straight ahead through the windshield at the black night. "Sort of grows on you."

"Maybe they went for a walk?" Ed said, referring to the Chapmans. Ed Montgomery was sixty-nine, hawk-nosed, gray-headed, and still as randy as a man thirty years his junior. He'd been an acclaimed chef when he was younger and had worked at some of the top vacation resorts in British Columbia (in the summers) and Florida (in the winters), where he spent almost as much time orchestrating romantic trysts with the guests as he did cooking meals for them. Nowadays he liked to remind people to call him "Monty," a nickname Sean Connery had allegedly bestowed upon him during a round of golf at a Tampa Bay country club. Nobody in the Lillooet Country believed this to be true, and so nobody called him Monty. Paul wasn't an exception. The old coot was, and always had been, Ed to him. Just plain old Ed.

"A walk?" Paul said thoughtfully, streaming a jet of smoke out the window. "Where are they going to walk, Ed? It's forest in every direction. And don't forget about the boy. You don't get all shaken up like that because your family goes for a walk without you."

"I'm not forgetting about him, Paulsy. I'm just throwing out ideas here. They obviously didn't drive anywhere. Car's right there." He tipped his head to the wood-paneled station wagon parked ahead of them on the driveway.

"Troy was some sort of middle manager, wasn't he?"

Ed nodded. "Ayuh. In a Canadian Tire. The one time I had a

drink with him at the sports bar—he was buying—he wouldn't stop talking about how good his goddamn pension was. So what?"

"Middle management isn't a seasonal job. He wouldn't be up here for the summer. Probably just up for the weekend to visit the missus and kids."

"So what?"

"Maybe they had two cars? One for Troy, one for Sally."

Ed was silent as he thought about that. "Maybe. But I've never seen Sally in town driving anything at all. And a Canadian Tire middle manager with two kids and a wife that doesn't work, I can't see a man like that affording two cars."

"He can afford a cabin on the lake."

"Nu-uh. That's something else we talked about at the bar. He inherited it from his pa. It's been in their family since it was built back in the Gold Rush days."

"So maybe he inherited money to buy a second car too?"

"Then what the fuck's he doing middle managing a Canadian Tire if he's got all this fucking money? C'mon, Paulsy. Let's not get carried away with speculating here."

Paul tapped some ash from his cigarette into the ashtray, took another drag, then snuffed the thing out. "So they didn't go for a walk in the woods. They didn't drive off anywhere. You think someone took them, Ed?"

"I'm not saying that. 'Cause you have something like that happen, you have a struggle, don't you? But there was no struggle. No sign of one, at least."

"Not inside," Paul said. "So maybe they were outside. Someone comes by when they were all already outside. The struggle coulda been outside. We won't know until we can look around properly tomorrow morning in the daylight."

Ed grinned. "Hey, Paulsy, maybe you got some of your pa's thinking inside you after all. I reckon that's a possibility. Someone got 'em when they were outside." Ed shifted his body a little so he could reach a pocket in his jeans. He produced a red apple and offered it to Paul. "Wanna bite?"

Paul frowned. He'd seen a bowl of fruit on the Chapman's Formica kitchen table. "Did you take that from inside, Ed?"

"So what?"

"It's evidence."

"Evidence, right. It's just a fucking apple." He took a loud, crunchy bite. He began chewing almost as loudly. Sinking back into the seat, he closed his eyes and kept chewing. Around a full mouth he said, "Wanna know what's messed up? When you close your eyes, you're still just staring straight ahead. Like right now, my eyes are closed, but I'm still just staring straight ahead. My eyeballs are just staring."

"It's time we get going, Ed. Get an early night. We'll come back tomorrow morning—"

A loud bang on the driver's side window made Paul jump. Ed choked, coughing out a pulpy piece of the chewed apple.

"Shit!" he gasped, slapping his chest hard.

Paul wound down the window all the way. A grizzled, bearded face peered in at him. A moment later the lone-wolf face of an Alaskan Malamute appeared next to its master's, its pink tongue lolling out of its mouth.

"How you doing, Paulsy!" Don Leech said. Squinting past him, he added, "You okay, Ed? You having a tough time eating over there?"

"You scared the shit out of me!" Ed sputtered, wiping his mouth with the back of his hand. "I'm sixty-nine, for Christ's sake. You trying to kill me? I oughta sue your ass for attempted murder, that's what I oughta do."

"Can't sue someone just 'cause you can't eat properly, Ed. It's a simple concept, really. Food goes in and down. You're doing it all backward."

"What's going on, Don?" Paul asked, scratching the dog between the ears.

"You tell me, Paulsy. If you and Ponch are on a stakeout or something, you're not being too discreet about it, parked right here in the driveway like you are."

Paul explained.

"Oh, jeez." The banter left Don's demeanor. "Is little Rexy all right? I just seen him the other day playing down at the lake. Him and his brother, Loge. I can see them from my dock."

"He's okay," Paul said. "Physically, that is. But he's not saying what happened. Did you hear anything, Don? Any shouting or… anything?"

Don frowned. "Don't think so. I mean, I'm five hundred meters down the road. You can't hear much from that distance. Sometimes I hear some things, sure. The boys shouting in play. Their mom shouting at them. But how do you know that kind of shouting from serious shouting from that distance?"

"Did you hear any of that earlier today?"

"Serious shouting? No, don't think so. Well, yeah. Maybe I heard Sally. I was dozing, and I remember thinking she better not wake me up with her yelling. But I thought she was just yelling at her boys again."

"How long was she yelling for? Did you hear anything specific?"

"Nah, it was just noise. I can't remember much, t'be honest. I was in that halfway place, you know, between sleeping and being awake, and I was trying hard at not being awake."

Ed threw his apple core. It flew past Paul's face and over the head of the malamute. The dog disappeared to track it down.

"Your aim's as bad as your eating," Don said.

"I wasn't aiming at you or your big dog, you twit," Ed snapped. "I was just getting rid of the apple. It was making my fingers all sticky. And you know what—maybe it was you."

Ed blinked, his tea-colored eyes confused. "Me?"

"Maybe you got Troy and Sally and the boy tied up over at your place. What do you think, Paulsy? Should we go check?"

Don snorted. "You're crazier than a bag full of raccoons, you know that, Ed?"

△△△

After dropping off Ed Montgomery at his meticulously kept bungalow at the end of Murray Street, which had unobstructed views of the back of the Chinese restaurant on Main, Paul returned to the century-old police station a few blocks away. He locked the front door behind him, which had one of those speakeasy peepholes at a little lower than eye level, so you could see who was knocking. His office was in the back of the building, in the same room as the three stone holding cells. He spent the next hour on the phone before he climbed the stairs to the second-floor constable quarters. *The Bob Newhart Show* was playing on the color TV. Rex Chapman sat in Paul's leather club chair, his knees pulled to his chest, his arms wrapped around them. He was facing the TV, but Paul didn't know if he was watching the show or staring off into his thoughts. Paul's wife Nancy was on the rose loveseat reading one of her mystery novels.

Setting the book aside, she got up, took him by the arm, and led him to the kitchen.

"How's he doing?" Paul asked in a semi-hushed voice.

"How he's always been doing since he got here. Hasn't said a word yet." Nancy had a cheerful, almost childlike face framed by chestnut hair and straight bangs. He'd known her since kindergarten but had barely said more than a handful of words to her over the years until he'd screwed up the courage to ask her to their high school prom. They were married two summers later, and now she was six months pregnant with their first child, the baby bump clearly visible beneath her luxe knit sweater. "Did you talk to Troy or Sally?" she asked. "What happened? Are they coming to pick him up?"

Paul shook his head. "They weren't at the cabin."

She frowned. "Weren't there?"

"Nobody was."

"What do you mean nobody was there? Somebody had to be there. They wouldn't just leave him."

"There was nobody there, Nancy," he said patiently. "I just

spoke to the captain of the RCMP's Whistler detachment. They'll be sending some crime scene guys out here tomorrow. I also got hold of Troy Chapman's brother. His name's Henry. If Troy and Sally don't turn up anywhere, he'll drive up from Vancouver in a few days and take custody of Rex for the time being." He shrugged. "There's nothing else more I can do right now."

Nancy appeared disturbed. "This isn't good, is it, Paul?"

"It'll work itself out," he said. "Just go on and take the boy to bed. He can sleep in the spare bedroom. I need to get some sleep myself. It's going to be a helluva day tomorrow."

Nodding hesitantly, Nancy returned to the living room, while Paul continued down the hallway to the master bedroom without bothering to stop in the bathroom to wash his face or brush his teeth. He changed into a pair of striped pajamas and was asleep before Nancy slipped beneath the covers next to him.

Sometime later he woke to a shrill, piercing scream.

Leaping to his feet, he rushed to the spare bedroom and threw open the door and flicked on the light.

Rex was sitting up in the single bed, his face a pale mask of terror, his eyes shiny and bulging, his mouth still open, still screaming.

Nancy burst past Paul into the room. She plopped down on the edge of the bed and pulled the boy against her breast, rocking him, hushing him. His scream became a moan, then a breathless sob, then nothing. He wiped the tears from his cheeks and laid back down, curling into a fetal position, facing the wall.

"You go on," Nancy said to Paul softly. "I'll stay with him."

"Do you want me to turn off the light?"

"No, I think we should leave it on, don't you?"

Paul returned to bed then, more bothered than ever by the boy's state of mind. As he drifted off to sleep for the second time that night, he wondered what answers tomorrow would bring—unaware that it would not be tomorrow, or the next day, or the day after that, but another thirty-eight long years before the monstrous truth of what happened to the Chapman family would come to light.

CHAPTER 1

38 YEARS LATER

"A nnnddddd...." Rex Chapman stretched the conjunction several seconds as they crossed the imaginary boundary line separating the towns of Blaine, Washington, and Surrey, British Colombia, before adding, "We're in Canada now!"

Bobby said from the back seat in his small five-year-old voice, "It doesn't *feel* any different."

"Well, there's nothing really to feel that's different, bud."

From next to him, Ellie, also five going on twenty-five, said, "Nothing *looks* different."

Tabitha, Rex's girlfriend of six months, turned in the front passenger seat of the sporty Mazda sedan to face the kids. "Nothing's going to feel different or look different, guys, because the United States and Canada share the same landmass. What will be different will be cultural things like—"

"Where are all the bears?" Bobby asked. "Dylan from school says there are lots of bears in Canada."

Rex glanced in the rearview mirror but could only see a golden cowlick sprouting defiantly from the top of Bobby's head, and to the right of him, the tips of Ellie's jet-black Sailor Moon hair buns. Bobby was his; Ellie, Tabitha's.

"There are bears in the States too, bud," he said, "especially in states like Washington."

"Are there owls here too? Owls are my favorite birds."

"Yup, owls too. But I doubt we'll see any. They're nocturnal."

"Owls aren't turtles!" Ellie said, giggling.

"I didn't say that. I said—"

"Where are the Indians? Are we going to see an Indian?"

"I'll let you field that one," Rex said, glancing sidelong at Tabitha. Turning forty next month, she was five years younger than he was. She had the same jet-black hair as her daughter, though hers was cut into a more mature jaw-skimming cut. Beneath her bold brows, her eyes were bright violet, her skin as smooth as porcelain. Despite the Elizabeth Taylor look, she saw herself only as a working single mom operating on too much stress and too little sleep, and if you told her that her beauty matched that of any Hollywood actress, she would most likely tell you where to stick it.

"Do you guys want to play I-Spy?" she said, sidestepping her daughter's questions.

"That's so boring!" Ellie complained.

"Why don't you watch something on your iPad then, sweetie?"

"Fine..." Music began to play. "Ugh. Jonas Hill again. He doesn't have many friends, does he?"

Mario music began to play also, indicating Bobby had gone back to his handheld Nintendo Switch.

Seeing the upcoming traffic light turn yellow, Rex accelerated through the intersection. He wasn't an impatient driver, yet they'd already been on the road for three hours since leaving Seattle, plus an extra half-hour wait at the border crossing, and they still had another three or so to go. So the less number of reds they had to sit through, the better.

It was late afternoon. The October sky was a washed-out blue, filled with fluffy clouds rimmed white that deepened to a slate gray in the center. Having been born and raised in the Pacific Northwest, Rex knew it wasn't a question of if it would rain but when. Being mid-October, it was the beginning of the rainy season on the coast, which meant they wouldn't be seeing much in the way of weather variation other than rain, fog, and moody skies for the next six months.

"Looks like it might rain," Tabitha said as if reading his thoughts.

"Hope it's just a drizzle," he said.

"You know it doesn't drizzle around here."

"You're right. It's going to be a downpour."

"A downpour that comes in sideways with the wind."

"A *torrential* downpour that comes in sideways with the wind."

"Umbrella-killing gale-force winds."

"Death and destruction all around."

"And we're going to be in a little cabin in the mountains." She smiled. "Sounds cozy."

"Sounds suicidal," he said.

"If you don't like the rain, you live in the wrong part of the world, mister."

"It's not the rain. It's the grayness. Everything's always gray. November to June. Gray. Don't you ever get tired of that?"

"Jeez, you're sounding glum."

"Yeah, Dad," Bobby said from the back, "stop being so *glum*."

"I'm just saying, some vitamin D sometimes would be nice."

"Don't listen to him, Bobby, he's just being the devil's advocate."

Bobby didn't reply, and Rex wasn't surprised. The boy didn't speak to Tabitha unless it was absolutely necessary. He was taking his mother's absence pretty badly, and from his erroneous perspective, Tabitha was to blame for the absence.

The silence in the wake of Bobby's pointed lack of reply lingered in the car. Rex rested a hand on Tabitha's thigh. She covered it with hers.

"What's a devil's abby cat, Mommy?" Ellie asked abruptly.

"It's someone who argues with you just to argue, hon."

"Why?"

"They just like to argue, I suppose."

"But why?"

"They just... Are you being a devil's abby cat right now,

sweetie?"

"No!" she replied.

"I think you are."

"Devil's abby cats are stupid!"

"Totally," Tabitha agreed.

"Hey, are you calling me stupid?" Rex said.

"Yes!" Ellie said.

Rex zipped through another intersection in the nick of time and felt absurdly proud of this accomplishment. On the left, a Tim Horton's coffee shop slipped past, followed by a Best Western with a neatly manicured garden of alpine flowers, and an auto repair shop hidden behind a phalanx of old tires. Surrey was one of Vancouver's southern suburbs, and like most suburbs, it consisted of wide roads, ample trees, a network of telephone poles and their corresponding wires, commercial shops, and pleasant houses, none of which were too big nor too small.

It took them roughly an hour to get through Vancouver before they were once again surrounded by raw nature.

"Any idiots out today, Dad?" Bobby asked out of the blue, with a confident nonchalance that made him sound ten years older than he was.

Tabitha laughed. "Does your dad call a lot of drivers idiots, Bobby?"

He didn't answer her.

Rex said, "Haven't run into any yet, bud. Hope it stays that way."

The Sea-to-Sky Highway continued north along the shore of the steep-sided Howe Sound, a network of fjords populated with small islands, and up into the Coast Mountains, where it cleaved through forested slopes and clung precariously to cliff walls, all to the backdrop of majestic ocean vistas.

While Tabitha and the kids oohed and ahhed at the sights —even catching a glimpse of a circling bald eagle hunting for its next meal—Rex remained focused on the road. With all the twists and turns, driving demanded his full attention. Still, now and then his eyes meandered to the rugged backcountry, and he had the same thought each time: there wasn't another freeway in North America, not even the I-70 through Colorado or the I-80 over the Sierra Nevada, which matched this remote, pristine beauty.

After another hour or so they reached the charming mountain town of Squamish, a haven for the outdoorsy types and renowned for its gushing waterfalls, stomach-dropping suspension bridge, and the Stawamus Chief, a huge cliff-faced granite massif towering seven hundred meters into the sky. Rex filled up the Mazda at a gas station, bought some candy bars for the kids to nibble on, and then they were off again.

"I want the Snickers!" Ellie said when he told them what he had.

"Can I have a Twik?" Bobby asked.

"You mean Twix, bud."

"No, I only want one."

He passed the Snickers and Twix back over his shoulder, then said to Tabitha, "Got a Mars and Kit Kat left."

"I'll pass," she said, patting her stomach. "Got to stay trim for this guy I'm seeing."

"Lucky guy, him. But I'm sure he'd like you just as much no matter your weight."

"He *is* a sweetheart."

"Eww!" Ellie said around a full mouth. "You guys are gross."

"Someday you're going to have feelings for boys too, sweetie," Tabitha said. "Just so you know."

"I already do have feelings, Mommy. I hate them."

Leaving the waters of Howe Sound behind and heading inland now, the Sea-to-Sky Highway continued its ever-upward ascent, snaking through hilly meadows, dense old-growth rainforests, and extinct volcanoes. It was a rollercoaster ride, the turns steep and sudden with some gradients approaching ten degrees. Rex had dreaded this part of the journey as a kid, not only because of the sickening blind corners and dizzying elevation but also because rockslides or accidents had been a regular occurrence, often trapping his family on the road for hours, which had always seemed like an eternity.

When they passed a turnoff to the ski resort town of Whistler Blackcomb, Tabitha remarked she would like to visit there someday, and Rex made a mental note to plan such a trip on their first anniversary, if they made it to that point, though he couldn't see any reason why they wouldn't, given how smoothly their relationship had progressed thus far.

Thirty minutes onward they entered the rustic town of Pemberton, which wouldn't have been out of place in an Old West movie, a consequence of its ranching and mining culture during the gold rush era.

"A McDonald's!" Bobby said.

"Can we stop?" Ellie asked.

Rex glanced at the McDonald's on the right: with its quaint cedar façade and covered walkways, it resembled a saloon from the 1920s. "We got our own stuff to make hamburgers, guys," he said. "Besides, we have a schedule to keep. Don't you want to reach the cabin before it gets dark?"

"Are there bears there?" Ellie asked.

"Well, yeah, but they won't come near us. They're more scared of you than you are of them."

"I'm not scared of them," Bobby said defiantly.

"Yes, you are," Ellie said. "Everybody's scared of bears."

"I'm not!"

"Are too!"

"Am not!"

"Guys—enough!" Tabitha said.

They drove through farmland for several kilometers before climbing once again into the snow-capped mountains for the final, and most treacherous, leg of the journey. Coniferous trees prevailed here, the blend of fir and pine in the lower elevations gradually giving way to spruce and aspen the higher they got. Nearly ninety white-knuckle minutes after this, they arrived at an intersection of deep gorges in the lee of the Coast Mountains where the tiny community of Lillooet was located. They crossed a wooden bridge over the Seton River, a tributary of the Fraser, and were immediately greeted by a totem pole carved from an enormous western red cedar. Bobby and Ellie yapped and pointed. Rex pulled to the side of the road so they could all gawk.

"It's huge!" Bobby said, pressing his nose to his window.

"It was there when I was a kid," Rex said, noting that it was even taller than he remembered, perhaps fifty or sixty feet from top to bottom.

"Why are the faces so scary?" Ellie asked, leaning toward Bobby's side of the car as far as her seatbelt straps would allow.

"They're just animals," Bobby said.

"One's a beaver," Tabitha said. "See its teeth?"

"The top one's a bird!" Ellie said.

"Looks like an eagle," Tabitha said.

"What's that one with the big nose?" Bobby asked.

He was referring to the face carved into the bottom of the pole.

"It's a mosquito," Rex said.

"I hate mosquitas!" Ellie said. "They bite!"

"Everyone hates them," Tabitha said. "That's why that one's at the bottom."

"That's not exactly true," Rex said, putting the car in gear and pulling back onto the road.

"You like mosquitos, Daddy?" Bobby asked.

"What I mean is, a lot of people think that the most important figure on a totem pole is placed at the top. But it's the reverse. The most important one is at the bottom to support the weight of all the others atop it. That, and it puts it at eye level with the viewer."

"I didn't know you were such a connoisseur of Native American art," Tabitha teased him.

"My father told me that one summer."

"What did grandpa do, Dad?" Bobby asked. "Was he a pilot like you?"

"No, he was a humanitarian."

"What's a human-tarian?"

7

"It's like a vegetarian," Ellie said assuredly. "But they eat humans instead of vegetables."

"Not quite, honey," Tabitha said. "It's somebody who helps others less fortunate than themselves."

They crossed the old CN railway tracks that served the Lillooet Railway Station, then made a right onto Lillooet's Main Street—and Rex was immediately clobbered with a myriad of nostalgic memories. The big Swiss-looking hotel that greeted them. The old pizza parlor with its hand-painted sign. The mom-and-pop convenience store, where he'd often spent his weekly allowance on gummy bears and sour keys. The House of Jade Mineral Museum, the Royal Canadian Legion where "EVERYONE IS WELCOME," and the Esso gas station. There was also the cinder-block supermarket where Rex had always checked the slots of the gumball machines for forgotten change. The pub that was still reminding people with its signage that it sold "Ice Cold Beer," and where his dad had always bought his cases of Labatt 50 and Coors Light. The I.D.A. pharmacy, the Canadian Imperial Bank of Commerce, and next to the post office with its Canadian flag flapping in the wind, the iconic Goldpanner Restaurant, which used to offer a weekend buffet, and perhaps still did.

In general, everything was as he recalled. Nothing had really changed. It was almost as if the tired community had remained locked in a time-bubble for the last thirty-eight years—

"I knew there were Indians here!" Ellie blurted.

Rex had no idea what she was talking about until he spotted four men standing in the parking lot of a budget inn, smoking cigarettes. They wore jeans and plaid lumberjack shirts. Their Native American heritage was evident by their dominant coloring, smooth features, and straight, dark hair.

"You shouldn't call them Indians, Ellie," he told her.

"Huh?" she said.

"They're called Aboriginals."

"Abo-what?"

"Aboriginals. That means they're the original inhabitants of this land."

"Abodidinal."

"Yes, that, or Native Americans. So try to use one of those instead. Okay?"

"Okay."

"Thank you."

Rex caught Bobby mumble, "You're so stupid," under his breath, which prompted Ellie to reply, "Like you knew! You're the stupidest stupid head in the world!"

The north end of the town deteriorated into a grungy industrial zone, which included an A&W restaurant that had been a teenage hangout when he was a kid, and a relatively new open-air strip mall he hadn't known existed until now.

"I need to go to the bathroom," Bobby said.

"Can't it wait, bud?" he said. "We're almost there."

"I really need to go!"

"He's going to pee his pants!" Ellie said.

"Am not!"

"Are too!"

"Am not!"

"Ay yi yi," Tabitha said with a sigh.

Rex was thinking about doing a U-turn to head back to the A&W when, ahead on the right, he spotted a rickety old A-frame house that, if his memory served him correctly, was a mining museum that also doubled as a tourism center.

He made a right into the parking lot, which was empty of any other cars. "Should be bathrooms in here if it's still open," he said, stopping before a maple tree resplendent with fall leaves. He killed the engine. "But let's not dally, okay?"

Everybody got out of the Mazda, four doors slamming in quick succession. Rex breathed in the cool, fragrant air, which was redolent with pine needles and wood smoke from a burning fire. He led the way to the log building that had VISITOR INFORMATION CENTER hand-carved into a thick slab of wood above the front door. A signpost next to the porch bristled with arrows indicating the distance to everywhere from Bangkok to

Paris.

"Hey, isn't that cool?" Rex said, indicating the post. "How far does it say Seattle is, Bobby?"

"I *really* need to go, Dad."

"Okay, okay, just hold on a bit longer."

The steps up the porch creaked loudly beneath his feet. A sign hanging in the door's mullioned window read CLOSED, though the lights were still on.

Rex rapped on the door and waited.

"Dad…"

"I know, Bobby. Hold on."

He rapped again, and the door opened a moment later. An elderly woman dressed in a brightly-patterned dress stood on the other side of the threshold. She was tall and delicately built with a short-cropped white perm, ski-jump nose, and sagging jowls. Bright red lipstick contrasted garishly with her sun-weathered leathery skin. Kind eyes probed Rex from behind tortoise-shell eyeglasses. "I'm sorry," she said, offering an apologetic smile, "we've been closed for a little while now. We'll be open again tomorrow morning—"

"My son just needs to use the restroom," Rex said. "Would that be possible? We've been driving all day."

"Oh, I see." The woman glanced at Bobby, who was dramatically cupping his genitals, and her smile became genuine. She gathered the fabric of her dress around her thighs and stepped back to allow them to enter. "Come in, please."

The interior of the museum/tourist center was one large dilapidated room with raked ceilings from which depended three antique brass fans. A smorgasbord of glass display cases contained all sorts of metals and minerals. Others held old mining tools, surveyor's instruments, and black-and-white photographs depicting life at the turn of the last century. In one dark corner stood an eerily life-sized exhibit of two haggard prospectors panning for gold over a creek bed. Nearby, a fire burned warmly in a stone fireplace.

"Restrooms are right over there," the woman said, indicating a set of doors at the end of a log counter stacked with tourist brochures.

"There you go, bud," Rex said, ruffling his hair with his hand.

Bobby took off.

"Mind you, there's no toilet seat!" the woman added.

Bobby hesitated at the door with the MEN decal, glanced back.

"It's okay, bud," Rex said. "Just don't fall in."

Bobby slipped inside and closed the door behind him.

"Wow!" Ellie said, staring up at the wall where an eight-point stag mount presided over them. "A deer head!"

"Ran right into the museum, that one did," the woman said with a lopsided grin. "It wasn't suicidal. Deers are rarely suicidal, you know. So it must have been real dark. But that's how I found it in the morning, head sticking through the wall, just like that."

"Was it okay?" Ellie asked, concerned.

"Dead as a mackerel," the woman stated bluntly. "So I lopped off the body on the other side of the wall and that was that. Been up there ever since."

Ellie was speechless for the first time all day.

Rex was too.

Crouching before Ellie, so they were at eye level, the woman continued, "But never-mind that. How do you like our little town so far, lovely?"

Ellie said, "We saw some Abodidinals."

"Aboriginals? Very good. A lot of young people often mistakenly call them Indians, but that's not correct. A long time ago, you see, Christopher Columbus set sail for what at the time everybody called India or the Indies. But then he accidentally landed on an island in the Caribbean instead, which is just south of the U.S.A. Thinking he was in the Indian Ocean, he called the people Indians, and the name stuck for all the different native people in North America."

"I knew they were Abodidinals because T-Rex taught me that."

"T-Rex?"

Ellie pointed at Rex. "That's T-Rex, my mom's boyfriend. And that's my mom. She looks like me when I get bigger."

"Oh—oh my, I see." The woman glanced up at Tabitha, who was blushing, then at Rex, then at their denuded ring fingers.

"I'm Rex," he said, not knowing what else to say. "This is my partner, Tabitha."

"Call me Barb," she said. Then to Ellie, "And you, little princess, are absolutely right. There are a lot of Aboriginals in Lillooet. In fact, just over half the town are St'at'imc. Do you know why?"

"Why?"

"You've seen the big river outside?"

Ellie nodded.

"That's the longest and most important river in British Columbia. Several streams converge with it right around here, making this area a great fishing spot. Aboriginals have been coming here long before Lillooet was called Lillooet, some archeologists think for thousands of years, specifically to catch migrating Chinook salmon."

"Huh," Rex said. "I didn't know that."

"Sure," Barb said, nodding her head sagely. "They also believe it's one of the oldest continuously inhabited locations on the continent."

Ellie scrunched her nose. "I don't like salmon, and I don't like mosquitas."

"Mosquitos?" Barb said. "No, not many people do, do they?"

"Abodidinals do."

Barb raised an eyebrow. "Do they now?"

"Because they made the mosquita face on the big totem pole, and T-Rex says the most important face is at the bottom, so that means they probably like mosquitas."

"Rex—or T-Rex, I should say—is exactly right. And you are too, in a way. The Aboriginals don't like mosquitos how you might like a cute puppy, with affection, I mean, but they certainly hold great respect for them."

"Why do they respect them?"

"Ellie," Tabitha said, "that's enough questions for now, I think. I'm sure Barbara has better things to do than—"

"Oh, not at all," Barb said. "I'm honored to have such an inquisitive young lady in my museum." To Ellie, "Would you like to hear a story, lovely?"

"Yes!"

Barb took Ellie's hands in hers and said, "A long, long time ago, long before there were white people in Canada, and when Lillooet was just a longhouse village, some of the St'at'imc were out on the river in their elm-bark canoes—"

"Fishing for salmon?" Ellie said.

"That's right," Barb said. "Fishing for salmon. Only that morning they didn't get a single bite in their usual spot, so they tried a new stream. They didn't get any bites there either, and so they paddled farther and farther into uncharted territory. Suddenly along the tree-lined bank there was a loud rustling sound and then"—she made an astonished gesture—"something thin and tall burst through the thick vegetation and snatched one of the men!"

Ellie covered her eyes with her hands. "Did it eat him?" she asked, peeking through her splayed fingers.

"Nobody knew what happened to him," Barb replied. "But back at the longhouse village, the chief wasn't happy. So the next morning he sent his best warriors to track down the creature."

Ellie lowered her hands reluctantly. "Did they find it?"

"They did. But they weren't strong enough to kill it. Instead, it took another one of the men and injured several others, who quickly fell sick and died over the next few days."

"Oh poo!" Ellie said, frowning in despair.

Rex cleared his throat. "Maybe we should pause the story there for now—"

"But I want to hear what happened!" Ellie protested, looking up at him with pleading eyes.

"I don't want you having nightmares tonight."

"I won't," she said. "I promise."

Rex glanced at Tabitha. Her daughter, her call.

Tabitha shrugged. "Ellie's a big girl. She can make her own decisions."

"Well," Barbara continued, picking up from where she had left off, "the chief wasn't just angry anymore. He was scared. What was this creature that could defeat his best warriors with such ease? He decided to send messengers to the neighboring St'at'imc villages to warn them about the creature—and much to his amazement, the other villages already knew about it. They even had a name for it. *Zancudo*. That means long-legged."

"Were there more like it?"

"Nobody knew. Nobody knew much of anything about it. Not where it came from, nor how many of them there were if there were indeed more than one. Only that it was very dangerous—and that the attacks kept happening. So after much worrying and consulting, the villages decided to work together. They organized the biggest hunting party yet. With their bows and arrows, war clubs and hunting knives, dozens of warriors tracked down the Zancudo, overwhelmed it with their sheer numbers, and chopped it up into pieces."

"They killed it?" Ellie said.

"They did indeed. But while they were celebrating, the strangest thing happened. Tiny little insects appeared in the Zancudo's spilled blood. Swarms of them took to the air, turning the sky black. Buzzing and biting, they attacked the warriors, killing many and driving the rest back to their villages—and returning every summer thereafter to seek their revenge." The old woman smiled. "And that, little princess, is the origin of hateful mosquitos, and why the St'at'imc people have a grudging respect for them."

Ellie scrunched her nose. "Is that true?" she asked skeptically.

"It's what the St'at'ime people believe."

"Is it true, Mommy?"

"You heard the woman, honey," Tabitha said.

"Little mosquitos came from a big one?" She chewed on this. Then, "Do other big ones still exist?" she asked worriedly.

"I have never seen one—"

The door to the men's restroom opened, and Bobby stomped out, fiddling with his belt.

"All good, Bobby?" Rex asked, happy that they could finally get going. There was something about Barb that bothered him in a vague and undefined way, almost as though she were in on a joke they knew nothing about.

"Yup!" Bobby said, coming over. "It was just me and my penis."

Rex cleared his throat. "A bit too much information there, bud. Now thank this lady for letting you use the bathroom."

"Thank you," Bobby said shyly.

Barb stood. "Where are you staying in town, if I may ask?"

"We're not," Rex replied. "I have a cabin on Pavilion Lake."

Her eyebrows went up in surprise. "Is that so?"

"I spent summers there as a kid. Haven't been back since."

"Rex... Rex *Chapman*," she said, her disposition changing in a heartbeat. Her eyes went to his prematurely white hair for just a moment. "Your parents were Troy and Sally Chapman."

Rex nodded tightly. This was the last conversation he wanted to have right then.

"I was in my twenties then," Barb said. "I remember...well, I don't remember too much. I heard..." She cleared her throat. "I never saw you after your family... They took you away..."

"Where did you go, Daddy?" Bobby asked.

"It's time we get going, guys," he said, placing a hand on each of the kids' shoulders and turning them toward the door. "Last one to the car's a rotten egg!"

Yelping and clawing at one another to gain the advantage, they bolted through the door and down the porch steps.

Rex placed a hand on the small of Tabitha's back and directed her outside after them.

"Mr. Chapman?" Barb's voice rose behind him, striking a concerned note. "Are you sure it's a good idea to go back to that cabin? Perhaps we could talk in private, please? Mr. Chapman? *Rex?*"

Without replying, Rex unlocked the Mazda with the remote

key and slipped behind the wheel. When everyone else was buckled up, he turned on the ignition. The engine cranked and started, purring loudly.

Tabitha frowned at him. "Are you okay, hon?"

He nodded, clicking on the headlights. "Fine," he said, though he felt far from fine.

"Did that woman know you, Daddy?" Bobby asked from the back seat. "When you were a kid like me?"

"I suppose," he said lightly. "Everybody knows everybody in a small burg like this, bud—and they all have long memories."

"But you don't remember her?"

"No," he said, pulling out of the parking lot and turning right onto Moha Road, into the darkening shadows of dusk.

CHAPTER 2

Paul Harris, who had become known affably by the townsfolk as Policeman Paul over the years, was not only the Chief of Police of Lillooet, but he was also the township's patrolman, detective, traffic cop, crime-scene investigator, and search-and-rescue guy. He had assumed all of these roles not by choice but by necessity.

He was the last man standing on the now one-man police force.

This had not always been the case. Paul's first deputy had been his father's old friend, Ed Montgomery, who had lived behind the still-standing Chinese restaurant. Since then Paul had gone through a handful of different deputies, the last one being a spunky mother of four named Fiona Marshall. Paul had gotten along great with Fiona. He would have liked to have kept her, but she moved with her husband and kids to Saskatchewan two months back to be closer to her sisters.

A few people interested in filling Fiona's role had approached Paul, but he hadn't made any decisions yet. He didn't want to choose hastily. Besides, it wasn't like Lillooet was drowning in major crimes. His duties were pretty mundane. He performed firearms inspections to ensure farmers were storing their guns according to regulations. He enforced traffic and attended collisions. He searched for hikers, mostly tourists, who ventured off the official trails and became lost in the wilderness. The two most serious offenses over the last six months had been illegal lighting of a fire during a fire-danger period and an opportunistic burglary.

Of course, Paul also dealt with all the day-to-day interpersonal drama that came with policing a township of fewer than three thousand people. Concerned mothers and fathers telling Paul to "have a word" with boys they didn't want their daughters dating. Bitter wives urging him to lock up their no-good alcoholic husbands. Those same husbands bitching to him about how their ungrateful wives were lazy cows that didn't lift a finger around the house. Others wanting him to settle boundary disputes with neighbors, gambling debts with former friends, or God knows what else. It was always something or other. And it never seemed to matter that "parent" or "marriage counselor" or "surveyor" or "fixer" weren't in Paul's job description. As the only cop within a hundred-kilometer radius, he had been nominated, whether he liked it or not, as the town's jack of all trades. So he listened politely to everybody's concerns, offered whatever support he could, and most importantly, remained objective in his actions. *Be friendly but not a friend* his father had once told him, and it was a mantra he now lived by.

Nevertheless, it would be nice to have a deputy along again for those domestic violence call-outs, Paul thought. These usually involved the same two or three families in town, mind you, who were generally more belligerent than violent...but you never knew. Sometimes it was the most ordinary folks who turned out to be the craziest in the head. Take Chad Burnett, for example, a charismatic sheep farmer on fifty acres a few kilometers north of town, who had also served as mayor between 2008 and 2012. He had been respected by everyone young and old, Paul included, so it was to Paul's great surprise when he gave his pretty wife Hula two black eyes, three cracked ribs, and a broken foot after she hid the TV remote because she believed he was watching too much pay-per-view porn. And let us not forget Maggie Williams, full-time muckraker and grandmother of four who once tripped out on a cocktail of anti-psychotic meds and Chardonnay and terrorized her neighbors by banging on their windows and tearing up their garden. She'd nearly taken off Paul's head with a steel-toothed hand rake before he and Fiona were able to cart her off to jail.

Maybe I should *start looking a bit more seriously for Fiona's replacement*, Paul mused as he rolled down the Crown Vic's window and lit up a cigarette

Inhaling deeply, tobacco crackling in the still air of the cab, he returned his attention to the sprawling hotel across the street. Two weeks ago, after Troy Levine plowed his Ford pickup truck through the pioneer cemetery out in front of the old Anglican Church, Paul had decided it was time to crack down on the drunken driving that he had mostly turned a blind eye to over the years. So last Saturday—the first of the month when the welfare checks came in and you couldn't find an empty seat in any of the town's licensed establishments between noon and midnight—Paul had staked out the same hotel he was now watching, which ran the town's largest and busiest pub, and busted a few patrons over the point-oh-eight threshold who attempted to drive home. Word had clearly gotten around because today the parking lot was only half full.

Paul took another drag on the cigarette, which set off a series of phlegmy coughs. A tickle in the back of his throat kept the coughs going for a good ten seconds.

The price you paid for smoking a pack a day your entire adult life, he supposed.

The back door of the hotel's pub opened, and a man beneath a cowboy hat emerged, his face hidden mostly in shadows, though he appeared unsteady on his feet. He disappeared around the west side of the building, and Paul figured he was either taking a leak or walking home when he returned a short time later in the saddle atop a chocolate Quarter Horse.

"Oh, for fuck's sake," Paul mumbled, flicking the cigarette out the window. He put the cruiser in gear and eased up behind the horse. He blurped the siren. The man glanced over his shoulder, and Paul recognized Sammy Johnson of Fraser River Meats.

Sammy reined the horse to a stop.

Putting the cruiser in Park, Paul got out and flanked the

steed. "Evening, Sammy," he said, looking up at the bleary-eyed butcher.

"Didn't see you out here, Paulsy," Sammy said, slurring his words. "Where you been hiding?"

"You been drinking, Sammy?"

"Had a couple, maybe."

"You want to blow into this for me?" He raised a small handheld breathalyzer.

"I got a medical condition that don't—"

"Hell you do, Sammy. Now let's just get this done with."

Scowling, Sammy leaned toward the device—and for a moment Paul feared he was going to topple head over heels to the ground. But he kept his balance, placed his lips on the device's mouthpiece, and blew.

"Harder," Paul said.

Sammy blew again.

After several seconds, Paul checked the digital readout.

"One-point-three, Sammy."

"Those things ain't accurate, you know that."

"Accurate enough. You're going to have to come to the station with me until you sober up."

"But I ain't even driving a car! It's a horse! And a *sober* horse at that!"

"I suppose technically that's only half a DUI then, but I still gotta take you in."

"Come on, Paulsy. We went to school together."

Paul got this all the time. "It's a small town, Sammy," he replied. "Everyone went to school together. There's only one damned school."

"Can't you just—"

"No. Now enough bullshitting. You're coming with me."

Paul helped the drunk butcher down off the horse, then tied the reins to the top rail of the fence that ran parallel to the sidewalk. He would come back later for the animal.

With Sammy in the back of the patrol car, bitching and moaning about his constitutional rights being violated, Paul drove the half-klick to the police station, pulling over at the curb out in front of it.

Built the same year Winston Churchill was born, the original wooden structure burned to the ground in 1926. The stone building that stood there now rose in its place, along with the iron-clad stables, long since demolished, and the constable quarters, which were still there, and which have housed every officer and his family since.

Paul led Sammy up the flagstone walk, stopping to pick up his grandson's bicycle, which had been abandoned on its side, kickstand be damned. The three stone holding cells were located in a room at the back of the building that also served as his office. Paul opened one of the barred doors and gestured for Sammy to enter.

"How the hell long do I have to sit in there for?" Sammy asked, though he nevertheless entered the six-by-eight-foot cell without protest and flopped down on the bed.

"A few hours, I reckon. Just try to get some shuteye. It'll be morning before you know it."

"You wanna call the wife for me then? Tell her you locked me up and I won't be home for supper?"

"I can do that."

"And, hey, Paulsy—you got any food?"

"Just get some rest, Sammy."

Paul closed the cell door, which deadlocked automatically. He went to his desk and sat down. By the time he had looked up Sammy's phone number in the white pages, and had spoken with his missus (who took the news of her husband's incarceration with bitter amusement), Sammy was already asleep and snoring loudly.

Hanging up the phone, Paul sighed while stretching his arms above his head. On his desk sat three plastic-framed photographs of his grandson. The boy had short black hair and dark, cynical eyes like Paul's (cop's eyes, Paul always told him proudly), as well as the Harris nose, which some would say was so big it distracted from the other facial features, though Paul had always considered a large nose to be distinguished rather than obtrusive.

A knock sounded at the front door.

Paul glanced at the wall clock: 6:12 p.m. His official hours might be nine-to-five like everybody else's, but he was unofficially on duty 24/7.

His sigh turned into a groan as he heaved himself out of his chair, returned to the front of the station, and answered the door.

Barbara McKenzie stood across the threshold, her craggy features bathed in the sepia tones of dusk. She pushed her tortoiseshell glasses up the bridge of her sharp nose and smiled at him.

"Evening, Paul," she said.

"Evening, Barb," he said. "Let me guess. Vandals again?" Kids had been spray-painting menacing-looking stickmen on the trunks of some conifers in the vicinity of the museum.

"No, no, not that. I wanted to tell you I had some interesting visitors at the museum just now."

"Oh?" he said, already thinking of an excuse to get out of the conversation tactfully.

She nodded eagerly. "It's about…well, you told me…this was several years ago…but you told me to let you know if I ever heard of anybody going down to Pavilion Lake."

"Oh?" he said again, his half-formed excuse immediately forgotten.

"You won't believe who it was either."

"Who, Barb?"

"*Rex,*" she said with an uncertain smile. "*Rex Chapman.*"

A sudden wash of unreality struck Paul like an open-handed slap. "That kid…" he said, frowning.

Barb nodded. "He's not a kid anymore…"

"Are you sure it was Rex Chapman?"

"Of course I'm sure! His hair was still as white as a snowflake. Not to mention he told me his name. He was with a woman—not his wife, I should mention—and two of the most adorable little children you have ever seen."

Paul ran a hand over the stubble surrounding his clenched mouth, the August night in '81 returning to him in a jumble of rusty images. After Rex Chapman was found wandering on the highway, he stayed overnight with Paul and Nancy, in the guest bedroom. Not that he'd done much sleeping. He'd woken up every hour, screaming at the top of his lungs. And by morning, his previously blond hair had turned completely white. Every goddamn follicle.

Paul had interviewed Rex a half-dozen times over the following two days, but the boy didn't remember anything, not what had frightened him so badly, nor what had happened to his parents and older brother, none of whom had ever been heard from again.

Barb was saying something.

Paul looked at her without comprehension, his mind still fogged up with the past.

"Paul?" she said. "Did you hear me?"

"What was that, Barb?"

"What are you going to do? You can't let them stay on the lake. Not with everything that's happened up there. The other families that have gone missing. The Petersons and—"

"The Ryersons. But, hell, that was a dozen years ago now. Nothing's happened since—"

"Because everybody else moved away!"

"Keep your voice down, Barb."

"Sorry, Paul," she said, casting a wary glance at the stairs leading to the second floor. "But it's just...I just...*you* were the one who told me to tell you if I heard of anybody going up to the lake."

"More than a decade ago, I did," he said, lowering his voice as well. "But whoever was down there, Barb, whoever was responsible for whatever happened to the Chapmans and the Petersons and the Ryersons...that person's gotta be at least my age now. He's long gone—"

"But—"

"Or more than likely he's dead. There's nothing to get all worked up about—"

"But what if someone *is* still up there?" she said. "What if something *does* happen? Those kids, Paul…"

He shook his head in frustration. "What do you want me to do, Barb? It's Rex's cabin. It's his right if he wants to go there."

"He probably doesn't know better. He hasn't been back since he was a kid. At least he hasn't been seen in town or spoken to anybody from town. So you have to at least tell him what's happened since he left."

Paul placed a hand on the door with the intent to close it. "I need some time to think this through, Barb. Thanks for bringing it to my attention." He started to close the door.

She held it open with both hands. "You have to go up there, Paul."

He sighed. "Yeah, I guess I do."

"Tonight."

"Let me think about it, okay?"

"Tonight."

"Yes, fine, tonight."

Barb sagged with relief. "Thank you, Paul. Maybe I'm overreacting. I know I'm probably overreacting. But I just keep thinking about those adorable little kids…"

"You go home now, Barb," he said. "Everything is just fine."

She stepped back, nodding, and then started away.

He closed the door halfway. "Barb?" he said.

She turned back toward him. "Yes?"

"Let's keep this between you and me for now. Can we do that?"

"Well, yes," she said. "That's probably a good idea. When are you going to go—?"

"Soon," he said and closed the door all the way. Standing with his back to the wood, staring down the long hallway that led to the holding cells, Paul felt the skin over his skull and arms tingle and tighten, as if it was suddenly one size too small.

"Paul?" Nancy's voice floated down the stairs. "Who was

that?"

"Barbara Moore from the museum."

"What did she want?"

"Nothing," he said, before adding, "At least nothing important."

CHAPTER 3

"That lady was strange, Mommy," Ellie said.

"Who are you talking about, honey?" Tabitha asked. They were passing through the northern stretches of Lillooet, looming foothills to the left of them, white-siding houses with wood-picket fences and scrub-filled lots to the right.

"The mosquita story woman."

"You mean Barbara? Why was she strange?"

"She just was."

Bluntly put, but Tabitha didn't disagree. Barbara's heavy-handed presence and melodramatic storytelling had been a bit over the top. A simple, "The restrooms are over there," would have sufficed just fine.

"Did the mosquito story scare you?" she asked her daughter.

"A little," Ellie admitted.

"You're not going to have nightmares, I hope?"

"No..."

"You're a scaredy cat!" Bobby said.

"Am not!" Ellie replied.

"Am too!"

"Am not—"

"Guys!" Tabitha said sharply. "Enough. Can't you think of something else to say?"

"Like what?"

Tabitha shook her head. They were five years old. They each had maybe a two-thousand-word vocabulary. How articulate did she expect them to be?

"Just…give it a rest," she said.

"What are you watching there, Ellie?" Rex asked.

"The Wiggles!" she said. "They're from Austwalia."

"Bobby?" he said. "How's your game? Kicking some Goomba butt?"

"Huh?"

"That's what those little brown mushroom creatures you stomp on are called."

"Goombas?" Bobby said doubtfully. "Are you sure?"

"Believe it or not, bud, *Super Mario Bros.* was around when I was a kid."

"Computers didn't even exist when you were a kid!"

"How old do you think I am?"

"Twenty-five?" Ellie guessed earnestly.

"Thanks, Ellie," he said, "but no, I'm a tad older than that. Forty-five."

"Forty-five!" she repeated, impressed. "So soon you'll be fifty. And after that, you'll be dead."

"Anyway, Bobby, I'm telling you the truth. My dad bought me a Nintendo when they first came out in 1985. They even came with a gun back then."

"A *real* gun?" he asked.

"No. It shot ducks."

"*Real* ducks?"

"No…Goombas… What was I saying?"

"I don't know, Dad."

"Me either," Ellie said, with exaggerated exasperation.

"Tough audience," Tabitha remarked.

"Tell me about it," he replied, chuckling.

They drove on in silence for a little. Roughly a kilometer outside of town they crossed a bridge over the Fraser River and reunited with Highway 99. The two-lane road passed through a gentle meadow with a meandering creek before switchbacking into a jagged gorge bordered by rugged peaks. Road signs warned drivers regularly to slow to thirty kilometers an hour around the tight bends and to be vigilant of rock slides.

"How much longer, Dad?" Bobby asked eventually.

"Not too much longer, bud," Rex said. "Just hold tight."

"I'm bored," Ellie said.

"I'm super bored," Bobby said.

"I'm boreder than you."

"Guys!" Tabitha said.

"What?" Ellie asked.

Closing her eyes, Tabitha tried tuning them out. When she was their age, she had been no less quarrelsome with her siblings. She was the youngest of three sisters. The eldest, Beth, was Rex's age now, and a dentist in Portland. Ivy was thirty-seven and a sex therapist on a radio station that broadcasted out of Olympia. Although Tabitha didn't visit as much as she would have liked, she had a good relationship with both of them.

Which hadn't been the case when they were kids. All she seemed to remember from those days was a lot of name-callings, hair-pulling, pinching, and double-crossing.

Long car trips had been especially...adventurous...with each sister valiantly defending the invisible borders of their seat space from errant thighs or elbows.

One car trip in particular stood out in her memory. It had been to Astoria, a three-and-a-half-hour drive from Seattle. There had been all the aforementioned sibling infighting on the way there, but as only children under a certain age were capable of, all was forgiven and forgotten as soon as they arrived at the campground where they were staying, which had featured a bouncy pillow, a playground with fast slides, a King Tut-themed mini-putt course, and a video game arcade. They ate lunch at a café/bakery that sold bread so fresh all it needed was butter. They stopped by the Goonies' house from the namesake movie, which had just been released the previous summer. They went swimming at Cannon Beach, explored the shores around the famous Haystack Rock, and when darkness fell, they cooked wieners and s'mores over a campfire.

I should try to get in touch more with Beth and Ivy, she thought.

Once or twice a year wasn't enough. Beth's two boys were growing up so fast. And Ivy was six months pregnant with her first. *Maybe I'll drive down to Olympia and surprise her next week,* she decided. *Ivy would like that. We'll go to that Italian restaurant she likes out on…where is it? No matter, I can google it…*

Tabitha opened her eyes and was surprised to find herself drowsy and disorientated. She had nodded off.

She blinked the sleep from her eyes. The half-tones of dusk muted the landscape. Shadows pooled in the nooks and crannies of the foothills. Streaks of vermillion and cotton candy pink colored the sky.

"Welcome back, sleepy-head," Rex said.

She stifled a yawn. "How long was I out?"

"Half hour."

"That's all? Feels like hours."

"Perfect timing." He pointed out her window. "Should be just around this bend…"

"Oh my," she said when the lake came into view. It was glass-smooth and perhaps a half-mile in diameter. Its mirrored surface, tinted red from the setting sun, reflected the forested slopes rising steeply from its far bank. "It's beautiful. Kids—"

"Wow!" Ellie said.

"Are we here?" Bobby asked.

"Just about, bud," Rex said.

A few minutes later they reached the northern tip of the lake. Rex turned off the highway onto a dirt lane, which followed the shore east. Almost immediately they were bumping up and down so violently to elicit gasps and cries from the kids.

Rex stopped the car. "The road was never this bad," he said, frowning.

"Looks like it hasn't been used in years," she said. "Yours isn't the only cabin on the lake, is it?"

"No, there are a half-dozen others…" He shook his head. "I wonder if they built another road in?"

"GPS is showing only this one," she said, consulting the navigation system in the center console.

He sighed. "Guess we're going to have to walk." He turned in his seat. "Sorry, guys. There's a little problem with the road. Are you okay with a short nature walk?"

"Do we have to?" Ellie asked. "My feet hurt."

"You haven't even walked anywhere yet!"

"They still hurt."

"Well, we can sleep out here in the car…"

"Can we?" she asked excitedly.

"No, sweetie," Tabitha said. "And we're not arguing the point. So pack up your bag."

"How far is it, Daddy?" Bobby asked.

"Not too far, bud," he said. "We should still get there before dark."

$$\triangle\triangle\triangle$$

Tabitha placed her hands on the small of her back and twisted her torso. The stretch felt good. How long had they been on the road? Five hours? Six?

Her gaze settled on the dirt lane that snaked away from them into a stand of impressive old-growth trees consisting of birch, Douglas fir, whitebark, pine, and spruce giants. The road was torn up with ruts and potholes and lined with knee-high grasses and weeds. The sight filled her with an undefined, uneasy dread. Nobody would let their road fall into such disrepair, which meant nobody likely lived, or even vacationed, out here anymore.

Why not? It was God's country, pristine and beautiful.

Rex noticed her frowning and said, "Shouldn't take us more than twenty minutes to get there."

"It's not that," she said. "It's just…" She shook her head. "Nothing. Ellie? Are you ready?"

Her daughter was trying to stuff her iPad into her pink Hello Kitty backpack. "It doesn't fit!"

"I'm sure it does."

"Bobby," Rex said. "No Nintendo. Leave it behind in the car, please."

Bobby looked like someone had just cracked an egg on his face. "But I want to bring it!"

"There are plenty of other things to do out here than play video games."

"Like what?"

"How about I take you fishing in the morning?"

"Really?"

"Sure."

Reluctantly, Bobby placed the Nintendo on the back seat.

"That's a good point," Tabitha said. "Ellie, I'd like you to leave your iPad behind too."

"Mommy, no!"

"I'm not arguing, sweetie."

"Mommy, I'm not joking, I'm not kidding, and I'm not playing. I *need* my iPad."

"No, you don't *need* it, Missy. Like Rex said, there are plenty of other things to do out here."

"I don't even want to go fishing! I hate fish!"

"Put it in the car, Ellie," Tabitha said. "I'm not going to ask you again."

Huffing, she tugged the tablet from her bag and tossed it onto the back seat. She didn't have to worry about damaging it as it was wrapped in a mango-orange shockproof case.

"Thank you," Tabitha said. Then, to Rex, "Does this apply to us too?"

"Why not?" he said, digging his phone from his pocket.

Tabitha produced hers from her handbag. "I need to make a quick call first—check on everything at home." She dialed her eldest daughter's cell phone number. It rang four times before going to voicemail. "Surprise, surprise," she said. "Vanessa's not answering."

"On purpose, you think?" Rex asked.

"That phone doesn't leave her person, ever. Definitely on purpose."

"She's having a party!" Ellie crowed.

"Better not be," Tabitha grumbled.

"Here." Rex passed her his phone. "She won't recognize my number."

"You don't think she'll find a second call right after the first suspicious?"

"Probably. But it could be a boy she likes. Would she risk not answering that call?"

Tabitha accepted the phone and dialed her daughter's number again.

"Hello?" Vanessa answered on the second ring.

"Hello, sweetie," Tabitha said.

"Mom!"

"What?" she said innocuously.

"Whose phone are you using?"

"I just called you from my phone less than a minute ago. No answer."

"I didn't get to it in time."

"I'm glad that's the case and you simply didn't want to talk to me."

"So whose phone are you using?"

"Rex's," she said.

"I should have known," Vanessa quipped. Vanessa, like many teenagers, could be at times selfish, rude, rebellious, and most of all, emotionally fragile. When Tabitha had first begun dating Rex, Vanessa had acted as if he were the devil incarnate and had done her best to make him uncomfortable whenever the two of them came face to face. Rex, to his credit, took the insults and snide remarks with remarkable poise, and he could usually turn the awkward situations into merely uncomfortable situations with self-deprecating wit. Eventually this humor won Vanessa over, and she was now on the record as admitting he was "an okay guy." Having said this, Rex was still the "boyfriend," and Vanessa could often and easily fall back into the I'm-not-supposed-to-like-him mindset.

"Anyway, sweetie," Tabitha said, "I'm just checking in to make sure everything is okay."

"It's like six o'clock. Why wouldn't everything be okay?"

"It's a little past seven."

"Is it? So?"

"What time does the party start?"

Silence. Then: "What? What are you talking about?" A bit panicky.

"Ellie thinks you're having a party."

"Tell Ellie to mind her own damn business—and change her diapers while she's at it."

Tabitha glanced at Ellie, who was bent over a wildflower, sniffing it, perfectly content in the moment, and Tabitha felt a pang of sadness. Vanessa had once been equally innocent. When had she changed? When would Ellie change? When would she stop being "her little girl?"

"I was serious when I told you no parties," Tabitha said. "You know the rules when I'm away."

"Dad would let me!"

A dial tone.

Sighing, Tabitha handed the phone back to Rex.

"Sounded all right," he said.

"You only heard my end of the conversation."

"She wasn't happy?"

"She hung up on me."

"Is Ness having a party?" Ellie asked.

"That doesn't concern you, honey."

"I bet she is."

"She's not."

"How do you know?"

"Ellie, enough."

When all the electronics were deposited in the Mazda, Tabitha grabbed her shoulder bag, which contained the toiletries, while Rex retrieved four bags of groceries, leaving the heavier two bags behind. They would come back for them and the remaining backpack tomorrow morning. Then he locked the car with the remote key.

"Are we all ready then?" he asked.

"Why are there so many holes in the road, Daddy?" Bobby asked.

"It hasn't been taken care of."

"Why not?"

Rex shrugged. "When I used to come up here as a kid, your grandparents paid a fee to keep the road serviceable. All the families with cabins along the road did. But it seems everybody's stopped paying that fee. So the rain and snow have caused all that damage."

"Why did everyone stop paying? Did they run out of money?"

"That I don't know," he said.

"Ow!" Tabitha said and swatted her bare left bicep with her right hand. "Mosquito."

"Unfortunately, they don't go away until the first freeze."

"Ow!" Ellie said. "One got me too!"

"Ow!" Bobby said. "Me too!"

"We better get moving then," Rex said, "or we're going to be eaten alive."

△△△

Following a little distance behind T-Rex and her mom, Ellie was trying to figure out what she was going to do for two whole days without her iPad. All her *stuff* was on her iPad: her songs, her movies, Peek-a-Zoo, Elmo's Monster Maker, Hungry Caterpillar. All the pictures her mom let her download from the internet. Her sticker album. *Everything.* She might only be five, but she had collected a lot of stuff in her life so far, and it wasn't fair for her mom to not let her play with that stuff.

"I hate fishing," she told Bobby, who was trudging along beside her.

"Huh?" he said.

"I'm not going fishing with you tomorrow."

"So?"

"Your dad's going to make me."

"No, he's not.'"

"He will, and I hate fish."

"You can help me catch bugs."

That sounded sort of fun. "What kind of bugs?"

"I dunno yet. Whatever I find. Probably a lot of ants."

"I like butterflies."

"They won't fit."

"Fit where?"

Bobby dug an empty Tic Tac container from his pocket. "My dad gave it to me. He brought it all the way back from Gurmamy."

Ellie frowned. "Where am I going to put my butterflies?"

"Dunno. But you can't use my case. They won't fit."

"Mommy!"

Her mom glanced back over her shoulder. "Yes, honey?"

"Where am I going to put my butterflies?"

"What butterflies?"

"That I'm going to catch."

"Oh…well, we can figure something out. We'll have a look around the cabin for something when we get there."

"It has to be big so they have room."

"Okay. We'll have a look."

"My mom's going to help me find something better than your case," Ellie told Bobby happily.

He shrugged. "Your mom sounded mad before."

"When?"

"When she was talking on the phone."

"That's because my sister is having a party, and she's not allowed to have parties." Ellie thought of something. "Why don't you like my mom?"

Bobby shrugged again. "I never said that."

"But you never say anything to her."

"So?"

"So…why don't you like her?"

"I never said that."

"You already said *that*."

"Stop talking to me."

"I can talk if I want to."

"I'm not listening anymore."

"You're a stupid sad head."

"I'm not sad."

"You're going to cry, and your tears are going to drown us."

"Dad!"

Rex turned around. "What's going on, guys?"

"She's teasing me!" he complained.

"No, I'm not!" Ellie protested.

"You two are going to have to start to learn to get along better —"

"But Bobby's a stupid head—"

"I know I am but what are you?"

"You're a stupid head!"

"I know I am but what are you?"

"A stupid head!"

"Ha! You're a stupid head!"

"Am not!"

"Am too—!"

"Guys!" Rex bellowed.

Ellie clamped her mouth shut. She knew when she "went too far," something her mom would often tell her she'd done, and by the angry look on T-Rex's face, this was one of those times.

∆∆∆

Bobby knew his dad wasn't really mad at them. He was just pretending to be so Bobby and Ellie would stop arguing. Still, he lowered his eyes to the ground and tried to look like he was sorry, which he was. He didn't like making his dad angry, regardless of whether it was real anger or make-believe.

When his dad and Ellie's mom started walking again, Bobby followed, though he kept his distance. He even let Ellie get a little bit ahead of him, so they wouldn't have to walk side by side, and so she wouldn't call him any more names.

He hated her. She was so mean to him all the time. He wasn't sad. Well, that wasn't true. He was sad inside his head sometimes. He was sad that his mom was gone. She'd been gone for so long now he almost didn't remember what she looked like unless he looked at one of his pictures of her. But he still missed her.

His dad told him that she was only going to be away for a short time. She wasn't dead, which was good, so he would be able to see her again. But the "short time" seemed like a really long time. Bobby had been in preschool when his mom left, and he was in kindergarten now.

Why didn't she come home for a visit? Why didn't she Facetime him?

Did she not love him anymore? Did he do something wrong? He might have. He was just a baby when he was in preschool, and his memory wasn't as good as it was now. So he might have done something to scare her away. But what?

He asked God every night when he said his prayers to send his mommy back. But God was busy, and He never replied to Bobby's prayers. Bobby was probably at the bottom of his list, just like Chris Zukowski was always at the bottom of Mrs. Janet's list at school when she called out everybody's name.

And maybe Ellie's mom was praying to God too, asking Him not to send back Bobby's real mom so she could stay around as his fake mom forever. She probably was because she liked Bobby's dad. This was why Bobby didn't like her. She was blocking his real mom from coming back.

Bobby would be really happy if everything was like it had been when he was in preschool. His mom and dad loving each other and living together. Ellie and her mom going back to their house on Mercy Island or whatever their island was called and never coming back to Newcastle, where his house was. That would be *rad*, a word that Dylan from school had taught him. Then he would have his mommy back, and he wouldn't have to listen to Ellie making fun of him all the time either.

God, he thought, squeezing his eyes shut as tight as possible to make the wish stronger, *if You're still listening, can you please do that? Make everything go back to how it was? I promise I'll be really good. I promise I'll love my mommy and daddy as best as I can. Just please send my mommy back.*

"Bobby?"

Bobby opened his eyes. It was his dad calling his name. Bobby must have been walking slowly because everybody was way ahead of him now.

"Yeah?" he called back.

"You're dawdling, bud! Let's pick up the pace a bit."

"Coming!" he said, and began to run, all thoughts of his moms, both real and fake, forgotten.

∆∆∆

When Bobby caught up to them, Rex dropped to his knees and told his son to climb on his back. Bobby latched on, and Rex stood.

"How's the view from up there, bud?" he asked.

"Go faster, Daddy!"

"No can do. This is my top speed. The groceries are heavy. You don't want me to slip and fall. I might land on top of you. And you know what that would make you, don't you?"

"A pancake?"

"A *squashed* pancake."

"Am I next?" Ellie asked, tugging at Rex's pant leg. "I want to be next!"

"You let Bobby have his ride, sweetie," Tabitha said, taking her daughter's hand and leading her away. "You're doing a good job walking on your own."

"But I want a piggyback too!"

"You heard me."

"Poop head," she mumbled.

"Excuse me, young lady?" Tabitha said sternly. "What did you call me?"

"Poop's not a bad word."

"As a matter of fact, it is a bad word when you use it as an insult like you just did."

"I didn't. I said… *snoop* head… Like Snoopy."

"Now you're fibbing, and that's getting you in even deeper trouble."

"I'm not fibbing!"

"She's going to cry," Bobby said into Rex's ear.

"Stay out of this, bud," he replied.

"You're fibbing about not fibbing," Tabitha continued. "That means there's no dessert for you tonight—"

"No!" And now the tears came.

"You know better than to tell fibs."

"I didn't!" she wailed.

"Keep it up, Ellie, and you can go to bed early too."

Ellie's face had gone red, and her wet eyes simmered with indecision: remain combative or submit to her mother's authority.

Reason prevailed. She sniffed resignedly and wiped an arm across her eyes.

"That's better," Tabitha said.

Ellie took off ahead of them.

Tabitha sighed and followed. Rex did a couple of circles, making Bobby squeal in fear and delight, and joined her.

The road wound into the dense rainforest, pushing deeper and deeper into the thick vegetation rife with moss, lichen, ferns, and epiphytes. They passed a towering cedar twice as thick as the other cedar and spruce and hemlock around it, and Rex was amazed to discover he had a childhood memory of it, of asking his father why it was so big. He didn't recall what his father's answer had been, but the tree remained as impressive now as it had been then.

All around them warblers, finch, and sparrows sang their late afternoon songs, and Rex inhaled the mountain air deeply. He felt good. The best he had in a while, and that was saying a lot, as he was currently experiencing one of the most trying periods of his life.

Last month Rex caught the flu and called in sick to work on the morning of September 14. It proved to be a fateful decision that would save his life, because on that same evening, at 11:36 p.m., nine hours into Flight 2026's journey from New York to Frankfurt, Frederick Johnson, his First Officer of five years, began an unscheduled ten-minute descent that concluded with the Airbus A320 colliding into a mountainside in the French Alps, killing Frederick and all one hundred and fifty-nine souls on board. When crash investigators recovered the cockpit voice recordings, a chilling suicide speech by Frederick blamed depression for his final and barbaric act.

Investigators uncovered email correspondence between Frederick and the airline's Flight Training Pilot School several years earlier in which Frederick had requested time off due to an episode of severe depression. Per protocol, the flight school should have kicked Frederick out of the program. Instead, they allowed him to resume his training to obtain his pilot's license, eventually issuing him a medical certificate confirming his fitness to fly.

Consequently, the airline was now facing charges of criminal gross negligence, which could result in criminal prosecution. To save their asses, the top brass went looking for a fall guy, and that guy turned out to be Rex. The argument was that Rex, having worked with Frederick for so many years, had been derelict in his duty as Captain for not observing and reporting any suicidal tendencies that his First Officer, in light of the magnitude of his depression, must have surely exhibited at one point or another.

In any event, while the investigation and litigation played out, Rex had been grounded, and his distinguished twenty-five-year career was now at best tarnished with a stain that could never be completely cleansed, and at worst in jeopardy of being irrevocably destroyed in one fell swoop.

To get away from all the bullshit, Rex had decided to come up to Canada for the week, to visit the old family cabin he hadn't been to since his childhood, even if it meant confronting an entirely different closetful of ghosts. He had originally planned to bring only Bobby with him, but Tabitha had the weekend off and insisted she and Ellie come as well, to which he happily agreed.

His back and arms starting to ache, Rex set Bobby down on the ground. "Looks like Ellie has found something, bud," he said, referring to the fact she was kneeling in the middle of the road thirty feet ahead of them. "Why don't you go find out what it is?"

Bobby obeyed, running in that silly, uncoordinated way kids do.

"Hope it's not some animal's...poop," Rex said lightly and laughed.

Tabitha frowned at him. "You think I was too hard on her?"

"Nope. I think you did exactly the right thing."

"She's not like Bobby, you know. He's so well-behaved. Ellie's like a female version of Dennis the Menace sometimes."

He shrugged. "She's just mature for her age."

"You know her school sent me a letter the other week informing me she said poop in class?"

He arched an eyebrow. "She called someone a poop head?"

"The letter didn't specify the context. When I asked Ellie, she said she used the word when she asked the teacher if she could go to the bathroom."

"What does the school expect her to say? *I need to defecate, Miss.*"

"That's what I thought. Her teacher was just being hyper-liberal. But now...maybe Ellie did direct the word at another student. That would better justify the letter. So what concerns me is not Ellie's language, exactly, but whether she's lying to me. She's five. Do other five-year-olds lie? Vanessa never did. She had been an angel—well, until she reached her teens, that is."

"As I said, Ellie's mature for her age. That means typical five-year-old rules don't apply to her. She thinks she can get away with things others her age couldn't. That includes manipulating others."

"Great, so she's not just a liar, she's a manipulative liar."

"All liars are manipulative, by definition. But what I mean is, look, it's not a bad thing. Not at her age. She's just…smart, I guess is what I'm saying."

"That has a better ring to it than a manipulative liar."

When they approached the kids, Ellie spun around and said, "Mommy, look! A baby squirrel."

Rex and Tabitha bent over for a better look. It was a chipmunk, Rex noted, not a squirrel, and it was just lying there, barely moving.

"What happened to it?" Tabitha asked.

Rex glanced at the branches crisscrossing the sky above them. "It must have fallen out of a tree," he said.

"Can I keep it?" Ellie asked.

"Definitely not," Tabitha said. "It's a wild animal. It might bite you."

"But it's just a baby! *Please.*"

"I think you should leave it right there."

"But it will die."

"Everything dies, sweetie. And chipmunks aren't exactly an endangered species."

"It's not a squirrel?"

"Chipmunks are smaller than squirrels, and brown, with a stripe down the back, like this one."

"Do they still eat acorns?"

"They love acorns."

"More than human food?"

"They *hate* Mexican food," Rex said lightheartedly.

Ellie eyed him suspiciously. "Well, I love chippymunks just as much as squirrels. So can I keep it?"

Tabitha said, "I've told you—"

"I promise I'll take care of it!"

"I'm allergic to chipmunks, honey. At least hamsters and gerbils. So probably chipmunks too."

"You can sleep outside."

Tabitha rolled her eyes and looked at Rex.

He shrugged. "She's right. It's going to die out here. I think a turkey vulture already has an eye on it." He nodded at the sky, where he'd spotted a large bird circling.

Tabitha saw the vulture too. "I guess maybe we can take the chipmunk to the cabin," she relented. "And if it lives until Monday, we can take it to a vet in town. But," she added quickly, holding up a finger. "And this is a big but, sweetie. It stays with the vet. It's absolutely not coming back to Seattle with us. That's the deal."

"Deal!" Ellie said, reaching for it.

"Whoa, hold on," Rex said. "Not so fast. I don't think chipmunks carry diseases, but it's best not to touch it. Here." He shrugged off his windbreaker and carefully scooped the rodent into it.

"Can I carry it?" Ellie asked.

"Be gentle." He passed her the jacket and its cargo.

Ellie held the injured creature against her stomach as if it was the most precious thing in the world. She started walking, Bobby in lockstep, peeking over her shoulder, asking excited questions.

"I wouldn't be surprised if the poor thing dies of a heart attack with those two ogling over it like that," Tabitha said.

"One summer up here," Rex said, "I found a baby bird. I nursed it back to health before letting it go again. I felt pretty proud of myself as I watched it fly away. This might be a good life experience for those two if they can do the same for that chipmunk."

"You mean chippymunk."

"Right."

The road rounded a bend, and on their left, hidden behind a phalanx of hemlock, pine, and Douglas fir, was a brown-painted cabin with white trim and green shingles on the roof. The mailbox leaned drunkenly askew. The driveway was more weeds than gravel.

"That was an old couple's place," he said, pointing it out. "The McCleods."

"Good memory," she said.

"I only remember them because Mr. McCleod—I never knew his first name—was a crazy bastard who once sicced his little... Yorkshire terrier, I guess it was...on Logan and me when we came down this way."

"You were scared of a Yorkshire terrier?" she teased.

"I was five or six. Any yapping dog regardless of size is terrifying at that age."

"Why'd Old Man McCleod do it?"

"No idea. Loge and I never really left the immediate vicinity of our cabin. There was no reason to really. With the lake, we had everything we wanted right there. But one day we went 'exploring.' Ten minutes down the road was pretty far for us. We saw Mr. McCleod out in front of his place using a broom to get rid of spider webs or something around his eaves. He yelled at us, saying," —Rex assumed a crackly voice— "'What are you up-to-no-good-kids doing down here? I know your father. I'm going to tell him you've been snooping!' At least, it was something along those lines. Then he said, 'Blixy? Blixy?'"

"The Yorkshire terrier?" Tabitha said.

Rex nodded. "The dog came roaring around the cabin, and then Mr. McCleod was telling it, 'Go get 'em, girl! Get 'em!' I'd never run so fast in my life."

"What an awful old man," she said. "I thought Canadians were supposed to be polite."

"Not him."

"Why did your parents decide to buy a place up here in the first place?"

"My great-grandfather jumped on the gold-mining train in the eighteen hundreds. He worked a claim on Cayoosh Creek for a decade and found a fair bit of gold. When the claim was exhausted, he retired in Lillooet. You might not guess it now, but at that time Lillooet was considered to be the largest town in North America west of Chicago and north of San Francisco—which was maybe why my great-grandfather ended up building the cabin out here. A little place to get away from everybody. I don't know what happened to his place in town, but the cabin got passed down to my father."

In the distance, Rex thought he heard a car engine. He stopped and listened. Yes, a motor, approaching from the highway.

"Guys!" he called to Bobby and Ellie. "Move to the side of the road! A car's coming."

He watched them move to the margin. "A little more."

"We'll be in the woods!" Bobby said.

"Better than road kill!"

They stepped back farther.

The engine grew louder, then a rusty old pickup truck came bouncing around the bend—the high axle allowing it to traverse the ruts and potholes that scarred the road.

"Maybe it's Mr. McCleod?" Tabitha kidded. "Come back from the dead?"

"Blixie's revenge."

But Rex could see into the cab of the truck now. The driver was a middle-aged man with a long beard and a Stetson hat pulled low over his face, keeping his eyes in the shadows. In shotgun was a younger woman with blonde hair. She waved at them as the vehicle crunched by.

Rex and Tabitha returned the gesture. Bobby did too, while Ellie kept both hands securely cradling the chipmunk against her chest.

Then the truck was gone around another bend.

"Well," Rex said as the sound of the motor dwindled, "at least now we know we're not the only people out here."

CHAPTER 4

They arrived at the cabin just as the sky began to spit small and icy droplets of rain. The cabin stood twenty feet from the road, surrounded by a variety of mature evergreens and deciduous trees, the leaves of the latter blazing fiery colors.

In an age of pre-fabricated building material where everything was perfectly square or symmetrical, the idiosyncrasies of the cabin afforded it an old-world charm: the stacked logs with their rough axe cuts and corner notches, the slapdash gray chinking to seal the spaces between the logs, the hand-peeled porch railings, the crumbling stone chimney.

Tabitha clutched Rex's arm. "Oh Rex, it's lovely."

"Amazing what you can do with a broad axe and mallet," he said.

"Can we go inside?" Ellie asked.

"That's the plan," he said.

They swished through a carpet of browning leaves to the covered porch. The wood planks moaned loudly beneath their footsteps. Rex stopped before the door and tried the cast-iron handle. It turned with a rusty gargle, and the door swung inward.

"Glad it's unlocked," he said. "I don't have keys."

"You're kidding?" Tabitha said.

"I haven't had anything to do with this place since I was seven."

"What would you have done if it was locked?"

"Broken a window, I guess."

Rex stepped inside the cabin. He scrunched his nose at the dank, musty odor.

"Ewww," Ellie said, pushing past his legs. "What's that smell?"

"It will go away when we open some windows, sweetie," Tabitha said.

Rex glanced around the room, surprised by how familiar it was to him. The teak sofa upholstered in drab earth tones; the Edison-style light bulbs in the brass fixtures; the rocking chair where his mother had read him C.S. Lewis's *Prince Caspian* on a particularly rainy weekend; the wood-paneled television set, which had required bunny ears to pull in its only channel. The pair of antique ice block tongs he'd once taken off the wall and used to terrorize Logan. The little tin sign that read AN OLD BEAR LIVES HERE WITH HIS HONEY.

A hand-carved bookcase held several foxed paperbacks and hardcovers bookended between art deco flying geese. On the uppermost shelf were three silver-framed photographs. The first was a studio shot of his parents, his mother's auburn hair fashioned into a perm, his father's parted neatly down the side and the same rich brown as his mustache. The second was of Logan wearing a Gobots tee shirt and smiling to reveal the gap between his front teeth. And the third was of Rex who, with his blonde hair and blue eyes and dimples, bore a more-than-passing resemblance to Bobby.

Swallowing tightly, Rex looked away.

"Where can I put my chippymunk?" Ellie asked, stopping in the center of the room.

Rex retrieved a hand-painted wooden box from next to the sofa, dumped the stack of dusty magazines onto the teak coffee table in front of the television, and set the empty box next to the magazines. "That should do," he said.

Ellie gently set the chipmunk into the box, then passed Rex back his windbreaker. He hung it on a wall-mounted coat rack fashioned from a barn-red bucksaw.

Ellie studied the rodent closely. "Is she going to be okay, Mommy?" she asked.

"How do you know it's a 'she?'" Tabitha asked.

"Because boys are dumb, and I want it to be a girl like me."

"I think she'll be okay for now. Once we're settled in, we'll get her some water and a little bit of food to nibble on."

"Where's my bed?"

"There's a small second floor," Rex said. "You and Bobby will sleep up there."

"Where are the stairs?"

"In the next room."

"Beat you to them!" Bobby said, darting around the afghan hanging in the doorway that separated this room from the next.

"No fair!" Ellie said, giving chase. "You got a head start! No fair!"

"Be careful!" Rex called after them. "The stairs are steep!"

Tabitha dumped her shoulder bag on the floor. "This place is perfect," she said. "It really is."

"Can't believe it's just been…here…unoccupied for so long." He shrugged. "Better take the groceries to the kitchen."

The adjoining room featured a stone fireplace, a roughly hewn timber staircase that led to the attic, and a seventies-style kitchen complete with linoleum floor tiles, Formica counter tops, and an ergonomic dining table complete with four tubular steel stools. There was a harvest-gold Kelvinator refrigerator, a stove the same horrid color with a stacked-stone backsplash, and an avocado-green toaster.

"Whoa," Tabitha said. "I wasn't expecting Carol Brady's kitchen."

"I remember my father doing the 'upgrades,'" Rex said. "He and my mom had been pretty proud of the finished product." He set the groceries on the table and opened the cupboard above the sink. It was stocked with plates, bowls, and glasses, though these were all littered with mouse droppings.

"Good thing we bought paper plates and plastic cutlery," Tabitha remarked.

Rex tried the sink tap. Not a drop of water.

"I'm guessing there's no electricity either," Tabitha said, opening the fridge door with a sticky pop of the gasket seal. She immediately spun away, a hand going to her mouth.

Rex caught the stench a second later and glanced inside the fridge. It was filled with all sorts of different-shaped items—everything covered with a layer of putrefied mold and mildew.

He slammed the door shut.

"Gross!" he exclaimed, then, seeing the green look on Tabitha's face, couldn't help but laugh. "Guess we're not having leftovers."

"It's not funny!" she said. "I hope I didn't breathe in any of those spores."

"We're going to have to lock up the fridge somehow so the kids don't go opening it."

"I can still smell that stench. It's like..."

"Maybe it's time to air out the place."

They spent the next few minutes opening all the windows, letting the stale air out and the fresh alpine air in.

"Much better," Tabitha said, inhaling deeply.

"After we light some candles, we'll be all set."

"Dad!" Bobby yelled from the attic.

"What is it?" Rex asked, facing the staircase.

"Which bed can I have?"

"There are only two. You choose."

"This one!"

"I want that one!" Ellie challenged.

"I called it!" he said.

"I called it first!" she said.

"Did not!" he said. "Dad!"

"If you two can't work it out, then you'll have to flip a coin."

Silence. Then their voices lowered as they entered serious negotiations.

Tabitha said, "I'm a bit scared to ask, but if there's no water, what do we do for a toilet?"

"Right." Rex scratched his head. "Well, water used to get

pumped up from the lake. But the pump needs electricity. There's a big old diesel generator in the shed we used to use for electricity. Hopefully it will fire up. I was going to have a look at it tomorrow. For now, I'll go fetch a couple of buckets of water from the lake. Pouring it slowly into the bowl should make the toilet flush."

"And if I can't wait…?"

"You need to go that badly?"

She nodded. "I should have gone when Bobby did at the tourist center."

"In that case, there's an outhouse not too far away…"

She groaned. "I was worried you might say that." She tugged free the KittenSoft toilet paper from one of the grocery bags, tore the plastic packaging open, and grabbed a roll.

They went outside. The sky was still spitting, though the droplets didn't have enough weight behind them to be anything more than a cold nuisance.

Rex pointed. Fifty feet away the outhouse loomed rickety and ominous in the gathering dark.

"Inviting," Tabitha said.

"You can go behind a tree," he said.

"I love having a choice."

"I'll be back up in a few."

ΔΔΔ

Holding her arms in front of her to deflect branches from her face, Tabitha made her way through the trees toward the outhouse. It was a fair hike from the cabin, she thought, but the location made sense. You didn't want a stinking hole in the ground near your residence, did you?

Tabitha experienced a sudden swelling of warmth in her chest—for Rex, for the cabin that time forgot, for the opportunity to be here with Ellie and Bobby for the weekend.

Getting away from the city was not only what Rex needed,

but what she needed too. The untangling of her life from her ex, Jacob, had been taking an enormous emotional toll on her, to the point where the stress of it had caused her to break down in spontaneous tears on more than a few occasions of late.

When Tabitha and Jacob had first met, Jacob had been a software developer for Microsoft and had often traveled to conferences around the country. In the early days of their relationship, Tabitha had missed him terribly on these occasions. Then the weekends away turned into three or four days away, then full weeks at a time. Jacob told her the increase in travel was due to a promotion he'd received, and she bought that for a while. But then his attitude toward her began to change. He became aloof, easily annoyed. Communication seemed an effort. Tabitha was convinced he was having an affair, and she confided this to Cindy Chew, a friend she'd known since college. Cindy ended up asking her husband Danny if he had any dirt on Jacob, because Danny also worked at Microsoft's headquarters in Redmond, though in a different department. The dirt relayed back to Tabitha had been heartbreaking and mindboggling: Jacob was a notorious womanizer who had hit on half the women working in his department. The mindboggling part: several of these women had filed sexual harassment suits against him, and he had been fired more than a year ago now. Tabitha confronted him that evening, they fought, he became violent, and she left with the girls, fearing for her safety. The following day she hired a divorce attorney—and in the process of sorting through their financial situation, she learned Jacob had been manipulating their books behind her back, and they were effectively broke.

Tabitha had always suspected Jacob had a gambling addiction (though he'd done well to hide or downplay it over the years), and she instinctively knew it was this addiction that had swallowed their life savings. However, knowing something and proving it in court were two very different things. The judge overseeing the custody litigation wanted evidence, not accusations, and that evidence was proving to be frustratingly circumstantial and elusive. Tabitha had retained the services of a private investigator in the hopes of tailing Jacob to one of his gambling dens, but either Jacob was aware of the tail or at least suspected it, and he was refraining from gambling in public, or he had moved his habit online, which he could do in the privacy of wherever he was living these days.

Currently the investigator was combing the accounts of multiple online bookies and gambling operations. So far he'd found no links to Jacob, and if this didn't change before the divorce proceedings began in a fortnight, Jacob could win joint legal and physical custody of the girls, which would throw their lives into chaos—

No, Tabitha thought angrily. *I'm not going to think about this now. I'll deal with everything in a couple of days when I'm back in Seattle. Not now. This is my time with Rex and Ellie and Bobby.*

Jacob isn't going to ruin that.

Tabitha stopped before the outhouse. It was a humble and utilitarian structure that appeared to be one push away from falling over. Horizontal wooden planks had been nailed, Band-Aid-like, over gaps where vertical boards had fallen away.

After a brief hesitation, Tabitha creaked open the door, which featured a star cut-out to allow ventilation and light into the stall. Cobwebs dusted the dank ceiling and walls, but a perfunctory glance did not reveal any eight-legged creepy crawlies. The toilet seat was nothing but a piece of wood with a hole in the middle of it. She peeked down the hole into the pit latrine. There was no smell, as any untreated waste would have decomposed years ago.

Did she really have to sit over that? But what other option was there? Go behind a tree as Rex suggested? That was almost preferable...

Carefully, Tabitha laid out toilet paper on the seat. She undid her belt and pushed down her jeans and underwear. She couldn't hear her urine hit the bottom of the pit, which made her wonder as to the depth of the hole.

What if some animal was down there? A family of raccoons

or rats? What if she was peeing on them? What if they climbed up and...?

What? Bit her in the butt?

Suddenly and alarmingly, a sharp crack sounded outside the outhouse, the distinct sound of a branch splitting in two.

Her bladder froze.

"Hello?" she said.

Nobody replied.

"Rex?" she said, knowing he wasn't out there; if he was, he would have announced his presence.

An animal then?

Would have to be a pretty large animal...

A bear?

God, she hoped not!

She finished her business, yanked up her jeans, and secured her belt. She inched open the door and poked her head out. The forest was dark and cold and silent. The gray sky continued to spit rain. She looked to the left, the direction where the sound had originated.

Nobody was there. No animals either.

But she hadn't imagined the sound.

Folding her arms to ward against a chill that had nothing to do with the foul October weather, she hurried back to the cabin.

ΔΔΔ

After collecting two plastic buckets from the shed behind the cabin, Rex picked his way down the pine needle-covered hill to the lake, following a path that was no longer visible but that he remembered vaguely from his youth. The massive conifers he passed beneath eclipsed the darkening sky and made him feel small and unimportant, a reminder that they had been standing here long before he had been born and would remain long after he had died.

When he emerged from the last of the saplings and

sagebrush, he stopped to take in the view of the still lake, which, in the dying minutes of dusk, spread away from him like a narrow black abyss. A dock supported by pontoons had once floated on the water a little way out. Now it was gone, likely destroyed by the ice that scabbed over the lake in the wintertime. The only indication it had ever existed were the skeletal remains of the gangway pilings that had linked it to the rocky shore.

In the distance, the haunting wail of a loon echoed over the dark water, sounding eerily like the howl of a wolf. A different wail answered it a moment later, though this one more closely resembled the crazy laugh of a hyena.

Man, I've missed this place, he thought to himself as a kaleidoscope of memories rose to the forefront of his mind. All the summer afternoons he had spent down here as a kid with Logan on inflatable rafts and tires that always seemed to lose their air. Snorkeling with their ill-fitting rubber fins and cheap K-Mart scuba masks, the head straps of which had all snapped so you had to rely on air pressure to keep it suctioned to your face. Fishing for sturgeon and trout, char and steelhead. And just goofing off in the sun doing kid stuff while their mom watched on from beneath a rainbow-colored parasol.

Pushing aside the nostalgic images before they overwhelmed him, Rex continued to the lake where he filled both buckets with ice-cold water. He scanned the rocky shore to the west until he spotted where the pump's black intake pipe emerged from the water. He followed it with his eyes to the pump house twenty feet or so inland. He went to the small structure, pleased to note it appeared to have weathered the years well, keeping its four walls and shingled lid intact. He set the buckets on the ground and opened the lid. His optimism that the pump might be serviceable went up in smoke. The pressure tank and valves and pipes were so covered in rust they looked like they might have been salvaged from the *Titanic*. He tried a valve, and it snapped off in his hand.

Guess nobody's going to be showering this weekend, he thought with a sigh as he picked up the buckets of water and returned up the hill.

He found Tabitha sitting with Ellie in the front room of the cabin, both of them studying the chipmunk.

"How's it doing?" he asked. "Sorry—*she*?"

"She won't eat," Ellie said. "We gave her some banana and peanut butter, but she won't eat. She won't drink her water either."

"She's probably just a bit overwhelmed by everything that's happened to her. Imagine if a family of giants picked you up and brought you to a strange place."

"Come on, Miss Chippy! Get it together!"

"Whoa there, sweetie!" Tabitha said. "Cut the little critter some slack. One of her legs might be broken. Each time she tries to get up, she falls over on the same side."

Rex had a look at the chipmunk. It lay on its belly. "Broken leg's not good," he said. "But the vet should be able to do something about that."

"Do we *have* to give her to the vet?" Ellie asked.

"We had a deal, Missy," Tabitha said pointedly.

"But if we give her away," Ellie complained, "I won't ever get to see her again. But if we let her go here, then she'll be here when we come back again, and I can be friends with her every summer until one of us dies first."

"I hope it's the chipmunk that dies first," Rex remarked amusedly.

"I hope it's me," Ellie said, "so I won't be so sad when she dies."

"Don't say that, sweetie," Tabitha said with a note of motherly concern in her voice. "You're going to live much longer than a chipmunk. And you're being a bit presumptuous to think that Rex will want us to come up here every summer. He might never want us to come back."

Tabitha kept her attention fixed on the chipmunk, but Rex sensed the statement was for him as much as it was for her daughter.

"Of course I'd like you guys to come back," he said.

"That's good news!" Tabitha said playfully. "Isn't that good news, sweetie?"

"Do we have to wait all the way to next summer?" Ellie asked. "I'll already be six by then."

"To be honest, I haven't given it any thought, Ellie," Rex said. "But if that's too long to wait…how about Christmas?"

"Really?" Tabitha said, looking up at him.

"Why not? The fireplace would heat the place. We could bring up some portable gas heaters too if we needed to make it extra toasty."

"But will Santa be able to find us here?" Ellie asked skeptically.

"Don't worry about Santa Claus, sweetie," Tabitha said. "He has a list with the addresses of every child in the world. He'll find us."

"Does he use Google Maps?"

"His list is much better than Google Maps."

"Okay!" she decided. "Then let's have Christmas here! We can even use a Christmas tree from right outside."

"Let's not get ahead of ourselves, hon. Christmas is still a couple of months away. It's not even Halloween yet."

"Can we have Halloween here too?"

"You've opened Pandora's Box," Tabitha said to Rex with a smile.

"My bad—do people still say that? Oh—and now for some genuinely bad news. The generator looked fine in the shed. I think it should fire up tomorrow. But the pump down at the lake has gone kaput. Which means we'll probably have electricity, but we won't have any water except what we lug up from the lake in buckets."

"So I don't have to have a bath tonight?" Ellie asked happily.

"Or tomorrow," Rex said.

"Yeah!"

"But that also means when you need to use the potty," Tabitha said, "you're going to have to pour water into the bowl to make it flush. I'll show you how before bedtime."

"Speaking of toilets," Rex said, "how was the outhouse?"

"Ugh," she said. "However, I did appreciate the star cutout in the door. Bit of a change from the usual crescent moon."

"Ah," Rex said, holding up a finger, "here's something that might come in handy on your next trivia night..."

"Our resident armchair polymath," Tabitha remarked.

Rex would consider himself more of a humble trivia buff than an armchair polymath, but in any event, he did love learning, and one of his favorite studies of interest was how mundane things people took for granted in the present originally came into being. He said, "The tradition of carving symbols into the doors of privies began in the early eighteen hundreds because back then most of the population was illiterate."

"What's illyate?" Ellie asked.

"Illiterate," Tabitha said, "means you can't read or write."

"I'm not illyate. I know uppercase *and* lowercase."

"A sun was usually used on the men's door," Rex went on, "and a moon on the women's. But over time, when restrooms with plumbing began to replace outhouses, the outhouses that were first to be torn down were the men's, because they were never as well kept up as the women's. Eventually the only outhouses left were women's with the moons on the doors. These became unisex—and the reason why the crescent moon is the symbol for all outhouses today."

"Where do you read this stuff?" Tabitha said, shaking her head.

"Gotta read something on the long-haul flights. Like everybody says, planes fly themselves these days."

"So you have yourself an original gem out there?"

"The outhouse? I suppose so. Maybe I should put it up on eBay? Where's Bobby?"

"He's upstairs in bed," Ellie said, her attention once again on the chipmunk. "He doesn't like being here with just my mom when you're not here too."

"*Ellie*," Tabitha said sharply, color rising in her cheeks.

"I'll go check on him," he said.

Rex went to the next room and climbed the steep staircase,

deciding that he'd block off the top with cushions from the sofa later on, so the kids didn't inadvertently stumble down them if they got up during the night.

The attic was an oblong triangular-shaped room. A window at each end allowed light during the daytime. The hodgepodge collection of furniture included a chest he knew was filled with children's books, an old dining room set in a corner, a rocking horse in another corner, a metal filing cabinet, and a small dresser. A threadbare red rug of Native American design covered part of the floor.

Bobby lay on his belly in one of two handmade beds, the LED flashlight he kept on his single-key keychain clutched in one hand, the bright beam illuminated a book open before him.

Rex crossed the room, bending so he didn't smack his head on the exposed beams of the pitched roof. He sat on the edge of the bed.

"What're you reading, bud?" he asked.

Bobby showed him the cover. "Sesame Street."

"Good?"

"So-so."

A few other books from the chest were beside him. Rex picked up the top one. *The Secret of the Old Mill*. The 1950s-illustrated cover showed Joe and Frank Hardy peeking between a gap in the floorboards of the eponymous old mill—and if Rex's memory served him correctly, the plot had something to do with counterfeit money.

"Isn't it a bit early to be up here in bed?" he asked his son lightly.

"I'm not sleeping," Bobby said. "Daddy?"

"Yeah, bud?"

"Why do my little things hurt when I squeeze them? My intesticles? They're not even attached to my body."

Rex blinked. That certainly hadn't been the question he'd been expecting. "Well, first of all," he said, "I think you're mixing up your testicles and intestines. Your testicles are down by your penis, while your intestines are inside your stomach. As to why your testicles are so sensitive, I don't know. Maybe it's your body's way of telling you not to go get them all banged up, because they're important in making babies."

"Do you have to kiss a girl to make babies?"

"You have to do a bit more than that, bud. But let's leave that discussion for another time. Ellie and Tabitha are trying to feed the chipmunk downstairs. Do you want to come back down and feed it too?"

"No," he said simply and lowered his eyes.

Rex considered giving him another lecture about his mother, how she would be coming back soon, how Tabitha wasn't taking her place and never would. But instead he said, "Want to see something cool?"

Bobby perked up. "What is it?"

"It's a surprise. It's outside."

"*What is it?*"

"I'll show you. C'mon."

Rex led the way back downstairs to where Ellie and Tabitha were still fussing over the chipmunk.

"He eating yet?" Rex asked them.

"No," Ellie said despondently.

Bobby pulled on his shoes. "I'm getting a surprise!" he said.

"What is it?" Ellie asked, alarmed she wasn't in on the know.

"My dad's going to show me something *cool*."

"I want to see it too!"

"This is only for Bobby now, Ellie," Rex said. "You can see it tomorrow."

"That's not fair!"

"That's enough, Ellie," Tabitha said. "You can stay here with me. Rex said he'll show you tomorrow."

"But I want to see it *now*."

"We won't be long," Rex said, retrieving from his overnight bag the Maglite flashlight he'd packed. "And when we get back we'll roast some wieners over a fire. How does that sound?"

"Poop head!"

"*Ellie!*" Tabitha said, stunned.

"Come on, bud," Rex said softly, ushering Bobby outside to escape the inevitable melodrama that was about to play out.

He closed the door just as Tabitha told Ellie she had lost her iPad privileges during the car ride home, and Ellie shrieked in indignation.

Rex took Bobby's hand and led him away. It had stopped raining, and a damp heaviness weighed over the forest.

"Is she going to cry again?" Bobby asked gleefully.

"That's not for you to worry about."

Playing the flashlight beam ahead of them, Rex picked a path through the dense growth of trees, the ghostly trunks of which all looked the same in the black of night. He thought he was heading in the right direction, but after a hundred paces or so, with each step taking them deeper into the woods, he began to second-guess himself.

Then he saw it.

"There!" he said, aiming the yellow beam at the wreck.

"What is it, Daddy?" Bobby asked.

"Let's go have a closer look."

"A car!" Bobby exclaimed as they drew closer. "It's a car!"

It was indeed a car—some type of Ford, according to the hood ornament and badge, and one probably dating back to the 1920s or 30s.

The years had certainly not been kind to it. Rust had eaten large holes through much of its body, which appeared to have once been painted tan. At some point someone had taken its four tires, so it sat flat on the axles and black fenders. The fifth wire wheel remained mounted to the trunk. Only tattered scraps of the canvas convertible top remained .

Rex hiked Bobby into his arms so he could see inside the car —though there was little to see save for the aged steering wheel and the brown seats spilling their guts of foam and springs.

"What do you think, bud?" he said. "Pretty cool, huh?"

"How'd it get way out here?" Bobby asked, clearly in awe.

The story Rex's father had told Rex and Logan went something like this: The car belonged to an old prospector named Barry White. Barry had amassed a small fortune during the Cayoosh Gold Rush, but his wealth had turned him paranoid over time. Believing his partner was planning on robbing him, Barry invited the man over for dinner one evening and sunk an axe in his back. Barry dumped the corpse into the trunk of his car and went looking for a spot to bury it. Unfortunately for him, he drove off the road and crashed into a tree. Injured but alive, Barry left the wreck where it was and resumed his life as normal. And to this day—cue the *dun dun dun*—the remains of his partner could still be found in the trunk of the car.

Unsurprisingly, the Legend of Barry White had given Rex and Logan nightmares for the rest of the summer, and Rex wasn't going to make this same mistake by passing on the story to Bobby, so he simply said, "There used to be a road—more of a dirt path—through the forest. The driver of this car crashed into a tree and left it right here. Over the years the woods grew up around the car and the road disappeared."

"Can we open the trunk?" Bobby asked.

Rex frowned. "Why would you want to do that?"

"Maybe there's gold inside?"

"Oh, well—no. We don't need to do that. The metal's all sharp and rusted. If it cuts you, you could get tetanus—"

Something loud and large crashed through the undergrowth perhaps fifty feet away. Rex whipped the flashlight left and right in alarm, throwing yellow ribbons through the night.

"Daddy?" Bobby said, worried.

Rex barely heard him.

A deer? A bear? A cougar?

Jesus Christ, where did it go?

"Daddy!"

"It's okay, bud," he said in a harsh whisper. "It was just a deer. But we should probably start back now."

Holding Bobby tightly against his chest, Rex heeded his own advice, resisting the urge to run.

CHAPTER 5

Tabitha had set the Oscar Meyer wieners and buns out on two paper plates on the kitchen counter, and she was dicing onions and tomatoes when Rex and Bobby returned.

Bobby burst past the afghan into the room, saying, "We saw a deer!" When he found only Tabitha in the kitchen, he clamped his mouth shut.

"Ellie's having a Time-Out right now," Tabitha said.

"Can I come down?" Ellie called from the attic.

"Are you going to be polite?"

"Yes!"

"Then I suppose so."

Footsteps darted across the ceiling, then down the stairs. Ellie skidded to a stop before Bobby. "You saw a deer?" she asked excitedly. "Like Bambi?"

"We didn't actually *see* anything," Rex said, pushing past the afghan. "We *heard* one."

Tabitha frowned as she remembered the sound outside the outhouse. Was that what she'd heard too? A deer? The same one? But wouldn't it have made more noise than the snapping of a single stick?

"It was really noisy!" Bobby said, as if in answer to her thoughts. "It was like..." By the expression on his face, he didn't seem to know how to replicate the sound, and instead he ran in circles around the room, mimicking the sound of a motor by blowing air through his pressed lips.

"So—the deer was the surprise?" Tabitha asked, confused. How did you organize to hear a deer in the wild?

"No, there was a car—" Bobby said before realizing to whom he was speaking.

"A car?" Ellie said.

Tabitha looked questioningly at Rex. He nodded. "It's been there for close to a hundred years. You guys can see it tomorrow. But right now let's get cooking. It's stopped raining, and I'm starving."

Rex carried the wieners and buns outside, Tabitha the onions and tomatoes and condiments. They set everything on the ground next to a ring of weathered stones that would serve as the fire pit. Rex collected the stringy shavings from the bark of a nearby cedar, which he rubbed quickly between his hands to create a small fluff ball. He used this as tinder, as well as the papery bark from a birch, to encourage a few nascent flames into existence, over which he added scavenged twigs and sticks for kindle, as well as larger deadwood. Ten minutes later they were sitting around a decent-sized fire, roasting wieners impaled on sticks.

"Smell that air, guys," Rex said. "How fresh is that?"

Ellie sniffed exaggeratedly. "Smells like the beginning of the world," she said straight-faced.

Rex and Tabitha laughed.

"What?" Ellie asked.

"You're beyond your years sometimes, sweetheart," Tabitha said.

"Can I have some Coke?" Bobby asked.

"I left the bottle in the car, bud," Rex told him. "It was too heavy to carry with all the other groceries. I'll go back and get it tomorrow."

"Can we roast weenies tomorrow night too?"

"That's the plan."

"What's for lunch tomorrow?" Ellie asked.

"Tuna fish sandwiches," Tabitha said.

"Do we have pickles too?"

"No pickles."

"I think your wiener's done, Bobby," Rex said. "Better pull it out or it's going to fall off."

Tabitha snickered at the double entendre. Bobby carefully removed his stick from the flames, but before he could get the wiener to his paper plate it slipped loose and fell to the ground.

"Oh no!" Bobby said, a look of devastation on his face.

"It's okay," Rex said quickly. "Have this one." He lowered his wiener over Bobby's plate. "Just pluck it off with your fingers. But be careful. It will be hot."

"Ow!" he said.

"I told you it will be hot."

"Yuck!" Ellie blurted, making a face.

"What's wrong?" Tabitha asked.

"I don't like that mustard!" She pointed to the bottle of Dijon mustard on the ground next to the regular mustard.

"That's adult mustard, honey. It's a bit stronger, that's all."

"I-I-I hate it," she sputtered, her cheeks coloring, her jaw setting, her eyes glowering—all the telltale signs of one of her temper tantrums. "And now. My life. Is ruined."

To avert a total meltdown, Tabitha said, "Guess what we have for dessert, guys?"

Silence.

Bobby was clearly curious but wouldn't speak to her.

Ellie seemed torn between curiosity and defiance, but put her concern over her ruined life temporarily on hold and asked, "What, Mommy?"

"S'mores! They're a kind of marshmallow sandwich."

"There's no such thing!"

"There sure is, sweetie. I had them all the time when I was your age."

"When were you my age?"

"A long time ago."

"When you were just like me but smaller than now?"

"That's right. Anyway, make a new wiener with the normal mustard, and I'll go fetch the ingredients we need."

While the kids finished up their dinner, Tabitha went inside and collected the graham crackers and marshmallows. Returning outside, she recalled she had banned Ellie from having dessert, but she decided to turn a blind eye to the punishment. This night was special for everybody.

She was just approaching the fire again when Ellie cried out, "Ewww!" She pointed at Bobby. "He's letting it bite him!"

"What's going on, bud?" Rex asked him.

"I'm letting the mosquita have dinner too." He held forth his right hand proudly to reveal a mosquito, plump with his blood, stuck to his wrist.

"Flick it off, Bobby," Rex said.

"Do I have to?" he said.

"You heard me."

"But I want to keep it as a pet."

"You can't keep a mosquito as a pet."

"Ellie got the chipmunk!"

"Not for keeps."

"I can put it in my Tic Tac container."

"How are you going to feed it? They only eat blood."

"I can give it mine."

"You're not a human blood bank, bud. Now flick it away."

Reluctantly, Bobby nudged the insect with his finger. It didn't move.

"It's too fat to fly!" Ellie crowed.

"Just give it a good flick," Rex said.

Bobby tried again. This time, however, he accidentally squished the bug flat, staring in surprise at the smear of blood it left behind on his skin.

"Gross!" Ellie said.

"And the moral of this story," Tabitha said, "is to not be greedy."

"Or risk getting struck down by a..." Rex trailed off.

Tabitha looked where he was looking and saw a light bobbing amongst the trees.

"Who could that be?" she said, frowning.

"Probably the neighbors," Rex said. "Must have heard us and are coming by to say hi."

"But the road... Do people still come out here?" She remembered the pickup truck. "That couple who passed us...?"

"Maybe," Rex said.

It would be an innocuous encounter, surely—this wasn't the city; people in the country were friendly—but Tabitha nevertheless felt a shiver of unease. "Kids," she said, "I think it's time to call it a night."

"But we haven't even had the S'mores!" Ellie said.

"We'll save them for tomorrow night."

"But you promised!"

"What did I promise? You can have the S'mores tomorrow, or none at all."

"Oh, crud!" she said, kicking at the dirt. "Tomorrow's *forever* away."

"The faster you go to sleep," Rex said, "the faster it will come."

"Is that true?"

"One hundred percent."

Ellie relented. "I guess I'll go to sleep really fast."

"That's a very good decision, sweetie," Tabitha said. "Now say goodnight to T-Rex."

"See you later, alligator," she said.

"In a while, crocodile," he replied, reciting their old joke.

"C'mon, guys, let's go brush our teeth." Tabitha looked at Rex. "I'll be back out shortly."

"Sure," he said. "I'll be here."

ΔΔΔ

Rex fussed with the fire, stoking the ashes with a stick to reinvigorate the winnowing flames, all the while keeping an eye on the foreign flashlight beam, which continued to move in his direction. He wasn't concerned by the neighbor's unexpected arrival. Inconvenienced was more like it. He wanted to spend the evening with Tabitha, not strangers.

When he could make out the silhouettes of two people, he rose from his crouch and faced them. It was indeed the couple from the pickup truck. The blonde woman wore a blueberry quilted jacket over a black turtleneck, tight jeans, and white high tops. The man had exchanged the Stetson for an oilskin mesh-back trucker cap. Despite the fact it couldn't have been any warmer than forty degrees out, he wore neither jacket nor sweater, only a black Metallica tee-shirt that revealed beefy biceps. A black belt that featured a flashy silver buckle held up stonewashed jeans. He gripped the flashlight in one hand, a tallboy can of Molson Canadian beer in the other. He had been limping, and now he stood with his weight favoring his left leg.

"Hi," Rex said. "I'm Rex."

"Hi!" the woman said, shaking. "Daisy." Her skin was icy cold.

The man made no effort to set aside the flashlight or beer can to shake his hand. "Tony Lyons," he said simply. His eyes were bright blue and serious.

"Saw you guys on our way in," Rex said. "Didn't know the road was going to be so bad. Forced us to leave the car behind and walk."

"It's been like that for years now," Daisy said. "Nobody comes out here nowadays."

"They don't like the view?" he said lightly.

She chuckled. Tony's face remained impassive.

"Are you next door?" Rex asked. "The place with the big deck...?"

"No, no," Daisy said. "Do you know the Williams' cottage? It's about two klicks down the road."

"Fair walk to get here," he remarked.

"We wanted to meet the one and only Rex Chapman," Tony said, smirking.

Rex hadn't told the man his last name, but he figured anyone who grew up in Lillooet would have heard about Rex—or more specifically, what happened to his family. Small towns talk, and remember. "Are you from around here?" he asked, guessing the man to be roughly his own age.

"Around," Tony said, draining his beer. He crushed the can in his fist and tossed it onto the fire, which irked Rex, as he would be the one picking the can out of the ashes tomorrow. "Spent a lot of time with the oil and gas companies up north. Tough as fuck work. People get injured. Some die. You living in Vancouver now, I bet?"

Rex studied Tony. The man's barb had been perfectly clear. He may as well have said, "You're a fruitcake office worker, I bet?"

"No, not Vancouver," he said.

"City boy?"

"You don't like cities?"

"Don't care much for the people from 'em. Pussies, most of 'em."

So the gloves were off, Rex thought. The question was why. What was this guy's problem?

He looked at Daisy. Her smile had faltered. He decided to remain pleasant for her sake. "And you? Are you from around here too?"

She nodded. "Lived all my life here."

"So you're friends of the Williams?"

"No, I never met them."

Rex frowned. "But you're staying at their place?"

"They're dead," she said with a shrug. "Been dead for a long time now. Their place just sits there empty, so sometimes we come down here for a bit of a vacation, I guess you would call it."

"You're *squatting*?"

"Oh, we don't stay long or nothing," she insisted. "We just come down for the night usually. We leave in the morning. We stayed at the Starr's place once. They're not dead. They just don't come out here no more. But we like the Williams' place the best. It has a fireplace and is practically right on top of the water. Don't worry though. We've never stayed here in yours!"

Rex was baffled. "Given the condition of the road," he said, "I figured people didn't come out here much anymore. But *never*?"

"Never ever," Daisy said. "Except us, course. You're the first person we've seen since we began coming..." She looked at Tony. "How long now, babe? Four or five years?"

"What do you do?" Tony asked him.

"I'm a pilot," Rex said, caught off guard by the abrupt change of conversation.

"You fly one of those commercial things?"

"An Airbus 380."

"I got me a single-engine Cessna. Use it to get to the oil and gas fields. You have to actually fly a Cessna. No autopilot bullshit."

Rex had had enough of the jerk's condescending attitude. "What is it?" he asked. "A 172?"

Tony nodded. "172RG Cutlass. Four-seat, single-engine."

"One-fifty, one-sixty horsepower?"

"One eighty," Tony said proudly. "Got the more powerful O-360 in her."

"Nice," Rex said appreciatively. "But not quite the same as having four eighteen-hundred-horsepower Rolls-Royce engines under you, is it? That's what? Eight thousand horsepower all told?"

Tony's eyes darkened.

"So—anyway!" Daisy said, intervening. "We just wanted to say hi. Meet the famous Rex Chapman! We knew right away it was you." She pointed to her head.

It took Rex a moment to realize what she meant. His white hair.

"Famous?" he said, unimpressed by the crass choice of an adjective. Did losing your family in a boating accident grant you celebrity status?

"Well, you know, because of everything that's happened," Daisy said. "You were the start of it."

Rex was dumbfounded. "What are you talking about?"

She seemed equally stunned that he was in the dark. "You mean...you don't know?"

"Don't know what?"

"Hey, Rexy," Tony said. "You gonna offer your guest a beer?"

"I don't have any," he said.

"Don't got no beer?"

"I don't drink beer."

"Ah, right. You a wine man?" That smirk.

"I don't drink at all."

"That so?"

"That's so."

"What you hiding?"

Rex blinked. "Excuse me?"

"All the teetotalers I know, they don't drink 'cause they got issues. They drink, and it all comes gushing out. All the tears and shit and everything. They just come fucking apart."

Rex had quit drinking after a night out at university. He'd drunk so much spiced rum at a frat party that he woke in the bushes behind the house with no memory of the preceding few hours. He'd been covered in vomit and knew if he'd passed out on his back and not on his front he likely would have choked to death. During the three-day hangover that followed this epiphany, he'd decided alcohol wasn't for him—and he'd simply never imbibed any more since.

Rex wasn't going to tell Tony this, of course, and so he returned his attention to Daisy. "What don't I know?" he asked.

"Everything that's happened since you left! The guy who... who got your family...he got—"

"*The guy who got my family?*" he said, incensed. Deciding he was the butt of a bad joke, he added: "I don't know what the hell you two are getting at, or what rumors have been spun about my family over the years up here in Hicksville, Nobody Cares, but nobody 'got' my family, and I think it's in extremely bad taste to come onto my property spreading such nonsense. They drowned in a boating accident. Now I think we're done here. You should both leave."

"Oh Rexy," Tony said, shaking his head. "How naïve do you think we are? Drowned?" He barked a laugh. "Where did the bodies go if they drowned? Pavilion Lake ain't the Pacific Ocean. They would've washed up eventually."

Rex frowned. The bodies were never found? He hadn't been aware of this. He'd only known what his Uncle Henry had told him when he came to Lillooet to take Rex back to Vancouver all those years ago. *They drowned, Rex. I'm sorry to have to tell you that, and I don't want you to think too much about it. There's no point thinking about what you can't change. You got a new life now to focus on.*

"If my family didn't drown," Rex said tightly, fighting the thick air of unreality washing over him, "do you want to tell me what happened to them? Who's this guy you mentioned?"

"We don't know exactly," Daisy said. "What I meant was, whoever got your family must have been a guy, a man. That's all I meant. No woman could, you know, make so many families just disappear."

Rex almost fell over. "Other people have gone missing too?"

She nodded. "That's what I was trying to tell ya. A whole lot of other people. I was only two years old when you left, so I don't recall anything that happened with your family and everything. I mean, I don't have *my* memories of that. Just what people told me when I got older. Like your hair and stuff. But I was eight when the Petersons disappeared. And I remember *that*."

"The Petersons?" Rex said, his heart pounding. They had been friends of his parents and had stopped by occasionally for cocktails. He seemed to recall Mrs. Peterson always having a cigarette in her hand.

"They were from Vancouver," Daisy said. "They only came up here in the summers. Always hosted a game of bridge on Friday nights. But one Friday they just weren't home. Car was there and everything, but they just wouldn't answer the door. Friends got concerned and called Paulsy who had a look around—"

"Paulsy?" Rex said.

"The police chief. He was still just a kid then. Didn't find any clues or nothing of what happened to the Petersons, and that got everybody talking. You know, because of how your family just disappeared six years earlier. Even the TV was talking about it. I remember everybody on my street going to one of the neighbors' to watch a story about it on the six o'clock news."

"There were no suspects?" Rex said. "No theories?"

"Suspects, no. Theories? Yeah, everybody had a theory."

"You got a theory, Rex?" Tony asked him.

"Me? My uncle told me my family died in a boating accident. I was seven. I believed him. And to tell you the truth, I'm still not sure everything I'm hearing right now isn't a big load of bullshit."

"We're not messing with ya," Daisy said. "It wasn't just the Petersons in '87 either. The Ryersons went missing in 1998. Rick, Sue, and their two teenage daughters. That time it was different. People heard them screaming. Paulsy found the front door wide open. Kitchen window was open too. Nobody knew if this was due to someone trying to get in, or the family trying to get out. Blood everywhere. In any event, all four of them were never seen again. And that was the tipper, I guess. When everyone decided to get the hell out of Dodge. One family disappearing, okay. Two families, well that's just weird, but it can happen, maybe. But three? Three families in what? Less than twenty years? On a lake that only a handful of people live on? That you can't ignore. The next summer every cabin out here went up for sale, but there were no takers. Not with what happened, and the rumors. A crazy mountain man. Ghosts. Bigfoot. Pavilion Lake got a reputation. A bad reputation. And, well, that hasn't changed. People just don't come here no more."

"So tell us what you know, Rexy," Tony said.

Rex clenched his jaw. "I told you—"

"Out of all the families that have been attacked and gone missing, nine people in total, you're the only one to have been part of that and survived. You want us to believe that's just one big coinkydink?"

Rex was incredulous. "You think I killed my own family when I was seven and have been coming back here to murder other unsuspecting families ever since? You're a fucking lunatic."

"I never said it was *you*. But I reckon you know who's responsible." Tony took a step closer and said in a threatening tone, "What did your pop say to you the night he killed your family?"

Rex was too shocked to speak.

"Come on, Rexy," Tony pressed. "You were there. Your hair turned white. That didn't happen 'cause you witnessed people drowning. You watched your pop kill your mom and brother, didn't you? Then he made you swear to never tell anyone what happened."

"Get the fuck off my property."

"It's the only thing that makes sense—"

Rex shoved Tony, hard. The bigger man shuffled backward two steps before regaining his balance. Rage flashed in his eyes, and he made to lunge for Rex, when Daisy grabbed his arm.

"Tony!" she cried. "Stop it!"

He tried to shake her off, but she held on.

"I'm sorry," she said to Rex, tugging at Tony. "We shouldn't have come."

Rex had balled his hands into fists. They were trembling.

Finally Tony let himself be led limping away, casting a final, furious glance back at Rex, who remained where he stood, sick to his stomach, his world suddenly turned upside down.

△△△

Holding up an apple cider-scented glass candle she'd brought from home, Tabitha peeked out the attic window and recognized the people speaking to Rex as the man and woman from the pickup truck that had passed them earlier. She felt relieved. She didn't know what had made her so skittish at the sight of the flashlight earlier. She supposed it had something to do with the fact it was after dark, and they were in a very isolated place.

Tabitha crossed the room to the two beds. Ellie was in the closest one, on her back, a white wool cover with candy cane stripes pulled to her chin. She'd folded her hands behind her head so she resembled a sunbather soaking up rays on a beach.

Bobby, in the adjacent bed, was scrunching his eyes shut the way he always did whenever Tabitha tucked them in.

She sat on the floor next to Ellie's bed so she was at eye level with her daughter. "Did you pick a story for me to read?" she asked.

Ellie produced a book from behind her head with a flourish. "This one!" she said.

"Were you hiding that?"

"Yes!"

"I was wondering why you were in such a silly position." She took the book and studied the cover. "...*I Love You, Broom Hilda*," she said, reading the title doubtfully. She thumbed through the pages of the thin paperback. "This isn't a novel, sweetie. It's a comic strip."

"But she's a green witch!"

"Who chain-smokes cigars and drinks whiskey, by the looks of it."

"*Please?*"

"We'll give it a shot, I guess. Can't be too bad if it was up here in the first place."

Tabitha spent the next twenty minutes reading to Ellie, and admittedly developing a soft spot for the cantankerous chubby witch and her eccentric friends.

When she closed the book, Ellie asked, "Can I be a witch like her when I grow up?"

"Absolutely not."

"How come?"

"Do you have a bent hat and striped socks?"

"No..."

"Well, that's why then." Tabitha kissed her daughter on the forehead. "Now try to sleep."

"Do I have to go fishing tomorrow?" she asked as she rested her head on the lumpy pillow.

"Not if you don't want to."

"T-Rex isn't going to make me?"

"When has Rex ever made you do anything you didn't want

to do?"

"He made me come to this house."

"He did not. I asked him if we could come. You don't like it here?"

"It's okay."

"Just okay?"

"It would be better if I was allowed my iPad."

Sighing, Tabitha stood. "Good night, sweetie. I love you."

"I love me too."

"Goodnight, Bobby."

At the sound of his name, Bobby scrunched his eyes together even more tightly, no doubt convinced he was pulling off an Oscar-worthy performance.

Tabitha returned downstairs and found Rex on the sofa in the front room. He'd lit the other three jar candles they'd brought, and the small flames filled the room with warm light and jittery shadows.

"That was a short visit," she said, referring to their company.

"Oh, hi," he said. He had been deep enough in thought he hadn't seemed to notice her standing there.

"Everything okay?" she asked.

"Yeah, sure," he said, and although she couldn't read his expression in the poor light, his voice sounded uncharacteristically melancholic.

"Did they want something?"

"Who?"

She frowned. "The couple you were talking to outside."

"No. They were just saying hi."

Tabitha wasn't sure she believed this, but Rex had always been very open with her, which meant there was likely a good reason for his reticence. She wasn't going to pry. "I'm going to get changed," she said. "Be back out shortly."

"Sure," he said.

Tabitha retrieved her shoulder bag and carried it to the small bathroom. Setting the jar candle and bag on the counter, she stripped down to her underwear and bra, unzipped the bag, and withdrew the pieces of her neatly folded flight attendant uniform. She pulled on the fitted navy skirt and matching jacket, and tied the colorful scarf around her neck, fussing with each end to perfect the bow. She studied her candle-lit reflection in the mirror and thought she looked pretty darn good for a forty-year-old mom of two. Despite the fact Rex was a pilot, and she a flight attendant, they rarely saw each other in their uniforms because they neither lived together nor worked at the same airport. She hoped he appreciated this little surprise.

She returned to the front room quietly so as not to disturb the kids. The last thing she needed was for Ellie to call for her, or worse, to come downstairs.

Rex still sat on the sofa. His eyes were closed now, his feet up on the coffee table. *Such a handsome man,* she thought, starry-eyed. Handsome, kind, patient, gentle, caring, successful. How had she ever gotten so lucky to meet him?

It had been a chance encounter. Her friend Leena had set her up on a blind date. She was to meet the date at a popular pub in downtown Seattle. Tabitha was punctual to a fault, and she showed up early. She went to the bar and ordered a gin and tonic. Rex was a few barstools down from her, drinking water. When she overheard him mention to the bartender he was a pilot, she told him she was a flight attendant. They started talking shop. Which airline do you work for? Which flights do you fly? This quickly devolved into what pilots and flight attendants liked discussing with each other best: gossip. You couldn't escape this when you worked in one of the most hardcore customer service jobs in America. So they exchanged their favorite stories, like the time when Tabitha had to inject a passenger with a sedative after he'd dropped ecstasy and began dancing in the galleys, or when severe turbulence turned the cabin into a mosh pit, causing luggage to rain down from the overheads, or when a woman on a red-eye flight had too much to drink and vomited her dinner everywhere, which had the domino effect of causing the entire last two rows of passengers to follow suit.

Rex, however, trumped all her stories with a truly terrifying tale. When he'd been ten seconds from landing at JFK one winter, he was forced to pull up at the last second to avoid colliding with the tail of a Boeing 747 that had crossed into his landing path without permission. He'd told her the disaster had been averted by a matter of feet.

"My God, Rex!" she'd said. "Were you scared?"

"I would have been screaming along with everybody else, but I was pinned to my seat with such force I could scarcely breathe."

In retrospect Tabitha didn't believe that modest statement. Rex was too calm, collected, unflappable. More than likely he would have exhaled deeply when the danger had passed, made a wisecrack to his First Officer about air traffic controllers getting too little sleep, and apologized over the loudspeakers to the passengers for the severe maneuver.

In any event, Tabitha and Rex had been getting along so well that evening that when her blind date eventually showed up, she huddled close to Rex and pretended to be together. Her date didn't look twice at them.

"Keep your eyes closed," she said now, adding a good dose of huskiness to her voice.

"Huh?" Rex said, turning.

"Eyes closed!" she said.

He kept them closed.

She stopped before him and cleared her throat. Was she about to make a total fool of herself?

"Okay, you can open them," she said.

He did—and stared in surprise.

"Well?" she said, striking a pose like a game show model and turning in a circle. "Do I compete with all those young flight attendants you work with?"

"Compete and defeat," he said and grinned.

"Good, because I feel like an idiot."

"You look stunning," he said, and she could tell he meant the compliment.

Stepping over his stretched legs, she straddled his groin. She leaned forward and nuzzled his neck, breathing in the spicy scent of his aftershave. She nibbled his earlobe. "We're going to have to be super quiet."

He kissed her on the cheek. She pressed her lips to his—but could tell right away he wasn't into it, which was a first in their relationship.

"Hey?" she said softly, pulling back. "What's wrong?"

"I'm just—I've got something on my mind."

"Those people... What did they...?" She shook her head, thinking of the boating accident that had taken his family. "It doesn't matter. Can we cuddle?"

"I'd love nothing better," he said.

She shifted off his lap and curled up on the sofa next to him, her head resting on his shoulder. "If you want to talk," she said. "I'm here."

"Thanks," he replied, but he said no more.

Tabitha closed her eyes, telling herself she would get up in a few minutes to take out her contact lenses and brush her teeth and make a proper bed on the foldout couch...but the long day quickly caught up with her, and almost immediately she drifted into a dreamless slumber.

△△△

In the quiet dark of the night, the only sounds were the susurrate whistle of wind on the other side of the cabin's sturdy log walls and, barely audible, the deep and regular rhythm of Tabitha's breathing.

Rex wrapped his right arm around her shoulder and pulled her more closely against him. She murmured but didn't wake. He pressed his nose into her hair, which smelled faintly of pears, and kissed the top of her head.

He would tell her in the morning about the conversation he'd had with Daisy and Tony. He needed some time to first digest what he'd learned, to try to make sense of it, or to debunk it, he didn't know which.

As he had been doing for the last while, he continued to scour his brain for memories of his father. Yet it was proving frustratingly difficult to recollect anything more than a foggy face and a few inconsequential impressions. He had been too young when his father had disappeared to conjure anything more concrete.

Which made it much easier to recast the man as a family-slaying monster.

The ease of which Rex could accept this possibility, at least theoretically, was frightening but not all that surprising. Because evil people existed in the world. They did horrible things to other people every single day. Somewhere some sick bastard was doing something unspeakable to someone right now.

So if Rex were to remain objective in the face of Tony's allegations, and not let his emotions cloud his impartiality, there was no valid reason for him to rule out that his father could not be one such sick bastard, innocent until proven guilty be damned.

Some humans were psychopaths.

Rex's father was a human.

Ergo, Rex's father could be a psychopath.

That was the syllogistic argument anyway, and if Rex were to go with the wild conclusion—and he was, for the time being, if only to prove it false—what then might have occurred up here in the summer of '81? Did Troy Chapman have too much to drink one night and pick a fight with Rex's mother, Sally? Did the argument spin out of control, and did he kill her in the passion of the moment? Did Logan and Rex witness this and try to flee? Did their father catch Logan and kill him to keep him silent? Did their father get rid of the two bodies so there would be no physical evidence of his crime if he were ever captured and charged? Did he disappear into the mountains to live the life of a hermit? But what of the other families? The Petersons and the Ryersons? Why kill them? Did he return to Pavilion Lake in 1987 to stock up on supplies? Did he play Goldilocks in vacant cabins?

Did the Petersons catch him red-handed in theirs? Did the same thing happen eleven years later in 1998 with the Ryersons…?

Rex massaged his temples with his thumb and middle finger. *This is ridiculous*, he thought. *Sitting here, thinking about this, playing Sherlock Holmes, turning his father into some murderous mountain man, ridiculous.*

The bottom line was that Rex didn't have any proof, Tony didn't have any proof, nobody had any proof of what happened to his family, the Petersons, and the Ryersons. Not one iota of proof. Whatever *did* happen would likely never be known, as was the case with the vast majority of unsolved murders—

Murders? he thought. *There I go again. Tony's poisoned my mind. Because without any bodies, who's to say a single murder was ever committed? Mom, Dad, Logan, the Petersons and the Ryersons, they could all be living in some backcountry utopian commune, sharing chores and clothes, husbands and wives—*

Something slammed into the cabin door, seeming to shake the entire room.

Rex shot upright. Tabitha, wide awake, seized his arm in a vice-like grip.

BANG! BANG! BANG!

Someone was trying to get in.

CHAPTER 6

Paul Harris climbed the staircase to the police station's second floor. The spacious constable quarters included a living room, kitchen, dining room, two bedrooms (which had originally been a single space filled with bunks for the unmarried troopers), and a large bathroom. Most of the building's original architectural features remained intact, such as the stone walls and chimney, double-hung sash windows, hardwood floors, and a high mansard roof. In the 1950s, an east-facing bay window was added in the living room to capture the morning light. More recently, the kitchen and bathroom received modern facelifts, with the latter getting a small laundry.

Paul stuck his head in the living room, expecting to find his wife, Nancy, curled up on the rose loveseat reading one of her mystery novels. She wasn't there. He continued down the hallway and heard the water running through the bathroom pipes.

That woman has more showers than anybody else, Paul thought to himself. One in the morning, one at night, and sometimes one in the afternoon if she was bored and wanted something to do. Perhaps she had been a fish in her past life?

For his part, Paul had little interest in water in general, aside from drinking it. When he took the family to Joffre Lakes to soak up the wilderness on a warm spring or summer day, he would remain on shore, or in the canoe if they brought it, while Nancy and their grandson, Zephaniah, splashed around in the shallows.

Why get wet? What was the point? You just had to dry yourself off again. One shower in the morning was enough for him. One every other day in the wintertime when the temperature dropped below zero.

Paul had clearly been no fish in his past life. Likely something from a temperate or tropical climate. An orangutan, maybe, or an armadillo. Yes, maybe an armadillo, from a South American rainforest. That sounded like the good life. Forage in the mornings, catch some Zs in the afternoon, forage a little more in the warm evenings...

Paul stopped outside Zephaniah's bedroom door. Zephaniah's father—Paul's forty-three-year-old son—had been in and out of jail since he was twenty, and he was now serving three years in a medium-security penitentiary for smuggling firearms across the border for a convicted felon. Zephaniah's mother died when he was two from a drug overdose. Consequently, Paul and Nancy had agreed to take custody of Zephaniah until his father was released from prison—though they were now planning to request permanent custody of the boy on the grounds that his father was an unfit parent.

Paul knocked on the bedroom door.

"Yeah?"

"Can I come in?"

"Yeah."

Zephaniah was seated at his desk, playing a video game on the computer. Paul pulled up a chair next to him and sat down. "What game's that?"

"Halo."

"Looks fun."

"It's boring."

"Then why play it?"

"This computer is really old. It can only play really old games."

The computer was a Dell Dimension from the late nineties. It had served Paul fine, as he had only used it for word processing. He had considered buying something better for Zephaniah to use but had been hesitant, not wanting to turn the boy into one of those zombie kids that sat inside all day and night, eyes glued to a screen.

"How was school?" Paul asked.

"Fine," Zephaniah said, pausing the game.

"That was polite of you."

"What was?"

"Pausing the game."

"I'm not good at multitasking."

"Me either."

"That's not true. You're good at everything."

"I'm flattered, Zeph. But, no, I'm not. Don't you ever wonder why only your grandmother cooks?"

"You can make pancakes."

Paul nodded. "I can do that." He shifted his weight on the chair. "I spoke with Mr. Jenson today." Mr. Jenson was Zephaniah's grade-five teacher.

Zephaniah looked down at his lap.

"Hey, you didn't do anything wrong," Paul said gently. "It was those boys who did the wrong thing. What are their names?"

"Steve Kozlow and Clay Parrish."

"They're older than you?"

He nodded. "They're in grade six."

"What were they teasing you about?"

"It doesn't matter."

"I'd like to know."

Zephaniah shrugged. "My nose."

Paul raised his eyebrows. "Your nose?"

"They called me a shoebill."

"What the hell's a shoebill?"

"It's a bird that always falls on its face because its beak is so heavy. Steve showed me a video on his phone of it falling over. Then they tried pushing me over too."

Paul clenched his jaw. "Did you push them back?"

Zephaniah seemed surprised. "Am I allowed to do that?"

Paul thought it over for a moment, then decided what the

hell. He wasn't going to stand for his grandson being bullied. "Usually I don't condone violence," he said. "But bullies are the exception to the rule. They need to be taught a lesson. It's the only way they learn."

"But they'll just push me back harder, won't they?"

"Maybe. But I'll tell you something else about bullies. They're usually big wimps. It's true. They're scared of a fair fight. That's why they go after kids smaller than themselves. So if those boys tease you again, you know what I want you to do?" He held up a fist. "You pop them one right in the mouth."

Zephaniah's eyes widened. "Really?"

Paul nodded. "That'll teach them."

"I won't get in trouble?"

"Not by me. And I'm the law."

"Cool! Thanks, Grandpa." He twisted his hands in his lap. "Can I ask you something?"

"That's what I'm here for."

"Can I get a nose job?"

Paul huffed. "Get real, son."

"But then nobody will ever tease me about my nose again."

"What's wrong with a big nose? Look, I have one too." He turned his head to profile. "It runs in the family. You'll…grow into it."

"But I don't want a big schnoz."

"Schnoz?"

"That's what Clay Parrish called it."

"He's just jealous of it. You know why? Because if you have a big schnoz, you don't ever have to worry about your sunglasses falling off."

Zephaniah rolled his eyes. "Grandpa…"

"And you'll never lose a photo-finish race."

"Grandpa!"

"Okay, okay. But look, Zeph. All I'm saying is there's nothing wrong with having a big nose. It makes you look distinguished."

"I just want to look normal."

"You do look normal. Don't ever think you don't."

Zephaniah nodded. "Can I play my game again?"

"Go for it." Paul messed the boy's hair, got up, and left. He found Nancy in the bedroom, wrapped in her housecoat, searching the closet for something to wear.

"Why do you like water so much?" he asked her.

"Excuse me?" she said, glancing back at him. At fifty-six, Nancy was still as beautiful to Paul as the day she'd accepted his invitation to the prom. A few more wrinkles, sure, some gray in her chestnut hair, but the same lively eyes and childish face.

"You take two or three showers a day."

She selected a pastel blouse and slacks, tossed them on the bed, and went to the dresser, where she rifled through her undergarments drawer. "I like being clean."

"You're clean after one."

"You're cleaner after two."

"What do you do here all day when I'm at work? Roll around in the mud?"

"When I'm not getting hot and sweaty with the milkman." She turned, holding a red bra and matching underwear against her body. "What do you think? Will he like them?"

"I think the milkman stopped delivering the milk in the sixties, when you must have been, oh, five or six."

"You're right. My mistake. I meant to say the pool boy."

"We don't have a pool."

"Maybe we should get one—you know, considering how much I like water and everything."

Paul laughed. "I have to go out for a little, so you and Zeph go ahead with dinner without me. What are you making?"

"Spaghetti Bolognese," she said. "Are you going to be sitting outside that bar all night again?"

"No, something else has come up."

Nancy frowned. "Something to do with Barbara McKenzie?"

"Sort of. Do you remember Rex Chapman?"

"Troy and Sally's boy?"

Paul nodded. "The one and only. Barbara said he stopped by the tourist center earlier. He was heading out to Pavilion Lake with a woman and two kids."

"Rex Chapman..." She shook her head. "My, my. He hasn't been back here since...well, why *is* he back?"

"No idea. I guess I'll find out when I speak with him."

"Why do you have to speak with him?"

"I don't *have* to. But he likely doesn't know what happened to the Petersons or the Ryersons. Barb thinks I should give him a heads up."

"But that's all... It must be twenty years since the Ryersons disappeared!"

"Twenty exactly," Paul said, nodding. "Anyway, I better get a move on it." He clapped his peaked hat onto his head. "I still have to find somewhere to stable a horse for the night."

CHAPTER 7

Bobby lay on his back in bed, looking up at the inky black ceiling. His nose and cheeks were cold, but the blanket pulled up to his chin, kept his body warm. The blanket smelled funny, like his grandma's house, where he stayed when his dad had to fly to different countries.

Bobby wished there was a nightlight up here in the attic like there was in his bedroom at home. It was too dark. He couldn't see much except the rafters above him and the shadowy outline of the furniture around him. Ellie told him there was a monster hiding under his bed, and if that was true, it might be thinking about coming out and grabbing one of his feet. He would scream if it did that. He didn't want to. He wasn't a baby anymore. But he would. His dad would come running up the stairs and fight the monster. Bobby couldn't picture this scene in his head. Maybe because he didn't know what the monster looked like in real life.

"It has big claws and big teeth," Ellie said from her bed a few feet from his.

"No, it doesn't," Bobby replied, and now he *could* picture the monster, and it made his stomach twist.

"Yes, it does," Ellie insisted. "And it's going to bite your head off."

"I'm going to tell my dad."

"Don't be a baby."

"I'm not a baby."

"You still suck your mom's boobies!"

"Do not!"

"Do too! And you always want your dad."

"You always want your mom."

"Not *all* the time."

Bobby swallowed and listened carefully. He didn't hear anything under his bed.

Should he turn on his little flashlight and look? But what if Ellie was telling the truth, and the monster grabbed him? What if it pulled him under? She probably wouldn't help him. She would be glad if a monster got him.

"I think it's gone," he said hopefully.

"No, it's still there," she said. "I heard it."

"I don't believe you."

"It's going to eat you."

"Shut up.

"*It's going to eat you.*"

"It will eat you too."

"No, it won't, because I'm almost six."

"I'm almost six too."

"But I'm older."

Bobby was getting frustrated—and scared.

"It will still eat you too," he said.

"Monsters only eat little kids."

"You're little too."

"I told you, I'm almost six. I can do anything."

"No, you can't."

"Yes, I can."

"Do a headstand."

Ellie was silent.

"See?" Bobby said happily. "You *can't.*"

But then he heard Ellie pushing off her blanket. He looked over at her. She was on all fours. She planted her head on the mattress, then kicked with her feet. She went straight up—and came straight back down.

"I did it!" she said happily, pushing hair away from her face.

"That doesn't count," he said. "You have to stay on your head for longer."

"How long?"

"One minute."

Ellie sighed and tried again. She came down just as quickly as before, only this time she fell sideways off the bed and hit the floor. Bobby laughed.

"Hey!" Ellie's mom called from somewhere downstairs. "What's going on up there?"

"Nothing!" Ellie replied, hopping back into her bed and slipping beneath the blanket.

"Go to sleep!"

Bobby remained perfectly silent, but when Ellie's mom didn't say anything more, he whispered, "Why do you always wear yellow?"

"I don't always," Ellie said.

"All your clothes are yellow. Your dress today was yellow. And your pajamas are yellow."

"I like yellow."

"Is your underwear yellow?"

"No!"

"What color is it?"

"I don't know." She checked. "It's white. What color is yours?"

"I'm not telling."

"I told you mine!"

"So?"

"Mommy! Bobby's not telling me what color his underwear is!"

"What?" her mom's voice came back.

"I told him mine, but he won't tell me his!"

"Don't make me come up there!"

"She's mad," Bobby whispered.

"We better go to sleep," Ellie replied.

"What about the monster? If we go to sleep, it can get us."

"I think it's gone to sleep already."

"You're sure?"

"Yeah."

Bobby was relieved. He closed his eyes, not tightly like he did to trick Ellie's mom into thinking that he was sleeping, but just normally. He thought about going fishing tomorrow morning with his dad. He had never been fishing before. He wondered if he would have to put the worm on the hook himself. That would be gross. And what would he do if he caught a fish? Would his dad make him eat it? That meant he would have to kill it, and he wasn't sure he wanted to do that. Maybe he would just let it go again.

Bobby kept thinking about fishing until he found himself thinking about bears. They lived out here in the woods. What if one came to the cabin? What if it busted down the front door? They could do that. He saw it happen in a movie. His dad had been on a date with Ellie's mom, and Ellie was having a sleepover at his house. They watched *Shark Tale*, but before it finished, Ellie and the babysitter fell asleep. Bobby watched TV way past his bedtime and found the bear movie on a channel he usually wasn't allowed to watch. The bear was going around killing people in the woods. It even knocked the head off a horse with its paw. So it could easily get through the front door of this cabin, no problem. It might have a hard time getting up the stairs—it would be fat and the stairs were narrow—but it would get his dad and Ellie's mom. He would cry if it got his dad, and he would probably even be a little sad if it got Ellie's mom...

Bobby slept. He dreamed he was wandering alone in the woods, and a bear was following him. He couldn't see the animal, but he knew it was there. It was a smart bear, and it was waiting for him to lead it back to the cabin, so it could eat not just him but everybody else too. Then somebody was shouting—

Bobby came awake. His dad and Ellie's mom were speaking quickly and loudly, and they sounded scared. Bobby knew right away what was wrong.

The bear had found them!

"Dad?" he cried. "*Dad?*"

ΔΔΔ

Rex jumped to his feet. "Jesus Christ!" he said, staring at the door in the candlelight.

Tabitha was beside him. "Who is it?"

"I have no idea." He thought immediately of Tony, but why would the guy be banging on the door at...what time was it anyway? Was he pranking them? Giving them a scare? Rex didn't think so. Tony was an asshole, but he was an adult. He wouldn't resort to juvenile games.

Tabitha said, "Is the door locked?"

"Yes."

"Are you sure?"

"Yes!" He clearly remembered engaging the deadbolt. Locking the door at nighttime was a habit he'd acquired from living in big cities his entire life.

"Dad?" Bobby cried. "*Dad?*"

Ellie called for her mom a moment later.

"Go upstairs and stay with the kids," he said.

"What are you going to do?" Tabitha looked panicked. "You can't go out there! We're in the middle of nowhere. It's nighttime. Someone just pounded on the door. That wasn't a polite knock."

"Maybe they need help?"

"Have they knocked again?"

The kids were shouting more loudly now.

"Go upstairs," he repeated. "Tell Bobby and Ellie everything is okay. Tell them to stay up there, then come back down."

"Don't go outside until I'm back."

"I'm waiting. Now go!"

She grabbed a candle and hurried into the other room. He heard her ascend the stairs rapidly. He glanced around for a weapon of some kind. The ice tongs on the wall? Too unwieldy.

He spotted a golf club in one corner. He grabbed it. A nine iron, the head rusted, the shaft wooden. His father had used it to chip golf balls off the dock into the lake.

Rex went to the window to the right of the door. He pressed

his nose to the glass but couldn't see anything outside except for the black night. His pulse was racing, his thoughts moving as equally fast, playing over everything Daisy and Tony had told him earlier.

"Can you see them?"

He jumped. Tabitha stood behind him.

"Can't see anything," he grunted, his mouth suddenly cotton-dry. "How are the kids?"

"Scared. Do you think it could be the people who came by? That man and woman?"

"No," he said.

"Then *who*?"

An axe-wielding mountain man?

"I'm going to find out," he said, going to the door. "Lock the door behind me."

"Rex, *please*," she said, grabbing his wrist.

He stopped. "What do you want to do, Tabs? Sitting around and doing nothing is going to be one hell of a long night."

"Rex—"

"I won't be long." He thumbed the deadbolt and opened the door. "Oh shit!"

Tabitha screamed.

ΔΔΔ

She's dead. She has to be. Look at all that blood!

Those three thoughts pushed everything else from Tabitha's mind as she stared in horror at the woman lying on her side on the porch. Her purple quilted jacket was slit open horizontally across the belly, which appeared to be where all the blood was leaking from.

Rex dropped the golf club and knelt next to the woman. A moment later Tabitha did so too, recording what she saw in crystalline detail. Wavy blonde hair, no dark roots, recently colored. Pale face, unnaturally so. Eyes closed. Eyelashes too thick and full to be natural. Blood on the left cheek. Mouth ajar. Fillings in the molars and two badly nicotine-stained front teeth. Silver studs in the earlobes. A birthmark on the underside of the heart-shaped jaw.

Tabitha said, "That's the woman…"

Rex said, "Daisy. Her name's Daisy." He patted her cheek. "Daisy? Daisy?" No response. He checked her throat for a pulse.

Tabitha swallowed with difficulty. "Is she dead?"

"Not breathing. CPR, quick."

Rex rolled the woman onto her back. He unzipped her ruined jacket.

Tabitha gasped.

Blood had turned her once white shirt bright red. It had been slit horizontally as had the jacket—along with the woman's flesh beneath. The grisly wound stretched the length of her abdomen, revealing the pink and wormy organs of her gastrointestinal tract.

"Oh fuck," Rex said.

He began CPR. Each powerful compression caused blood to squirt out of the terrible wound. Then the woman's bowels began to slip out too.

"Rex, stop!" Tabitha cried in disgust.

He stopped. His eyes were wide, wild. He felt her throat again for a pulse.

"She's gone," he said woodenly.

"What *happened* to her?" Tabitha said, looking around as if to find evidence of a car accident. Then an epiphany. She stiffened, aghast. "Did somebody *do this*?"

Rex was shaking his head. He seemed haunted.

"Rex? Rex!" she said. "What's going on?"

"We need to get out of here. Go get the kids." He retrieved the golf club and stood.

"What's going on, Rex?" she demanded, leaping to her feet to stand beside him. "Who did this? *Did someone do this?*"

"Get the kids! We're wasting time!"

ΔΔΔ

While Tabitha went upstairs to get Bobby and Ellie, Rex fetched the handmade throw quilt from the sofa and draped it over Daisy's corpse. He knew you were supposed to perform CPR for much longer than he had on a victim in cardiac arrest, but in this case there had been no point. It was clear Daisy was doomed even if she resumed breathing. Her goddamn guts were spilling out of her stomach. Maybe if they'd had a phone he would have kept performing the compressions, because at least then there would have been a chance, however unlikely, of help arriving in time to save her. But they didn't have a phone. It had been his crazy decision to leave them back in the car.

Rex went inside and collected the Mazda keys and the Maglite just as Tabitha and the kids came down the stairs. Tabitha was white as a ghost. Bobby and Ellie were sleepy yet alarmed.

Rex dropped to his knees so he was at eye level with the kids. "Listen up, guys," he said, trying to make his voice as no-nonsense and fatherly as possible. "There's been an accident. Someone's had an accident. So we're going to go get help. Which means we have to get to the car. We're going to have to move fast. Maybe even run when we can."

"Who had the accident?" Ellie asked.

"A woman. She's resting right now. But we need to go—"

"Did you cut your hands, Daddy?" Bobby asked.

Rex glanced at his hands, which were wet with Daisy's blood. "No, I'm okay." He stood and looked at Tabitha. "Should we carry them?"

"They'll be okay on their own."

Rex nodded. "Bobby, Ellie, you two stay right behind me. Tabitha's going to be right behind you. Okay? Okay."

Rex led them outside. The kids yelped in surprise at the sight of Daisy's body, for despite it being covered by the throw quilt, the shape was still clearly that of a person. Tabitha hushed them, saying the woman was only sleeping. Rex scanned the night. He didn't hear or see anybody. He dashed down the driveway, silently cursing the noise his footsteps were making on the mucky ground.

When he reached the road, he waited for a beat for the others to reach him, then he started in the direction of the highway, sweeping the flashlight beam back and forth before him. His heart was pounding in his chest, and he felt sick with dread. He told himself they were going to make it, yet deep down he had his doubts.

Three families had gone missing on this lake over the years without a trace.

He had been the only known survivor.

Was fate trying to rectify that mistake?

△△△

As she followed Rex down the dark road, Ellie was trying to figure out what happened to the sleeping woman. Why wasn't she sleeping in a proper bed? Why on the porch, without her head showing?

Ellie had tried sleeping like that once when she was allowed to take her afternoon nap in her mom's bed. The bed was huge compared to hers, and she climbed beneath the sheets and covers, holding them up with her head, so she sat in the middle of a little fort. She would have remained there for her entire nap, hidden away from the world with her imaginary friends, but it became really hot and hard to breathe. She remembered when she popped her face back out again how cool the air felt, even though it was probably the same temperature it always was.

She's probably okay with her head not showing because she's outside, Ellie decided. *It's too cold out to get hot beneath the cover.*

T-Rex was moving pretty fast. He wasn't running. He was only jogging, but because he was bigger than she was, jogging for him was like running for her.

She was pretty fast herself. They once had a hundred-meter-dash race at school for all the students. She ran against the other girls in grade one with her, and she had come in third place. This was good because everybody knew Sylvia Sanders, who came in first, was the fastest girl in their grade, even faster than most of the boys. And Laurie Miller, who came in second, started running before the gun went off, which was why everybody called her a cheater.

Still, Ellie had never tried running *far*—and the car was far. It had taken them forever to walk to the cabin. She didn't think she was going to be able to run fast all that way back to it without taking a break.

Bobby was running right next to her. He was crying, but silently, like when you don't want anybody to know you're crying.

Ellie wondered again what happened to the sleeping woman. Her mom told her the woman had an accident, but sometimes when her mom said "accident" she meant something else. Like when Ellie's real dad came over to the house and broke some things. Her mom and Ellie spent that night at Ellie's grandparents' house. Her mom had a bruise on her face and told Ellie she had an accident, but Ellie overheard her talking to Ellie's grandparents in the kitchen, telling them how Jacob, which was Ellie's dad's name, had hit her.

So did the sleeping woman *really* have an accident? Or did something else happen to her? Ellie wasn't sure what could have gotten her—

The monster under Bobby's bed!

Maybe it had a whole bunch of different doors in its house, and it could go through them to get to other people's bedrooms. After it left the space under Bobby's bed, it went to this woman's bedroom. It bit her or punched her or did something bad to her, and that's why she was sleeping on the porch. She was scared of going back to her bed!

Feeling proud she had solved the mystery all by herself, Ellie concentrated on running fast.

ΔΔΔ

Rex was terrified as he led Tabitha and the kids down the winding road into the unknown. He was terrified he had made the wrong decision to leave the cabin. Because they were now exposed and vulnerable. They had nothing with which to protect themselves save a rusty old golf club. If the murderer caught up to them and was well-armed, they were as good as dead.

But what could they have done instead? Remained bunkered down inside the cabin? They would have been sitting ducks.

At least now they were moving. It was only another ten minutes to the car.

Yes, that was right.

The car, safety.

Another ten minutes.

The night air on Rex's face and the adrenaline coursing through his veins was helping him to think straight. He began to rationalize the situation, dissect it, and in the process, temper the panic that had until then been dictating his thoughts and actions.

When he had first seen the dead woman on the porch, he immediately linked her death to the disappearance of his family. The person who had gotten them had returned for Rex and those close to him.

But this was silly, wasn't it? Theoretically speaking, say his father had been responsible for the kidnappings and, presumably, murders, over the years. He had been forty-four years old in 1981. That would make him eighty-three today. If he had spent the intervening decades roughing it in the mountains, living off a meager diet with no medicine or modern accouterments, his life expectancy would not be ideal. If not already dead, he would be frail. He had not attacked Tony and Daisy.

If someone other than his father were responsible for the kidnappings and murders, someone who had only been, say, twenty in '81, that would put him in his late fifties now. This person could very well have attacked Tony and Daisy.

Nevertheless, as Rex's panic continued to ebb, he asked himself a question that had eluded him until then.

Why did the tragic events of the past have to have anything to do with those of tonight? It had been nearly forty years since Rex's family went missing; twenty since the Ryersons went missing.

There was no connection between the past and the present.

The much more likely suspect in Daisy's murder, Rex decided, was her boyfriend, Tony. The guy was an asshole, that much was for sure. Did something happen that set him over the edge when they returned to their cabin? Did Daisy get a text message that made him jealous? Did she say something that pissed him off? Disagreed with him in some way? Perhaps an old argument came up, a touchy topic, money or an ex-boyfriend.

And then what? Rex wondered. Tony attacks Daisy with the knife he'd been using to dice onions? Uses it to slice open her gut? Did he take savage glee in this violence? Or did it occur in the passion of the moment? Did he immediately regret hurting her? Was he curled up on the kitchen floor in a puddle of his tears right now?

No, Tony was a dick. He had too much machismo to ever shed a tear for a woman.

So Daisy fled, hands on her stomach to keep her innards inside, and Tony gave chase. But he had that limp. He was slow. She reached Rex's cabin first. From the time she banged on the door to the time Rex and the others were on the road, on the way to the car, no more than five minutes had passed. The longest five minutes of Rex's life, but five minutes nonetheless. Tony still hadn't caught up.

So where did that put the guy now? Had he just discovered Daisy's body? If so, he would know Rex and Tabitha and the kids had fled. He would be coming. He wouldn't let any witnesses to his crime escape.

And all this was good news.

Because they had a head start. There was no way limping Tony could catch them. Even if he went back for his truck, he wouldn't reach them before they reached the Mazda. They would be zipping down Highway 99 toward Lillooet shortly. They would be at the police station in less than an hour, safe, nightmare over—

A light flashed between the trees.

From ahead.

Rex stopped in his tracks. He felt Bobby and Ellie bump into his legs. Tabitha stopped beside him and whispered, "He's out here!"

"Shit!" Rex said, flicking off his own flashlight, plunging them into darkness.

How had Tony gotten ahead of them?

Rex squeezed the golf club tightly in his right hand. It didn't instill confidence in him. Tony would be armed with something more lethal. The knife he'd used on Daisy. Or maybe even a gun. Canada had strict gun laws on handguns, but anybody could purchase a rifle from their local Walmart.

The light was coming closer.

"Rex?" Tabitha said worriedly.

Should they duck into the forest? No, they would make too much noise, especially with Bobby and Ellie. Tony would surely hear them and catch them.

Which meant the only option was to turn around.

They couldn't return to the cabin. But if they got far enough away from Tony, they could look for a proper spot to hide.

Until when? Morning?

One step at a time.

"We have to go back," he whispered.

△△△

Tabitha was totally freaking out as she followed Rex and the kids down the dark and winding road. She clenched her jaw to prevent herself from issuing unwanted sounds as she struggled to comprehend how abruptly her world had been flipped upside down. Just a few hours before they had been sitting around the fire, roasting wieners, happy and unharassed. Now they were being pursued through the night by a vicious killer.

They rounded a bend, and Rex slowed the pace from a stealthy jog to a hurried walk. Tabitha glanced back and could no longer see the yellow light from the flashlight beam. She gave Ellie and Bobby a reassuring shoulder squeeze.

"You guys are doing great," she said, bending over to whisper in their ears.

"Where are we going, Mommy?" Ellie asked in a hushed, conspiratorial voice, almost as if she were playing a part in a movie.

Tabitha wondered the same thing.

Where was Rex taking them?

Back to the cabin?

Tabitha didn't think this was the best idea. The killer knew they were staying there. It wouldn't take him long to realize the woman might have gone there for help.

Perhaps Tabitha and Rex could hide the body, blow out the candles, and make it look as though they were all sleeping, unaware of what the killer had done.

He would leave them alone then, wouldn't he?

No, she decided immediately. He wouldn't. A pool of blood stained the porch. There was no way they could clean that up in the short time they had. There was no way the killer would miss it either.

So did they lock the doors and windows and barricade themselves inside the cabin? Until when? Morning would bring no salvation. Nobody was going to come and rescue them. Almost nobody knew they were there. The woman at the tourist center did. But why would she give them any thought?

And all Vanessa knew was that they were visiting Rex's cabin somewhere in Canada. Tabitha and Ellie weren't supposed to be home until Sunday evening. Even then, Vanessa likely wouldn't get worried enough to call the police until Tuesday or Wednesday. That was more than half a week away. They couldn't hunker down in the cabin for that long with the scant food and water they had.

"Don't worry about that now, sweetie," she said in answer to her daughter's question. "Just keep up with T-Rex, and we'll get where we're going soon."

The road continued straight for the next hundred yards through the old-growth rainforest, which had been so alive and green during the day but was now silent and ominous. After another hundred yards, Tabitha made out the white, canted mailbox at the end of the McCleods' overgrown driveway. She pictured Rex and his brother Logan as kids running wildly for their lives from a yapping Yorkshire terrier, arms and legs browned from long days in the summer sun flapping madly, mouths pulled into rictuses of fear.

If only it was a toy dog we were running from now.

"Ow!" Bobby cried out.

Rex stopped abruptly. Tabitha did too.

"What is it?" Rex whispered between pants.

"I stubbed my toe. The one that went to the market."

"Do you want me to carry you?"

"I think I'm okay."

"Where are we going, Rex?" Tabitha asked. "We can't go back to the cabin."

"We're not." He hesitated. "We're going to *their* cabin."

"*Whose* cabin?"

"Where Tony and Daisy are staying."

"The guy chasing us?" she said in disbelief.

Rex nodded. "He didn't see us. He doesn't know we're out here."

"He will when he gets to our cabin. And you want to hide in *his* cabin? That's—"

"Not *hide*. I want to take his truck."

She blinked. "His truck?"

"Hopefully he left the keys behind. Then we can drive right out of here."

Tabitha considered this. "What if they're in his pocket?" she asked.

"Do you keep your car keys in your pocket when you're relaxing at home? Anyway, even if we don't find them, we might find one of their phones. We can call for help."

Call for help.

The wonderful warmth of hope filled her chest, and all at once she felt woozy with relief.

They had a way out of this nightmare after all!

Tabitha scooped Ellie into her arms, kissed her daughter on her button nose, and allowed herself the briefest of smiles.

"How far is it?" she asked.

CHAPTER 8

The Crown Vic's high beams flashed on the late-model Mazda coupe parked alongside the dirt road. Frowning, Paul Harris pulled up behind it and put the patrol car in Park. Leaving the engine idling and the headlights on, he climbed out, his hand on the butt of his holstered pistol. He walked to the Mazda and peeked in the driver's side window. Empty. He continued a few feet past the vehicle's hood. In the swath of yellow cast by the Crown Vic's high beams, the road was clearly visible, including all of its starkly outlined ruts and potholes. This explained why Rex Chapman had abandoned his car here, if the Mazda was indeed his car, though he couldn't fathom to whom else it might belong.

One mystery solved, Paul thought sardonically. *And one new dilemma.*

Because without a four-wheel-drive vehicle, he wasn't going to be able to drive down the road either.

Tugging his pack of Marlboro's and lime-green Bic lighter from his hip pocket, he lit up, rocked back on his heels, and studied the overcast night sky.

Although the Lillooet Country's boundaries were only loosely defined by cartographers, anyone who lived in the area would tell you they encompassed the land within the Fraser Canyon from Church Creek and Big Car Ferry in the north, to a spot known as the Big Slide on Highway 12 south of Lillooet. They'd probably agree the summit of Cayoosh Pass near Duffey Lake on Highway 99 was the western "border," if you wanted to call it that, and the summit of Pavilion Mountain Road the eastern one.

Pavilion Lake was located just inside this northeastern demarcator, putting it in Paul's jurisdiction.

Paul had first come up here to investigate the Chapman family's disappearance in 1981, and again to investigate the Peterson's and Ryerson's subsequent disappearances in 1987 and 1998 respectively. Over the years he fished on Pavilion Lake and hiked in Marble Canyon. His most recent recreational visit, however, must have been…well, it was before the Ryersons went missing. So that would make it probably twenty years or so ago. Maybe even twenty-five. He would have been in his thirties.

Jesus Christ, where did the time go?

Paul took a drag on his smoke, his eyes going back to the derelict road.

Pretty much undrivable, he thought. A good enough reason to turn around and head home. Then again, undrivable didn't mean unwalkable. How far was it to the Chapman's cabin? Three kilometers? How long would that take on foot? Twenty minutes? The rain had stopped for the moment, and it was a pleasant enough evening. Walking never hurt anybody; the exercise would do him good.

Taking a final drag on the smoke, Paul flicked the butt away and returned to the cruiser. He killed the engine and retrieved the Streamlight tactical flashlight from the glove box, which was more powerful than the smaller version he kept in the holder on his duty belt. He clicked it on and started down the poorly kept road. Soon tall conifers and broad-leaf deciduous trees loomed above him, their shadowed boughs blocking out the sky. The air smelled of wet soil and pine needles and wildflowers. Gravel crunched beneath his footsteps, and he did his best to avoid the water-filled potholes.

Tucking the flashlight beneath an armpit, he lit up another cigarette. He would miss his police work when he retired in two years, he mused, cold, wet nights included. He would only be sixty years old, but he wanted to spend more time with Nancy and Zeph. Go camping on the weekends. See more of the province. Hell, maybe even more of the country. Travel like that was never an option when you were on duty seven days a week.

Paul would have preferred to spend the rest of his days in the police station's constable quarters. He had lived there his entire life. But the old has to make way for the new; that was how the cookie crumbled. If his son Joseph had followed in his footsteps and become the next police chief, Paul and Nancy might have remained put. But Joseph had not followed in his footsteps. Not even close. He had chosen to walk the other side of the law.

Paul often wondered where he'd gone wrong with the boy. He had been a good father, he thought. Certainly better than some of the other fathers in town whose kids had turned out all right. So why did Joseph turn out so rotten?

Drugs were the easy answer. Joseph got into them after high school when he went to work as a snowboard instructor at Whistler Blackcomb. A lot of partying went on there among the staff, many of whom were backpackers from as far away as Europe and Australia. Most kids experimented with drugs at one point or another in their adolescence. Some decided they weren't for them and steered clear in the future. Some continued to use them recreationally. And some, unfortunately, developed a habit. Joseph got a taste for heroin. Within a year of leaving home he was nearly unrecognizable from his old self. Gaunt, pale skin, puffy eyes, pinpoint pupils. Paul confronted him during the Easter weekend when he came back to visit, which was probably the wrong tactic because Joseph never returned. Instead, he turned his efforts to building himself a pretty extensive criminal record. Then he went off the radar for six years before turning up in the news as one of two suspects charged with a string of burglaries in the Okanagan Valley. He was found guilty and spent the following two years in prison. Over the next decade he rose through the ranks of a well-known criminal gang until he was sent behind bars once more for cocaine trafficking, and then again, most recently, for smuggling weapons across the border.

If his son ever wanted to turn his life around, Paul would

be there for him, but this seemed like wishful thinking, and Paul had long ago decided he would not waste any more of his time worrying about someone who clearly did not worry about anybody but himself.

A few minutes and another cigarette later, Paul came upon the Ryerson's driveway. It was completely overgrown with weeds and scrub and bush. Paul only knew it was there from memory. He played the flashlight beam over the trees before stopping on a dilapidated white slab of wood nailed to the trunk of a cedar. The black, hand-painted letters spelled THE RYERSONS. He aimed the beam in the direction he knew the cabin to be. He couldn't see it through the thick vegetation.

Ahead, down the road, he spotted a flash of light.

In the next instant it disappeared.

Despite Paul standing statue still for a full minute, it didn't return.

His imagination? The reflection of his flashlight beam off the lake, or an old road sign?

Someone else out here with him?

Who? Rex Chapman? But why would he be skulking through the woods at this hour?

Paul resumed walking. The Chapman's cottage was still more than a kilometer away, and suddenly he wanted to get this courtesy call over with as quickly as possible.

CHAPTER 9

"There it is," Rex said, pointing to the rusty red pickup truck parked out in front of the Williams' dilapidated cabin. They were standing fifty feet away from it, to the side of the road, hidden in the shadows of the trees.

"Are we going to drive it?" Bobby asked.

"If I can find keys, bud," he said.

"It looks scary," Ellie said.

"It's not scary, sweetie," Tabitha said. "It's just a truck."

"It *looks* scary, like a ghost truck."

"You and Bobby are going to stay here with your mom," Rex told her. "I'll go check it out, make sure there are no ghosts. When the coast is clear, I'll wave you over. Got that?"

"Look in the back seat too," Ellie said. "That's where I sit."

"Will do," he said. Hunching over, Rex hurried toward the truck, trying to make as little noise as possible. Nobody should be in the cabin. Only Tony and Daisy had been in the pickup truck when it passed them on the road. There were no other vehicles parked out here. Still, too much was at stake right now not to be extra cautious.

He stopped at the truck and tried the passenger door. It was unlocked! He swung it back with a groan of metal and hopped up on the bench seat. The cab smelled of engine oil and grease. No keys dangling in the ignition. They weren't behind either of the sun visors. He checked beneath the seats and in the glove box with little hope. If Tony had left the keys in the truck, it would have been for convenience's sake. He wouldn't be hiding them, not out here.

Unsurprisingly, all he discovered was an empty Mountain Dew can, the vehicle's logbook, and some tools.

He exited the truck. Looking back the way he'd come, he couldn't see Tabitha or the kids. It was too dark. Regardless, he knew they were there, watching him. He waved them over.

Shadows moved. Then Tabitha materialized, holding the kids' hands.

"Did you find them?" she whispered when they reached him.

"No," he said. "They must be inside."

Her face fell as she looked at the cabin. He looked too. It featured a shingled roof, clapboard siding, and an overgrown garden. Candlelight illuminated the windowpanes.

"I'll go get them," he added. "You guys wait in the truck."

△△△

Sitting in the front of the pickup truck, behind the steering wheel, Ellie snuggled closer against her mom's warm body, breathing in the familiar smell of her perfume, which made her feel safer.

She wished they had never come to T-Rex's stupid cabin. It had been fun for a bit, but now it wasn't fun at all. She would much rather be back in her house, playing with her Barbie dolls on the carpet in her bedroom. She had just gotten Barbie's Dreamhouse for being good when her mom had to run errands on the weekends and Ness had to look after her. The horse could walk and nod either yes or no when you asked it questions. You could also feed it the carrots that had come in the package (but not real carrots, she'd discovered). And when she got bored of the horsey, she could play with her Lite Brite. Right now she was making a picture of a train, but she was missing some of the pegs to finish it. They might be under her bed. That's where everything that didn't want to be found seemed to go. Last time she had been under there she had recovered two of her black-and-white penguin bath toys.

"I want to go home," she murmured.

"We'll be going home soon, sweetie," her mom said, kissing the top of her head.

"Can I have ice cream when we get there?"

"Sure."

"In a cone?"

"Okay."

Her mom sounded strange, and Ellie looked up. Her face was sad, and she was crying.

"What's wrong, Mommy?" she asked, concerned.

"Nothing, hon." She kissed the top of Ellie's head again. "I'm happy."

"But you're crying."

"It's happy-crying."

Ellie frowned. Happy-crying?

"Like when it rains when it's sunny out?" she asked.

"Yes, like that. You're such a smart little girl."

"Smarter than Bobby?"

"You're both very smart."

"But I'm smarter because I'm older—"

"Ellie!"

"What?"

"You know what."

Ellie didn't. Really, she didn't. But she stayed quiet anyway.

Her mom might start angry-crying, and she didn't want that.

△△△

When Rex stepped inside the Williams' cabin, he expected to find evidence of a violent struggle in the form of overturned chairs, splattered blood, and a general air of helter-skelter. To the contrary, however, the scene that greeted him seemed perfectly innocuous. A half-dozen candles flickered silently, while embers glowed warmly in the stone fireplace. The sturdy log pine furniture was all upright and where it should be. The rustic décor—everything from the heavy curtains to the well-worn rugs that covered the knotty wooden floorboards incorporated wildlife motifs—appeared undamaged. A bear-sculpture end table held a spread of crackers, cheese, olives, and dips. On the dining table, a bottle of wine chilled in an ice bucket, next to two half-filled champagne flutes and a deck of Bicycle playing cards, dealt into two hands.

All the trappings of a romantic evening, Rex thought—so what the hell happened to change that?

He didn't waste time speculating. Instead, he moved quickly through the room, eyes darting to and fro, each passing second feeling like a knife twisting deeper into his gut.

If he'd been wrong to come here...

If Tony caught up to them...

Shoving aside these thoughts, Rex entered a narrow hallway. The first door on the right opened to a small bedroom. The single bed was neatly made, not slept in. A dated Tom Clancy hardback novel, a bookmark protruding from the pages, sat expectantly on the night table as if waiting for the absent reader to return and pick up again where he or she had left off.

He didn't see keys or a phone anywhere, so he moved on.

The next room was locked.

Rex drove his shoulder into the door to no avail. He looked up. All of the interior walls rose only three-quarters of the distance to the open rafter ceiling. The unusual architectural decision was likely made so the heat from the fireplace could warm every room in the wintertime.

In any event, it would allow him access to the room.

Rex proceeded to the kitchen. Vegetables waiting to be sliced and diced sat in a bowl on the roughly hewn countertop, along with a package of croutons, a head of lettuce, and a jar of pasta sauce. A glance inside the pot on one of the stovetop burners revealed a clump of cooked spaghetti in about an inch of boiling water.

He clicked off the gas to prevent a fire, then grabbed a chair from the set around the drop leaf table. Back in front of the locked room, he set the chair against the wall and stepped onto the seat. His head was now level with the top of the partition, though he couldn't see over it. Tucking the flashlight inside his jacket, he hooked his arms over the top beam and tried to hoist himself up, kicking his legs feebly. This didn't work, and he touched his feet back down on the chair seat. On his second attempt he placed one foot on the brass doorknob, using it as a step.

This time his head and shoulders cleared the partition, and he peeked into the locked room.

CHAPTER 10

"Hello?" Paul called, sticking his head inside the Chapman's cabin. "Rex? Rex Chapman?" he added, not expecting an answer. Empty residences emitted their own uniquely forbidden vibe, and he was feeling that vibe right now.

Paul turned around, looking down again at Daisy Butterfield, who lay in a pool of thick blood on the porch. When he'd removed the quilt that had covered her a few moments ago, he'd expected to discover the body of Rex Chapman, or his lady friend. Not poor Daisy, who Paul had known since she was a kid selling lemonade from a handmade stand out in front of her house on Hangman's Lane. She left Lillooet after high school, earned a teaching certificate from the University of Victoria, and found work in a private school in West Vancouver. When her mother, Darla Butterfield, had a stroke four years ago (widowed a year or so before that when her husband, Joe, died of natural causes in his sleep), Daisy returned to Lillooet to become her full-time nurse while also teaching at the elementary school.

Paul pulled his eyes away from Daisy and surveyed the wet, black night, fighting the urge to flee back to the patrol car. It wasn't finding the body of someone he knew that was spooking him so badly. It wasn't even that the body had been opened up like a can of beans, though this was certainly unnerving. It was the fact the body was on the doorstep to Rex Chapman's cabin, where Rex Chapman's family had disappeared so mysteriously almost forty years earlier.

Could that be a coincidence? If so, it was one hell of a big one, and a lifetime of policing had made Paul cynical enough to not put much stock in coincidences.

Which left...what?

A sicko playing games?

A copycat killer?

Tony Lyons?

Paul focused on that last thought. *Tony Lyons*. Sure—why jump to outlandish conclusions when nine times out of ten the culprit of a domestic murder was a spited spouse or lover?

Tony Lyons had wandered into Lillooet a little over a year ago, and he'd been keeping company with Daisy for maybe half that time. Paul had taken an immediate disliking to the man. For starters, Tony had one of those bulldog faces that made him look as if at any moment he might hit someone. And his terse personality didn't help his image. Unlike the majority of residents of Lillooet who were more than happy to stop and have a yak with Paul when they saw him around town, Tony never offered a word or even a nod of recognition when they crossed paths. This had led Paul to believe the man might be prejudiced toward cops, perhaps due to a criminal past, and so he ran Tony's name through the National Canadian Police Information Center, discovering he had a laundry list of misdemeanor convictions, as well as three felonies for aggravated animal cruelty, mail and wire fraud, and sexual assault.

Which made him a prime suspect in what happened here tonight.

Moreover, Paul thought, Tony would be somewhere in his mid-fifties, which, in 1981, would put him in his late teens.

Plenty old enough to commit kidnapping and murder.

"Jesus and Mother Mary," Paul mumbled. He set the flashlight on the porch railing and took his cell phone from a pocket. British Columbia contracted policing responsibilities in small villages and rural towns, and even some of the larger cities, to the Royal Canadian Mounted Police. The nearest detachment was in Whistler. They could be here within three hours.

Before Paul dialed a single number, however, a whining, buzzing noise from behind the cabin froze him stiff. It sounded like an electrical tool, a circular saw, perhaps, or a drill.

It lasted for maybe two or three seconds, then abruptly stopped.

Swallowing the hard knot of fear suddenly clogging his throat, Paul shoved the phone away and snatched the Streamlight from the railing. Gripping it as you would an ice pick, he held it beneath his pistol so his hands were back to back and the flashlight and weapon were aimed in the same direction —toward the back of the cabin.

"Tony? That you?" he asked, working saliva into his mouth. "It's Paul here. Police. I'm armed. Best thing to do would be to come out with your hands up."

Paul forced his legs to move, taking one cautious step after another. He stopped at the corner of the cabin. He listened. He didn't hear anything aside from his quick, susurrate breathing.

Now or never.

He stepped around the corner, sweeping the flashlight and pistol from side to side.

Nobody there.

He had not imagined that sound—

Bzzzzzzzzzzzzzzzzzzzzzzz

Looking up, Paul's eyes bulged and he opened his mouth to scream, but a black terror the likes of which he had never experienced muted his voice, and all he issued before the attack came was a pitiful, wheezing, "*No...*"

CHAPTER 11

Bobby kept his eyes glued to the pickup truck's window, which looked directly toward the rundown cabin. On other more normal days, he would have found it weird sitting next to Ellie's mom in such a tight space like the front of a car. He couldn't think of many times when it was just Ellie's mom, Ellie, and him, without his dad around too. There were nights like when Ellie's mom tucked them in at bedtime, but he didn't have to speak to her then because he always pretended he was already asleep. He didn't have to speak to her now either...but the other really weird thing was that he sort of wanted to speak to her. He felt sick on his inside—not like when he had a cold; more like when he knew he was going to get in trouble for something—and he thought maybe by talking to her, that sickness might go away a little.

He looked down at his hands fidgeting in his lap. "Ellie's Mom?" he said, not knowing what else to call her. He didn't have a nickname for her like Ellie did with his dad.

"Yes, Bobby?" He felt her eyes on him, though he wouldn't meet them.

"Is Barry coming after us?" he asked.

"Barry? Who's Barry, sweetheart?"

"The man who crashed his car in the woods."

"What man, Bobby?"

"He crashed his car a long time ago. My dad showed me the car, remember? It's all broken and everything. So maybe Barry couldn't get home and is still in the woods?"

"I think your dad was just telling you a story, Bobby."

"But I saw the car!"

"Didn't your dad say it was close to a hundred years old? That means whoever once owned it—this Barry—died a long time ago."

"Is he in heaven, Mommy?" Ellie asked.

"If he was a good man, yes," her mom replied.

"Is he watching us right now?"

"I don't think so."

"Why not?"

"He probably has other things he wants to do."

"And it's nighttime!" Bobby told her. "He can't see in the dark!"

"Maybe he had special glasses."

"He doesn't."

"You don't know that. You're not God!"

"You're not either!"

"Guys!" Ellie's mom said, sounding more scared than angry. "Quiet!"

"When's my dad coming back?" Bobby asked after a moment.

"Soon, hon."

"What if he doesn't find the keys?" Ellie asked.

"He will."

"But what if he doesn't?"

"We'll think of something."

Bobby tried to think of something himself. They couldn't walk back to his car because Barry—despite what Ellie's mom said, Bobby still thought it was Barry coming after them—would catch them. They couldn't stay in the truck either because Barry would probably check it. Bad guys always found where the good guys were hiding. So they'd have to run into the woods, and this was the last thing he wanted to do. Because bears lived in the woods, and they came out at nighttime, and they might eat all of them, and this was way worse than what Barry would do to them. He might only tie them up and say mean things like he was going to cut off their heads. But he probably wouldn't do this, because he would go to jail—

Bobby sucked back a breath as a new thought struck him.

"What's wrong, honey?" Ellie's mom asked.

Bobby looked directly at her for the first time. Her eyes were wide, and she looked really pretty, even in the dark. She always looked pretty, and she always smelled nice too.

"Maybe the monster's following us?" he said.

"There's no such thing—"

"It's not!" Ellie said, cutting off her mom.

"Why not?" Bobby demanded.

"Because," she stated.

"Because isn't an answer," he said, using the comeback Marty Phillips from school always used.

"Because it can't live outside from under the bed!"

"You don't know that!"

"Do too!"

"It can live anywhere it wants."

"*You* don't know that—"

"Ellie, *enough*," her mom said.

"But Bobby started it!"

"*Enough!*" She lowered her voice. "We need to be quiet, okay? So...no more talking until Rex comes back."

"What if he doesn't come back for an hour?"

"Ellie, I'm not telling you again."

Bobby heard Ellie huff like she always did when she got in trouble. But she was smart enough to stay quiet. Otherwise, she might get grounded for a week, or maybe a month. Her mom was a lot stricter than his dad was.

A short time later Ellie said, "Mommy?"

"Yes?"

"What did I earn for being good today?"

"My affection."

"I don't want that!"

"Well, that's what you got."

"Mommy, you're not my friend anymore."

"Ellie, shush—" Suddenly she sat up straight, alarmed.

Bobby heard something too. A loud bang. It came from inside

the cabin.

"What was that?" Bobby asked, forgetting that he wasn't allowed to talk.

"I don't know," Ellie's mom whispered. "Shit!"

"Mom!" Ellie said. "You swore—"

"Bobby, open your door. Let me out." She reached in front of him and opened the door. The cold night air blew inside.

She slipped over his lap and stumbled as she climbed out, but then she was standing on the ground, looking in at them.

"Mommy, don't go!" Ellie cried.

Bobby wished the same thing, but he was too surprised by everything happening to speak.

"I'm not going to go for long, sweetie. I promise. I just have to check if Rex is okay. You two stay here. Keep your heads down, below the windows. Keep the doors closed and locked. I'll be right back."

Before either Bobby or Ellie could reply, she slapped the lock knob down and closed the door. Through the window, she pointed to the ground and mouthed the word, "Down."

Bobby ducked his head. Turning it sideways, he saw Ellie was ducked low on the seat as well.

"Maybe you're right," she whispered to him.

"About what?" he asked.

"The monster. It got out from under the bed, and now it got your dad."

ΔΔΔ

Tabitha dashed toward the cabin, instinct dictating her actions, telling her that only two things mattered: helping Rex and protecting the kids. There was no hierarchy to these imperatives. They both simply had to be done.

She burst into the cabin, stealth be damned. Her eyes took in the rustic room in a heartbeat.

Deserted.

"Rex?" she hissed urgently.

"Tabs?" his voice came back from the hallway.

She skirted through the room. Rex stood next to a chair facing a closed door. He appeared shocked and skittish.

"What's going on?" she demanded, some of her fear ebbing at the sight of him unharmed. "What was that noise?"

"That was me," he said. "I'm trying to get into this room."

"What's in it?"

He seemed about to answer, then shook his head. He brought his knee to his chest and drove his foot into the door. The bang seemed to shake the cabin. Wood cracked and splintered.

"Rex!" she said. "Quiet!"

He kicked the door once more.

It burst open in a firework of splinters.

Rex entered the room first, Tabitha following on his heels, curiosity mixing with dread. Two overnight bags sat open on a double bed. A lamp fashioned from snowshoes and garlanded with pinecones stood on a night table. A dresser/mirror combo lined one wall, next to a stiff-looking armchair.

And a body lay facedown on the floor, surrounded by blood.

"Oh!" Tabitha gasped, her hands going to her mouth in surprise.

Rex played the flashlight over the face.

"It's Tony," he said woodenly.

Tabitha's mind spun. "But how...? Then who...?"

"I don't know," he said flatly. He went to the body, careful to avoid stepping in the blood. He crouched and felt for a pulse.

"Is he alive?" Tabitha asked, knowing the answer.

Rex shook his head in the negative. He patted down the rear pockets of the man's jeans. Then, with some effort, he rolled the deadweight body onto its back.

A monstrous incision opened his belly from side to side, nearly identical to the one Daisy had suffered.

Tabitha felt momentarily faint.

Rex rifled through all of the man's pockets, swearing loudly.

"They're not here!" he added, referring to the truck keys.

"They have to be somewhere!" Tabitha said, fighting her ballooning panic. *We need to go, we need to go, we need to go,* she kept thinking over and over while struggling to understand who had been out on the road if Tony had been lying here dead the entire time. "They must be in another room—"

"I've checked everywhere!"

"Phones?"

Rex shook his head, running a hand through his hair. He was about to get back to his feet when something in his demeanor changed. He stiffened and became solely focused on the body. He directed the flashlight beam at the smiling, lipless wound. "What in God's name…?" He extended his hand.

"Rex!" she cried. "What are you doing?"

His hand hovered above the gash for a moment before he plunged it into the bloody tangle of organs.

He's gone crazy! she thought. *He's lost his mind!*

"Rex!" she repeated, though the word was so hoarse with dismay that she could barely hear it herself.

Rex removed his hand and held high something shiny pinched between his red fingers.

The truck keys.

CHAPTER 12

Rex stared in shock at the bloody keys. Someone was playing with them. Whoever had killed Tony and Daisy, the jackass was playing with them. He knew Rex and Tabitha and the kids were here on the lake. Somehow he'd known they would head to the Williams' cabin. Because the keys weren't for the cops to eventually discover. Why would the cops care about a set of keys to a rusty old pickup truck? The only people the keys mattered to were Rex and present company so they could escape—and the sick bastard knew this!

"What's going on, Rex?" Tabitha asked in a voice near hysterics. "Why would someone do that with the keys? He must know we need them." She was backing out of the room, her face a ghostly white in the backsplash of light from the flashlight. "This is fucked. This is so fucked, Rex. He knows! *He knows we're here!*"

Rex wasn't going to argue that point. He snapped to his feet—and stepped in the puddle of blood. He spun in a pirouette before grappling one of the bed's end posts, reaffirming his balance. "Shit!" Watching where he stepped next, he exited the room. He gripped Tabitha's hand and led her quickly from the cabin.

For a moment his heart seemed to stop when he didn't see Bobby or Ellie in the cab of the pickup truck, but he breathed again when he opened the passenger door and saw them crouched in the footwells.

"Daddy!" Bobby said, the terror on his face morphing into joy.

"Up on the seat," he said, already rounding the hood.

He slid behind the steering wheel at the same time Tabitha climbed in the passenger door.

"I'm squished!" Ellie protested as she was pressed tightly between Rex and Bobby.

Rex barely heard her above his pulse thumping inside his head. He jammed the key in the ignition and turned it. The engine coughed, then turned over.

"Are we going home now?" Ellie asked.

"Yeah, honey," Tabitha said, her voice tight with emotion. "Hold tight."

Rex flicked on the headlights, then took a moment to familiarize himself with the truck's controls. He engaged the brake pedal, depressed the clutch, and shifted the stick into first gear. The engine revved and the truck jumped forward. Startled, he let off the clutch. Gears crunched. The truck lurched to a stop and stalled.

"What happened?" Bobby asked.

Rex looked at Tabitha. "Can you drive a manual?"

She shook her head. "Try again! You can fly a jumbo jet, you can drive a silly truck!"

Rex started the vehicle a second time and managed to shift into first without popping the clutch.

"Yay, Dad!" Bobby said as they chugged forward.

"Faster!" Ellie said.

"Shush, guys!" Tabitha said. "Let him concentrate!"

Rex knew he was revving too high. He clutched in and gassed off and shifted from first to second. Gears ground, but not too badly, and then the truck was picking up speed along the dark road.

"Piece of cake!" he said, grinning riotously. He accelerated.

"Not too fast, Rex!" Tabitha cautioned.

He shifted to third. The speedometer needle crept past forty.

With the headlights carving a tunnel through the darkness, Rex kept his eyes glued to the gravel road, doing his best to avoid the worst of the ruts and potholes. Even so, the truck was bumping and shaking on its worn-out suspension hard enough to rival some of the worst turbulence he had experienced in the skies.

He eased a little off the accelerator.

"Thank you," Tabitha said, and a glance in her direction revealed she was bracing her arms against the roof and the dash. Bobby and Ellie were hugging each other so neither flew off the seat.

Rex slowed a little more.

"Sorry," he said. "Just want to get the hell out of here."

"Let's get out of here in one piece," she said.

Rex realized he was as rigid as a statue. He exhaled and felt his entire body sag.

"You guys okay?" he said casually, wanting to signal a return to normality.

"Yeah," Bobby said, letting go of Ellie.

"Yeah," Ellie agreed, pushing Bobby's legs off her. "But can we change cars when we get to the other one? I like it better."

"In two minutes, sweetie," Tabitha said.

Remaining in third gear, Rex navigated the beat-up road with general success, tapping the brake and gas pedals when needed to avoid the hazards.

"Cabin should be coming up on the left," he said.

A few moments later, beyond a phalanx of gray tree trunks, the cabin came into view—at least the cabin's windows, backlit as they were with the yellow glow of candlelight.

"Watch out!" Tabitha cried.

Rex returned his attention to the road and saw two figures crossing it, one standing, the other lying on his or her side —being dragged? The standing figure spun around just as Rex swerved hard to the right.

The truck roared into the forest. Vegetation slapped the windshield. The steering wheel spun loose from Rex's grip. He stamped the brake with his foot, though it was too late. The truck crashed into a tree and came to a bone-crushing halt.

∆∆∆

In his dream Rex was in the Captain's seat of the doomed Airbus 320 that would crash into the French Alps in nine hours. As the large aircraft climbed into the sky after taking off from JFK airport, he flicked on the autopilot to allow him to scan for other aircraft nearby. He set the altimeters to standard pressure and turned off the landing lights. After confirmation from the high-altitude controller that no pilots in front of him had experienced turbulence, he switched off the seatbelt sign.

Rex turned to his First Officer in the seat next to his. "Good weekend, Freddy?" he asked.

Frederick shrugged. "Didn't do anything special."

"Jeanne's well?" Jeanne was his wife of close to two years now.

"She's fine." He seemed about to add something but didn't. "How are you and Tabitha?"

"Good. We're very good."

"She seemed nice."

"She liked you too," Rex said, referring to the time the three of them had a drink at a bar at Sea-Tac Airport.

Below them, New York City disappeared as they coasted out over the Atlantic Ocean. Soon they wouldn't have any ground-based navigation facilities to rely on, so they performed the final checks to make sure the computer was accurately tracking their position.

With this done, Rex was going to phone the cabin crew on the upper deck to bring them coffee when Fred blurted, "She's leaving me."

Rex blinked. "Jeanne? Ah, shit, Freddy."

"She's met somebody."

"I'm sorry, man."

"Some fucking vet. Not even a real doctor."

Rex noticed the First Officer clenching and unclenching his right fist.

"You'll be fine," he said. "There are a lot of other women out there."

"She's kicking me out. She wants to keep the house we bought together."

"There's no working things through with her?"

Frederick shook his head. "She says we don't have anything in common anymore. She says she's bored. She actually told me that. The bitch." He was still clenching and unclenching his fist.

"Hey, Freddy—you okay?"

The First Officer looked at him. "What do you think, man? My wife is leaving me."

"Yeah, but I mean… You want to take some time off to deal with it?"

He barked a laugh. "You don't trust me up here with you?"

Rex shook his head. "I just mean—why not take some time off? Go on a vacation or something. Clear your mind."

"Jesus, Rex. I'm not going to fly the plane into a goddamn mountain."

"Well, I'm here if you want to talk."

"Thanks."

This was the conversation Rex and Frederick had verbatim a week before Frederick took his life, along with the other one hundred fifty-nine passengers on board Flight 2023.

Which raised the haunting question: Had Rex indeed been derelict in his duty as Captain by not reporting this conversation? Rex had asked himself this a thousand times since the crash, and the conclusion he had come to was that, no, he didn't believe so. He didn't know then that his First Officer had suffered previous episodes of depression. In fact, before that day, Freddy had never displayed any odd or depressed behavior whatsoever. To Rex and the entire flight crew, he had always been a happily married twenty-seven-year-old doing a job he loved doing. Everyone was entitled to feeling down now and then. Frederick, he'd thought, was just having a down period.

Someone began banging on the flight deck door, shouting to be let in. Suddenly Rex became aware of screaming and pandemonium in the cabin. Then he realized Frederick had started the unscheduled descent that would kill them all. His first thoughts: *It's too early! We're still over the ocean!*

"Fred!" he said, his stomach dropping. "Don't do this!"

"No can do, Captain."

Rex tried to pull back on his yoke to gain altitude, but he found he couldn't move his arms.

"Fred!" he croaked. "Don't do this!"

The aircraft continued its eighty-degree death plunge, accelerating, corkscrewing, nose rocking. The white clouds parted. The horizon was nowhere to be seen. Just the ocean, sparkling blue, coming at them far too fast.

So this is what it feels like to know you're moments away from dying.

An image of Bobby flashed in Rex's mind, and Tabitha and Ellie, and then—

∆∆∆

Ellie's head hurt just as bad as the time she was riding her bicycle without a helmet and lost her balance and swerved into a telephone pole. She not only smacked her head into the pole but also fell off her bike, skinning her knees and palms.

She almost started crying now, but she knew that probably wouldn't be a good idea. The monster would hear her and eat her. Maybe if she stayed quiet it would just leave her alone and go away.

But what if it didn't?

What if it was coming for her right this moment?

She opened her eyes. She was lying on top of Bobby on the truck's seat. When they crashed she must have hit her head on the dashboard and bounced back onto the seat again. No wonder her mom always told her to wear her seatbelt.

Her mom.

Ellie looked up and saw her mom slumped forward, her head

resting against the dashboard.

"Mommy," she whispered. "Mommy, wake up."

She didn't.

Ellie tugged her sleeve. "Mommy!"

Why wasn't she waking up?

Ellie turned and saw T-Rex. He was slumped forward too, his body draped over the steering wheel. The windshield above his head was cracked. It looked like a big spider web.

Ellie didn't think he was going to wake up, so she pushed herself off Bobby and shook his shoulder. "Bobby! Bobby!"

Bobby's eyes opened. He looked at her dazedly. He felt a bump on his forehead and made a face like he was going to cry.

"Don't cry!" she said. "It will hear us!"

Now he saw her, and his crybaby's face became worried. "You mean the monster?"

Ellie nodded.

"Did you see it?" he whispered.

She nodded again. "Did you?"

"Not really."

"Me either," she admitted. "Should we check?"

"Check?"

"See if it's waiting for us?"

"I don't want to."

Ellie sat a bit taller and peeked over the dashboard. The truck's headlights were still on, illuminating the green-black forest. She realized she was facing the wrong direction. The road was behind them. She turned around and looked out the back window. The road was right there, not far away.

And in the red glow of the taillights she saw the monster.

It was crouched over the person lying on the road, unmoving. Ellie didn't know what it was doing, and she couldn't see anything more than its big black outline, but it frightened her terribly.

"Do you see it?" Bobby asked.

"Yes," she breathed.

"Is it coming?"

"No."

"What's it doing?"

"Just sitting there." She had a new thought. "Maybe it's eating the other person!"

"Let me see!"

Bobby pushed up beside her. He gasped. "Is that person dead?"

"I don't know."

"We need to tell my dad." He shook T-Rex. "Dad! Dad! The monster's eating someone! Dad...?"

"He's sleeping like my mom," Ellie stated.

"Why won't he wake up?"

"I don't know."

Bobby looked back at the monster. "What should we do?"

"We need to help the person."

"How?"

"We need to scare the monster away."

"How?"

Ellie was thinking. She didn't want to get out of the truck, because then the monster might get her and eat her for dessert. She could yell. Tell it to shoo like you do to barking dogs. But it might not listen to her because she was just a little girl.

"Do you know how to use the horn?" she asked suddenly.

"What horn?" Bobby asked.

"The car horn."

They both looked at the steering wheel.

"My dad's in the way," Bobby said.

"You can reach under him and push the button."

Bobby frowned. "What button?"

"The horn button."

"You do it," he said.

"He's your dad!"

"So? You're closer."

Frowning, Ellie stuck her arm under T-Rex's chest. She felt the hard plastic of the circular steering wheel. Wasn't the horn button right in the middle of it? Her hand followed a spoke until she felt a smaller circle. She pressed it.

Beep!

Ellie jumped in surprise.

"It heard!" Bobby said. "Honk again!"

She pressed the button a second time.

Beeeeeeeeeeeeeep!

"It's standing up!" Bobby said.

"Is it running away?"

"No! It's coming to us!"

"To get us?"

"I think so!"

Ellie pressed the horn again, holding it for several seconds.

T-Rex groaned.

Ellie let go of the button. "Your dad's waking up!"

"So's your mom!"

Ellie glanced at her mom, and she was indeed sitting up, rubbing her head.

"Mommy!" she cried.

"Daddy!" Bobby cried.

With a groan, T-Rex slumped back in his seat. Blood covered his face, and the whites of his eyes seemed very bright in the darkness.

"It's coming, Mommy!" Ellie jabbed her finger at the back window.

The monster had stopped and was just standing there, staring at them.

Her mom frowned strangely at Ellie like she didn't even know who she was!

"Mommy, look!"

The monster turned and disappeared into the night.

△△△

"We need to get to the cabin before he comes back," Rex said quietly but urgently. He had gotten out of the pickup truck and now stood in the forest, peering into the cab.

Tabitha was thinking the same thing. Whoever that man was, he had already killed two people, possibly three, and they needed to return to the cabin ASAP until they figured out what the hell they were going to do.

She shoved open her door, the movement causing pain to flare where she'd struck her head in the crash. Grimacing, she climbed out, her jellied legs nearly collapsing beneath her.

"Come on, Ellie," she said, reaching for her daughter. "Give me your hand."

They met Rex and Bobby back on the road. Rex shone the Maglite on the person lying unmoving on his stomach on the wet mud and gravel.

"Jesus, it's a *cop*!" he exclaimed.

"What's he doing out here?" Tabitha asked. Then with a surge of hope: "Could he know about the maniac? Did he come to help? Are there others?"

Rex didn't reply, and the deep silence of the night seemed to answer that last question.

"Is he dead?" Bobby asked timidly.

"Don't look at him," Rex said.

"Bobby, come here," Tabitha said. When the boy joined her, she turned him and Ellie around so they faced the forest.

"Why can't I look, Mommy?" Ellie asked.

"You don't need to," she said simply.

Tabitha heard Rex roll the police officer onto his back. She glanced over her shoulder. The man was in his late fifties, with a lived-in face and a rather large nose. His Eisenhower patrol jacket, zipped to the neck, had been torn open across the abdomen and appeared to be stained with blood.

Rex checked for a pulse and said, "He's alive!"

Tabitha said, "What should we do?"

"Take the kids to the cabin. I'll be right behind you."

"We're not leaving you—"

"Go! I'll be right behind you."

"Guys, come on," she said, ushering Ellie and Bobby along the road. She could see the candlelit windows of the cabin blinking in and out from behind the trunks of the trees they passed. They had been moving at a swift trot, but when they reached the driveway Tabitha's nerve left her, and she led Ellie and Bobby at a full sprint until they reached the rickety porch. The woman's body, she saw in horror, was no longer covered by the quilt. Thankfully the kids didn't immediately notice this in the dark, and she got them inside before they did.

"What if the monster comes back here too?" Ellie asked, her cheeks flushed.

"That wasn't a monster, sweetie," Tabitha said, trying to catch her breath. "It was just a bad man."

"Do you promise?"

"Monsters aren't real."

"This one was."

"No, it wasn't. Now I want you and Bobby to go upstairs and… get under your beds."

"That's where the monster lives!" Ellie protested.

"Ellie, for the last time, monsters aren't real!" Tabitha clamped her mouth shut, knowing this was an argument she wasn't going to win. "Now listen to me, young lady, you and Bobby go upstairs and, well, just get in your beds if you won't go under them. But be very quiet. Because if the bad man does come back here, he might want to hurt you. So the best thing you can do is to go upstairs and not make any noise. Do you understand me?"

She nodded silently.

"Bobby?"

"It's dark up there."

"You have your little flashlight, don't you?"

He nodded, pulling from his pocket his keychain flashlight.

"Good," she said. "You can turn that on if it's too dark."

Suddenly Ellie burst into tears. She wrapped her arms around Tabitha's legs in a hug. "I don't want to leave you, Mommy!"

"Oh, baby, hush, hush," Tabitha said, crouching. "Look, I don't think the man is coming back here. And Rex is with the policeman. And the policeman has a radio, and a gun, so we're going to be okay. I just need you to go hide for me until help comes. Okay?"

Ellie sniffed, rubbing her eyes.

"Okay, sweetie?"

"Okay."

"Good. Now go on. I'll come up and check on you two shortly."

Tabitha waited until she heard the kids clamber up the staircase before she stuck her head out the door and scanned the night. She saw Rex immediately. He was coming down the driveway, bent over, his back to her, as he dragged the police officer by the arms. She went to help him, taking one of the man's arms. Together, they got the body to the porch, up the stairs, and through the door, which they deadbolted behind them.

"Where are the kids?" Rex asked, puffing heavily.

"Upstairs in bed," Tabitha replied.

"Okay," he said, his eyes glinting with concern. "Okay, we need to….we need to secure this place. Give me a hand."

They spent the next few minutes moving the bookcase and sofa and other pieces of large furniture in front of the door and windows. Anyone half determined could still get in, Tabitha knew. But at least they couldn't simply throw a rock through a windowpane and follow through the opening.

Back in the front room, Rex unzipped the police officer's jacket. His navy uniform was shredded and bloodied. The nametag above the breast pocket read PAUL HARRIS.

Rex unbuttoned the shirt's strip of buttons to examine the wound beneath.

"Not as bad as Daisy's," he muttered.

It wasn't, Tabitha noted thankfully, but that wasn't saying much. The police officer's guts might not be spilling out of the leering gash, but it was still an inch deep and at least six inches wide and bleeding freely.

She retrieved a cotton throw pillow they had tossed aside when they'd moved the sofa and said, "I'm going to try to stop the bleeding." She knelt next to Rex, pressed the pillow against the police officer's abdomen, and held it tightly in place.

"Rex! His gun!" she said, noticing for the first time that the man's holster was empty. "Where is it?"

"I don't know," he said, frowning. He engaged the quick-release buckle of the police officer's duty belt and slid it free from around the man's waist.

Tabitha glanced at the numerous pouches. "Shouldn't there be a radio? Where's his radio?"

"Handcuffs, spare magazine, keys, flashlight." Rex removed and studied an expandable baton.

"Where's the radio, Rex?"

"He must have dropped it. I'll go have a look."

"Go have a look?"

"Outside."

"You can't go outside! *He's* outside."

"We can't just sit here, Tabs. We need to call for help."

"A phone. Maybe he has a phone."

Rex searched the man's clothing and found only a worn wallet which contained a gold police badge and some bills. His eyes went back to the keys on the duty belt. One of them was for a Ford.

Tabitha knew what he was thinking and said, "He must have parked where we did and walked—

"Oh, Christ!" Rex said, cutting her off. "The light we saw on the road," he added, his face drawn. "It was this guy, walking here on foot."

And we turned back, Tabitha thought with a dose of black despair. *We were in the clear, and we turned back. But how could we have known better?*

"What are we going to do, Rex?" she asked, and it was almost a plea.

"Make a break for the car again?"

"We can't! *He's* out there! That crazy, sick…" She shook her head. "He'll be expecting us to do that!"

"Then I have to go look for the cop's radio. If he was surprised, caught off guard, he probably just dropped it. Same with his gun."

"Wouldn't the psycho have taken them?"

"I don't know. But I have to at least check."

"Who is it, Rex? What's going on?"

Rex shook his head. "All I can think is some copycat killer. He heard about what happened to the other families up here, and now he's—"

"*Other* families?" Tabitha blurted. "What other families?"

Rex summarized what Tony and Daisy had revealed to him earlier in the evening. "I swear I didn't know about any of this," he finished. "I've always believed Logan and my parents died in a boating accident. I never would have brought you guys here otherwise."

Tabitha sank back onto her butt, shocked and stunned, and cold, so cold, the sensation seeming to emanate from her bones.

"This is madness," she said in a daze as Rex took over applying pressure to the police officer's wound. "You know that, right, Rex? This is madness. What you're saying happened, what, twenty, thirty, forty years ago? Three families kidnapped and never found? That's bizarre enough. But what's even more bizarre, it's happening all over again, to *us*—"

"It's not!" he snapped. "Whatever happened then has nothing to do with what's happening now. Tonight's a coincidence. Nobody knew we were coming up here."

Tabitha felt as though her world was tearing apart at the seams. This was a nightmare from which she couldn't wake. All they'd wanted was a few days away from the city to relax...

"The kids, Rex," she said. "We can't let anything happen to the kids."

"Nothing's going to happen to them," he said decisively. "Press down on the pillow."

When she did as he asked, he stood.

"What are you doing?" she asked.

"I'm going to find the radio."

"No, Rex!"

"We can't just sit here doing jack shit, Tabs! We're sitting ducks!" He softened his tone. "I'm sorry, but we have to do something. So just hold tight. I'm not going to go far."

CHAPTER 13

Rex waited on the porch until he heard Tabitha latch the deadbolt on the other side of the door. Then, armed with the Maglite and a serrated knife he'd taken from the kitchen, he proceeded down the rickety steps. The rain started at the very moment he stepped from beneath the porch roof, increasing to a gentle patter to a hard fall in the space of seconds. The cold drops stung his face and eyes and caused him to squint. He held his hand gripping the knife against his brow in a salute and started along the perimeter of the cabin. The fresh, ozone-laced air filled his nostrils. His ears strained to hear any noise he didn't make. Every muscle in his body seemed tensed to either fight or run.

Rex stopped when he reached the corner of the cabin. He swept the flashlight beam across the ground in front of him, revealing matted pine needles and rivulets of running water and wilted, soggy autumn leaves. He raised the beam, poking the darkness between the crowding, craggy tree trunks. Silent lightning flashed overhead, momentarily stinging the sky purple-blue. In the distance, thunder rumbled menacingly. The wind whistled and moaned and fluttered his clothing.

Rex heard something behind him and spun around. There was nothing there. The sound had been his imagination.

Exhaling the breath that had caught in his throat, he told himself to keep his cool. He was just about six feet tall, fit, and had a knife. He was likely more than a match for whoever was out here with him. He couldn't allow himself to slip into the mindset of a victim. That's what this guy wanted. Predator versus prey. As long as Rex thought of himself as a predator also, then they were on a level playing field.

Maybe I should stalk him? Rex thought suddenly. *Or at least ambush him? I could lie up somewhere with a view of the cabin door. Wait for him to come out of hiding. Sneak up on him. Give the bastard a taste of his own medicine.*

This prospect was appealing. But he'd told Tabitha he would be back shortly. If he didn't return in a few minutes, she would get worried. She might even do something rash like coming outside to look for him.

Best to stick to the plan for now. Look for the cop's gun and radio. If he didn't find either, he would return inside and explain Plan B to Tabitha.

Rex started left along the lake-facing façade of the cabin. Unlike most modern cottages, only a single bay window looked onto the water. As Rex passed it by, he could see orange candlelight seeping between the window frame and drawn blinds, but that was all. He certainly couldn't see the bookcase he and Tabitha had moved in front of it.

The rain continued to pour down in buckets. Rex's hair was already as thoroughly wet as if he'd stepped from a shower. His green bomber jacket was holding up well, but his khaki trousers clung uncomfortably to his legs, and his feet felt clammy in his wet socks and boat shoes.

When Rex reached the far corner, he stopped again. He walked the flashlight beam back and forth revealing only trees, trees, and more trees. Lightning flashed. Through a break between the weeping boughs of two conifers, he glimpsed the briefly illuminated lake. Usually inky smooth, the surface boiled with peaks and white caps.

It was a dark and stormy night... he thought without humor.

Rex started down the back of the cabin. He passed another window shielded by closed drapes (and blockaded with a high chest of drawers in which his mother had kept her good china and silverware). Next came the chimney. It was made entirely of fieldstones and smaller rocks and protruded nearly three feet from the cabin proper. The top of the smokestack had succumbed to the elements years ago, and many of the stones were now scattered over the ground.

Rex rounded the next corner so the road was in the trees to his right. Beyond it, the foothills rose steeply up the slopes of the Fraser Canyon to the largely unpopulated inland forests and mountain ranges that stretched for hundreds of miles between here and Alberta.

Anyone could live out there, off the grid, for years or decades, he thought. *And Dad had loved the outdoors. Could he have taken Mom and Logan there? Were they still alive? Could his father have returned to Pavilion Lake now and then in the offseason to raid the cabins for supplies? Had the Petersons and Ryersons caught him red-handed? Had he killed them only to keep his secret?*

But what of Daisy and Tony and the police officer?

How did their attacks fit?

Rex had been so absorbed in these musings he almost walked straight past the pistol lying on the muddy ground. He stared at it for a moment in shock, blinking rain from his eyes. Then he promptly swooped it up.

His heart sang at the sight and weight of it in his hand.

Rex didn't know anything about guns, and it took him a few exploratory moments before he pulled back the slide and saw that the chamber was loaded—though in the process he pulled the slide back too far, engaging the ejector and expelling the round through the breech.

Stupid! he thought, fearful that might have been the last bullet. But to his relief, a second check revealed a new round from the magazine had been loaded in place of the first.

Rex picked up the ejected cartridge and stuffed it in his pocket. Then he searched the ground for the police officer's radio. He discovered the man's cylindrical flashlight, his gold-embroidered cap, and a few popped buttons. But no radio.

"Shit," Rex said. "Shit, shit, shit. *Where is it?*"

Not here, that was all he knew.

Doesn't matter anymore! a voice inside his head told him. *You have the gun! Get inside. Protect the others.*

He obeyed this sound advice.

∆∆∆

Rex hung his bomber jacket on the wall-mounted rack, then dumped the three items he'd found outside on the coffee table.

Tabitha, still kneeling next to the supine police officer, applying pressure to his abdominal wound, said, "The gun!"

He nodded. "Have you fired one before?"

"Not for a long time."

"But you have?"

She hesitated. "Yes."

Rex wondered at the pause, but he didn't press the matter. Sitting down next to her on the floor, doing his best to ignore the wet clothing chafing his skin, he said, "I didn't find his radio. No idea where it went. It's clear he was attacked behind the cottage. That's where he dropped his flashlight and gun. So what about his radio?"

"His name's Paul," Tabitha said. "Paul Harris."

"Paul," Rex repeated. Then, to the cop: "So help us out here, Paul. Where's your radio? It would be nice to know someone was coming out here to give us a hand."

"Someone *will* come," Tabitha insisted. "When he doesn't return to the station, and no one can get in touch with him, other cops will come. And look, I think he's important, like the chief or something." She indicated the rank insignia that adorned his shoulders: a gold crown above three gold pips.

Rex studied Paul Harris. His craggy face was pale and waxy, his eyes closed, his mouth ajar, his cheeks sunken, almost corpse-like.

He probably is the chief, Rex thought. He had seniority on his side, and a place as small as Lillooet probably only had a couple of cops on the payroll. A chief and a lieutenant, maybe. A part-time retiree who volunteered here and there, maybe. But that would likely be all.

So who was going to be missing him at this time of night? His wife? He wore a wedding band on his ring finger. Even so, couples who had been married for a long time often chose to sleep in separate bedrooms. His wife might very well be nestled snug in her bed, visions of sugar-plums dancing in her head, unaware that her husband had yet to return home from his last shift.

Moreover, given Paul's age, it wasn't inconceivable that his wife had prematurely passed on. He could be a widower wearing the wedding band out of obligation, or memory.

The only thing we know for certain, Rex decided gloomily, is that we know nothing for certain. Help could arrive ten minutes from now, or ten hours, or longer.

Chin up, soldier.

Rex blinked. For a startled moment, he thought Tabitha had spoken those whispered words, but they had been inside his head.

Chin up, soldier.

This was an expression his ex-wife, Naomi, had often used, usually to cheer up Bobby when he was down. A particularly vivid memory struck Rex of the three of them sitting around the dinner table, Bobby in a funk because he knew he couldn't leave the table until he finished the vegetables on his plate, and Naomi ruffling his hair as she carried dirty dishes to the sink, saying, "Chin up, soldier. There are worse things in this world than munching back a few of your mom's delicious veggies."

A not-unfamiliar ache rose inside Rex's chest. He had loved Naomi once, and although that love had faded, it had not disappeared altogether. Their divorce had not been poisonous as so many were. There had been no vulgar shouting or scandalous accusations or flying china or behind-the-back disparaging remarks to friends. They had been together for seven years, and despite having a son together, seven years had simply been enough.

Rex's job was largely to blame for their falling out, he knew. His constant traveling had been tough on Naomi. She came to equate his downtime in other countries with mini-vacations while she remained stuck at home dealing with backed-up toilets, car problems, and the like. He tried to paint a more realistic narrative of what he did, along with the downsides to living out of a suitcase, but these efforts were constantly undermined when a co-worker uploaded a picture to social media of him enjoying a cocktail at a hotel bar, or of the sun setting over Athens or Rome or whichever exotic locale his work took him. Moreover, as Captain, he was responsible for every major decision on every flight, which was mentally exhausting. As a consequence, when he returned home he usually wanted to do only one thing: decompress. So when Naomi handed him a to-do list of chores that had accumulated in his absence, he'd often put off doing them. When she made breakfast in the hopes that he'd join her, he'd often opt to sleep in. When she asked him where he wanted to go for dinner, he'd most likely tell her he didn't care (as long as it wasn't McDonald's, which was his go-to airport restaurant).

Although this tension between them over his work had been building for years, the final straw came when Rex got scheduled to fly to London during the family's annual vacation to Hawaii, despite having bid for a different route and date far in advance.

"Maybe I'll just go with Bobby, just the two of us," Naomi said tartly after he explained the change of plans to her.

"Maybe you should," he said sincerely. "Enjoy yourself. You don't need me tagging along."

"No, I don't," she replied in a cold voice. "In fact, I don't think I need you at all anymore, Rex." Her face flushed with anger. "I'm sick of going to Bobby's school functions alone, Rex. I'm sick of falling asleep in front of the TV because it's the only company I have, Rex. I'm sick of being lonely." Her face softened. "You're a good man, Rex, and I love you, but I think it might be best if we go our own ways from here on."

Deep down Rex had known Naomi was right. The only

solution to their marital woes would be for him to find a different job, and that would never happen. Like most pilots, he had a passion for what he did, it was in his blood, a part of his identity, and he couldn't change that.

So they quietly and amicably filed for divorce, drafting a parental plan to detail the custody arrangement of Bobby. The boy took the news of their separation rather well, even showing excitement at the prospect of having two houses and thus two bedrooms of his own. But then a month and a half after the divorce was finalized, in October of the previous year, Naomi struck and killed a sixty-five-year-old woman with her Toyota sedan. Too drunk to realize the extent of what she had done, she drove to a side street where she passed out. In the morning she called a body shop to fix her vehicle, telling the owner she had hit a telephone pole. Police, however, recovered a fog-light grill from the scene of the accident and matched it to her car. She was charged with the operation of a motor vehicle causing death, failure to stop at the scene of an accident causing death, and impaired driving causing death. She was released on $100,000 bail. During her court appearance, teary-eyed and apologetic, she explained she had been drinking heavily at the time of the accident due to a trifecta of converging events: her mother's death, her father's refusal to continue taking chemotherapy for his cancer, and her divorce to her husband of seven years. The judge, in her ruling, said she took into account these mitigating factors, as well as the fact Naomi had entered a guilty plea and had no prior criminal record, before handing down a five-year prison sentence.

That night, Rex and Naomi explained to Bobby what his mother had done and that she would be going away for a while. He took this news extremely well also, just as excited at the possibility of visiting his mom in prison as he had been at having two bedrooms. Nevertheless, his seemingly boundless optimism nosedived when Tabitha came into the picture. Her regular visits to the condo where Rex had been renting a unit, combined with Naomi's abrupt departure from his life, caused him to begin viewing Tabitha with suspicion, hence the commencement of the silent treatment he gave her.

For his part, Rex hadn't planned on dating someone so soon after the divorce, but he and Tabitha had immediately clicked upon meeting. As a flight attendant, she understood the rigors of working for an airline, and the baggage that came with the job, so to speak. He could talk to her without feeling defensive about his day, or guilty about providing her with a life she didn't want. For the first time in years he felt young and vivacious and happy.

And now it was all at risk. The new life he was building with Tabitha, Bobby, and Ellie was now all at risk of not surviving until morning—

Rex banished these thoughts from his head. He would not dabble with despair.

Wanting a distraction, he retrieved the pistol from the coffee table and flipped it over in his hands, getting a feel for it. The frame was polymer, not steel. At the top of the hand grip was, G L O C K, and above that, MADE IN AUSTRIA. He pressed a button that ejected the magazine.

A series of holes at the back portion of the magazine revealed it currently held six out of a possible seventeen rounds. Rex fished the cartridge from his pocket he'd ejected earlier and inserted it into the top of the magazine, making sure the rounded tip was pointing forward. He reseated the magazine in the hand grip with a satisfying click.

Tabitha was watching him. "Better disengage the safety," she said.

"Where is it?"

She pointed to a lever on the upper back portion of the firearm.

He pushed it down.

"A regular Dirty Harry," she said.

"'Do you feel lucky, punk?'"

"That's not the quote."

Rex returned the pistol to the coffee table. He wrapped an

arm around Tabitha's shoulders and kissed her on the top of the head. Then, seeing he was inhibiting her from properly applying pressure to the cop's wound, he released her.

They waited.

∆∆∆

Rain drummed on the roof of the cabin. Wind buffeted the sturdy log walls, moaning longingly as if to be let in out of the wet and cold. Thunder rolled across the sky, approaching ever closer.

Tabitha kept the pillow firmly pressed against Paul Harris's abdomen. The slip had been white to begin with. Now it was stained bright crimson. Her hands were sticky with blood.

As the minutes dragged on, she kept her ears pricked for the sound of a car engine approaching in the dark, or distant klaxons, anything that would signal the arrival of help.

All she heard was the damnable rain and wind and thunder.

To keep from totally wigging out, she entertained herself with positive future scenarios. She and Rex and the kids in the toasty warm Mazda, cruising along Highway 99, some cheery pop song on the radio, leaving this little slice of nightmare behind. Or the four of them in a hotel room in Squamish, or Vancouver, sitting by the pool, or eating a buffet breakfast, surrounded by other people, parents and their children, everybody laughing and smiling and enjoying themselves. Or back in Seattle, downtown amidst the bustle of the city, or in her house, or Rex's condo, or in a jet, in the sky.

Oh, what she wouldn't give to be thirty-thousand feet in the air right now!

Black scenarios inevitably crept into this thinking as well, such as one of the cabin's windows exploding inward, furniture toppling over, and the killer leaping into the room, brandishing a butcher's knife or machete or whatever his weapon of choice might be.

Thank God they had the pistol, she thought. The killer likely didn't know this. He would be surprised, caught off guard. Rex would fire off a volley of shots, and the bastard would be dead before he hit the floor.

And me? she wondered. *Would I be able to shoot the man if it came to that?*

Although Tabitha's father had been a Clark Griswold family man on the surface, who liked nothing more than embarking on road trips, barbequing steaks on the grill, and visiting wacky tourist destinations, he was also an avid firearms collector and champion marksman. As a consequence of this, guns had been an integral part of Tabitha's childhood and adolescence. By the time she entered fifth grade, she knew how to field strip, clean, and reassemble several types of revolvers, semi-automatic pistols, and rifles. She knew wadcutters from hollow points. She could distinguish on sight a Browning from a Heckler & Koch from a Smith & Wesson.

One of her earliest memories was of the first time her father had taken her to a gun range. It was a big concrete place with strings of light bulbs lining the ceiling and brass shell casings littering the floor. She couldn't see the shooters in the other booths, so each of their gunshots caught her by surprise, causing her to flinch instinctively, the cumulative effect an unrelenting jumpiness that kept her vividly alert.

After Beth and Ivy had their turns shooting, her father handed her his semi-automatic pistol. She assumed the proper stance, aimed at the paper target, eased her breathing, and relaxed her trigger finger. Then she fired, the gun leaping back up her hands. The spent shell, ejected from the chamber smoking hot, bounced off her bare forearm, shocking her with a quick sizzle. The tang of gunpowder wafted up into her nostrils.

When they got home later that morning, her dad immediately set out cloths, solvents, and oil, and Tabitha and her sisters dismantled the weapons they'd used, wiping the powder residue from the firing pins and the cylinders and pushing solvent-soaked cotton squares through the barrels until they could see the tiny spiral grooves inside. Then, like three little soldiers, they reassembled each gun with speed and precision that belied their young ages, each part joining with metallic clicks and ka-chaks.

Tabitha continued to visit the gun range with her father and sisters throughout elementary school, junior high, and high school. She went to gun shows and participated in shooting tournaments. She read each issue of the NRA's magazine, *The American Rifleman*, cover to cover the day it was delivered to their doorstep each month. When she moved away from home to attend Seattle University, she bought her first gun, a Colt Cobra .38 Special. She kept it in the drawer of the nightstand next to her bed, loaded with five bullets, the firing pin resting on an empty chamber so it wouldn't accidentally discharge. When she heard creaks or strange noises in the house she rented with a handful of roommates, she wasn't afraid. Knowing her gun was within easy reach, she felt empowered and in control.

Then two years ago she had been in downtown Seattle celebrating her thirty-sixth birthday. She and one of her girlfriends, Katy Pignetti, were the last to leave the bar. While they were wandering the empty city streets, looking for a taxi, a man in a hoodie brandished a 9mm snub-nose in their faces and demanded they hand over their purses. Instead of complying, Tabitha gripped the .38 in her handbag and fired three shots through the leather into his chest. She had not thought this action through. It had been an automatic response, as instinctual as looking both ways before crossing a street.

As the would-be robber fell to the pavement, mortally wounded, he got off one shot in return. The bullet struck Katy in the chest (Tabitha would later learn it nicked her aorta an inch from her heart). She died minutes later in Tabitha's arms.

Despite the police telling Tabitha she had acted in self-defense, despite her father congratulating her for her quick thinking, and despite her sisters praising her bravery, Tabitha blamed herself for Katy's death. In the days and weeks and months that followed, she suffered severe depression, punishing herself with *if-only* questions. *If only she hadn't been so rash... If only she hadn't tried to be a hero... If only she'd handed over her purse. If only if only if only...*

Then one day roughly one year after Katy's murder, Tabitha called in sick to work with the flu. It had been midmorning. The girls were at school. She'd been in her bathrobe, *Today with Hoda & Jenna* playing on the bedroom television. She'd been planning on drawing a bath, but instead she found herself standing in front of her walk-in closet. She was thinking she could take a belt dangling from one of the plastic coat hangers, slip it around her neck, and hang herself right there. The acidic guilt gnawing away at her insides each day would go away. All the shit she was going through with Harry would go away. She would have no more worries.

And she knew—without a doubt—that if it wasn't for Vanessa and Ellie, she would have done it, she would have hanged herself right there and then. Perhaps a bad gene ran in her family because her grandfather had committed suicide when he was still a young man, as did her Uncle Jed. And her mother very nearly died after passing out one evening after consuming two bottles of wine and far too many sleeping pills (she had always insisted this was an accidental overdose... though what other answer could she tell her daughters?).

So, yes, perhaps Tabitha did indeed have a bad gene inside her, because it would have just been so easy to have killed herself that morning.

The seductive and sick thought of taking her life never went away, not fully. It returned now and then as a passing suggestion —*you could drive right off the bridge, people would think it was an accident* or *you could tip the kayak, drowning would be quick, it might even be peaceful*—and she always shooed it away as quickly as possible in the event it grew roots and became a permanent fixture in her mind.

In any event, Tabitha no longer owned the Colt Cobra. She'd turned it into the police shortly after Katy's death for them to dispose of. And she'd sworn to herself she would never fire a gun again.

But this is different, she told herself. *This maniac isn't a two-bit mugger. He's a murderer. He's killed two people in cold blood.*

So if he comes after Ellie or Rex or Bobby—hell, yes, I'll shoot him. I won't hesitate to shoot him.

Rex stood up abruptly. Tabitha glanced at him. He started pacing, rubbing his hand over his five o'clock shadow. "We can't just sit here all night," he said. "He's coming. He knows we're here, and he's coming."

"But he can't get inside. The doors are locked, and we've barricaded all the windows."

"That won't stop him."

"But we'll know he's out there. We'll be ready."

"What if he sets the place on fire? Smokes us out? We'd run right into his waiting arms. If he has a gun, he could pick us off one by one before we knew where he was firing from."

Tabitha tried not to picture that. "What can we do?" she asked. "Where can we go?"

Rex didn't say anything for a few long moments, then: "I have to get the Mazda."

She stood next to him, alarmed. "You can't leave us, Rex."

"I can be back in twenty minutes. We can be out of here."

"We've already tried that—"

"And would have got away scot-free if we didn't get spooked and turn around."

"He'll know, Rex. He'll expect us to try to get to the car. He'll be watching the cabin. As soon as you leave—"

"You'll have the gun, Tabs. You'll be safe until I get back. Besides, he won't know I've left. There's a root cellar beneath the cabin. The trap door is in the other room, beneath the rug. There's another little bulkhead door that leads from the root cellar to outside, the back of the cabin. I'll leave that way. He'll never know I'm gone."

She considered this. "Let us come with you then. The kids and me. We'll go together."

Rex was shaking his head. "We can't go straight to the road.

We have to go through the forest for a bit until we're far enough away from the cabin not to be noticed. The four of us will make too much noise. It's best I go alone. When I reach the road, I'll sprint. I'll be back before you know it."

This plan frightened Tabitha to her core. The last thing she wanted to do was split up. But Rex was right. They couldn't just sit here like bugs beneath a rock, hoping the rock wasn't turned over. They had to do something unexpected.

"He'll hear the car," Tabitha said, even though she knew she had already conceded to Rex's plan, but wanting to exhaust all avenues of argument nonetheless. "He'll try to get us before we get in it."

"I'll drive it right up to the door. You just have the kids ready. Have the gun ready."

"It's risky," she said. "He could shoot you."

"We don't even know if he has a gun. He probably only has a knife. That's all he's used so far. And how's that going to help him if we're in a car?"

"But he *could* have a—"

"He's just a man, Tabs," Rex said, taking her bloodied hands and squeezing them between his. "We can do this. We can be out of here in twenty minutes. It will be over."

His words were too tempting for her to not believe, or to not *want* to believe, for Tabitha had never desired anything more in her life than for this night to be over with.

She nodded.

CHAPTER 14

Rex yanked back the throw rug with the flourish of a magician, revealing the trap door that hid beneath. Even had it not been covered by the rug, it would have been hard to see, as it was flush with the floor and made from the same thick planks of solid timber. There was no handle or latch, so he slipped the blade of the serrated knife he'd taken from the kitchen into the crack between the edge of the hatch opposite the hinges and the floorboards. He pried, and the hatch lifted easily.

Rex clicked on the police officer's flashlight and shone it into the hole. A short ladder descended four feet to hard-packed dirt. Stale, earthy air wafted up, carrying with it the scent of neglect and age.

"There's not much room down there," Tabitha said warily.

"It opens up," Rex assured her. "The ground slopes toward the lake. When you get beneath the front room, you can almost stand."

He shifted onto his butt, dangled his legs into the hole, then hopped down.

"Be careful, Rex," she said.

"I'll be back soon," he said.

Squatting, he swung the flashlight from side to side, scanning the dark cavity that opened away from him. The air was damp and cool. The ground, like he'd told Tabitha, sloped toward the lake, following the natural lay of the land. He crouched-walked forward, using his free hand like a third leg to balance himself until he was able to stand, though he had to hunch forward so he didn't whack his head against any of the beams or joists that supported the subflooring above him.

Rocks of all different sizes lined the root cellar's walls to help keep the cold air in and the warm air out during mild winter days. Wooden shelves eighteen inches deep protruded from the walls. In Rex's great grandfather's time, before the proliferation of refrigerators and canned food, the shelves would likely have stored apples, sweet corn, potatoes, and perhaps root crops such as beets, turnips, and carrots. Now they held rusty tools, broken toys, musty books, dented paint cans, camping gear, a set of dumbbells, and other miscellaneous junk, all of which was covered with dust, spider webs, and grime.

A lump formed in Rex's throat at the sight of Stretch Armstrong, his once beloved gel-filled action figure, poking out of the top of one toy-filled bucket.

"You okay down there, Rex?" Tabitha called, her voice sounding far away.

"Yeah," he called back.

Pushing aside a life jacket that dangled from an iron hook, which would have originally been used to hang smoked meat, Rex aimed the flashlight beam at the door that led outside. It was made of vertical wooden planks and was about three-quarters of the height of a regular door.

He started toward it—and had the scare of his life.

△△△

The suddenly molasses-thick air slowed down time and made it difficult to breathe. Rex stared at what lay against the rock wall in shock and dismay as a decades-old memory clawed triumphantly free from the depths of his subconscious where it had been buried for the last thirty-eight years.

Rex working on his Lego castle on the floor of the cabin when the door burst inward and his mother appeared, wild-eyed and ashen-

faced.

"Hide!" she told him in a voice so panic-stricken he barely recognized it as her own.

Rex leaped to his feet. "What happened, Mom?"

"He got your Dad," she said, and Rex noticed that her knees, bare below the cuffs of a pair of yellow shorts, were dirtied with mud, and her hands were shaking uncontrollably.

"Who got Dad, Mom?" he asked, his voice rising to soprano level.

"I don't know! We were just walking and he got ahead of me...and he screamed... I didn't see what happened... He was too far ahead. He just told me to run, I didn't see what... I didn't see..."

"Is Dad dead, Mom?" Rex asked, feeling as though his insides had just been scooped out with a giant spoon.

"I don't know, pumpkin, I don't know, I don't know, I don't know." She shook her head and seemed to snap out of the paralysis that had gripped her. "You have to hide!"

"Where's Logan?"

"Logan?" she said, turning in a circle as if just realizing he wasn't there. "He was with me. He was right beside me. Logan? Logan, baby?"

A moment later Logan staggered through the door. Rex thought he was smiling, perhaps about to burst into laughter (maybe tell him this was all a prank), but then Rex realized it wasn't a smile he was seeing on his brother's face; it was a grimace of pain. And then Rex noticed that Logan's hands, pressed against his tummy, were red with blood.

"Logie?" their mom said. "Logie? Baby? You're bleeding! What happened?"

"I tried to help Dad..." His voice was a whisper.

"Logie!" their mom all but screamed, dropping to her knees. She made to touch his wound, but hesitated, as though fearful to hurt him. "Is it bad, baby? How bad is it, baby?"

"It hurts," he moaned.

She started to lift his torn shirt. He cried out.

"Sorry, baby, sorry." She stood decisively. "You boys hide. Right now. Hide."

"Where are you going, Mom?" Rex asked.

"Take your brother, Rex, and go hide right now. You boys are good at that."

She went to the door.

"Mom!" Rex cried. "Don't leave us!"

"I have to lead him away." She pushed her dark hair from her dark eyes, which were looking at Rex but didn't seem to be seeing him.

"Hide with us," he pleaded.

Attempting a smile that trembled and became a frown, she left the cabin, closing the door behind her.

Rex turned to Logan, whose mouth was twisted in pain. "Did he have a knife?" he asked.

"It wasn't a person," Logan mumbled, and then he began sobbing.

"What?"

"I'm scared, Rex."

"What was it, Loge?"

"I don't know!"

Although Rex was the little brother, he knew he was going to have to make the decision of where to hide. Logan was acting way too weird.

Upstairs under their beds was the first spot that came to his mind. But he quickly dismissed this possibility. That was the first place where people looked when they wanted to find where you were hiding.

In the chimney?

Rex grabbed Logan's hand and all but dragged him into the connecting room. He stuck his head into the fireplace's firebox and looked up. The flue was too narrow. Neither of them would fit. When he pulled his head back out, Logan had already thrown the little rug back to reveal the trap door to the root cellar. Rex and Logan used to play down there. But then at the beginning of the summer their dad found that a family of raccoons had moved in and told them it was off limits, and they hadn't been down there since.

Logan jumped into the hole. "Come on!" he said, his head poking up above the floor.

Rex hesitated. If he went down too, who would put the rug back in place? Someone needed to, or the man who attacked their dad would easily find them (Rex couldn't believe that the person coming after them wasn't a person).

He started swinging the hatch back into place.

Logan stopped it with one of his hands. "What are you doing?"

"I need to put the rug back."

"Where are you going to hide?"

"I'll find a better spot."

Logan held his red-stained hands in front of him. "Am I losing too much blood, Rex?"

Rex shook his head. "I don't think so."

"I don't feel good."

"Just hide. Mom will be back soon."

Rex closed the hatch and pulled the rug back in place. With his heart beating so fast and loud in his chest he could hear it in his ears, he tried to think of a place to hide. In the stove? He was too big. Under the sofa? That was as bad as under the bed. In the closet? No room with the shelves. The bathroom? He could lock the door. No, the attacker would just break it down.

Outside, he decided. There were way more places to hide outside than inside.

Rex left the cabin. It was late afternoon, the sky dull and gray. The forest seemed especially quiet and still. His mind raced through all the places where he had hidden before when he and Logan played Hide and Seek—

His mom screamed.

She sounded like she was near the Sanders' place, which was next door but still far away. Maybe she was going there for help? No, it was late summer, and Rex and his family were the last people remaining on the lake. She understood that. She was just leading the attacker away—

(and he caught her)

Rex grimaced. His first instinct was to go and help her, but he knew he would be too late and too small to help. His second instinct was not to hide but to run. He could try to get to the highway, *and then to town. Even though nobody was on the lake, there were always cars on the highway. If he could reach it, someone would drive by and pick him up and—*

△△△

"*Rex?*" Tabitha called. "*Rex? What's happening?*"

Rex couldn't look away from the small skeleton that lay alongside the wall a few feet away from him. It was dressed in clothes he recognized from his childhood. Logan's green KangaROOS sneakers with the zipped pockets where he used to carry his pennies, nickels, dimes, and quarters. Logan's Hawaiian tiki-print jeans cinched around a non-existent waist. Logan's fluorescent green tee shirt clinging to his sunken chest, outlining the ribs beneath and revealing his denuded arms poking out from the short sleeves.

Perhaps the worst sight, the most ghastly, was Logan's skull. It had turned brown and brittle with age. The skin that still clumped to it was cracked and shriveled. Hair sprouted from the dome. Dried detritus filled the eye sockets. The unhinged jaw gaped unnaturally wide, revealing gaps in the teeth where an incisor or canine had fallen free of the rotting gums.

All at once Rex felt hot and sweaty and sick. He bent over, his stomach cramping, thinking he would throw up.

"*Rex?*" Tabitha called yet again, sounding frightened now.

A deep breath dispelled some of his nausea, and he replied more sharply than he'd intended, "*What?*"

"Why weren't you answering me? Is everything okay down there?"

"Fine," he said absurdly, still focused on the skeleton, thinking, *It's really you, Loge. You've been down here all along. Right down here, in the root cellar, the goddamned root cellar. Dead. Lying here dead for forty years while I've been going about living my life. Jesus Christ, I'm sorry, Loge. I'm so sorry.*

"Rex? What's wrong? Rex? You're scaring me. I'm coming

down."

Rex pried his eyes away from his brother's remains and shone the flashlight back the way he'd come. He saw Tabitha's legs dangling through the trapdoor.

"Stay there!" he shouted.

"What's going on?"

"Nothing. I'm at the door." For some inexplicable reason he didn't want Tabitha to see the skeleton. He didn't want her to freak out. But more than that, he wouldn't allow his brother's remains to become a spectacle to elicit horror and pity, like some schlock horror movie prop.

With a final glance back at Logan, telling himself he would mourn his brother properly at a later time, Rex went to the small door. He pushed against it but found it locked. He shoved harder. The latch and mini padlock on the other side of it, which he glimpsed between cracks in the timber, rattled but held firm.

"Come on!" he said, throwing his shoulder into the door. Wood splintered and cracked, and the door swept open. Rex's momentum propelled him into the storm. The driving rain splashed off his head and shoulders. The gale-force winds lashed his exposed face and hands and pulled wildly at his jacket.

Wiping rain from his eyes, Rex scrambled into the dark mass of forest that surrounded the cabin, his feet making little noise on the soggy leaf litter. He didn't think the night could get any blacker, but it did when the towering, swaying trees closed around him.

Moving blindly, he felt his way forward with his hands, pushing water-logged branches and other vegetation aside. He tripped over what he guessed to be a large rock, his arms pin-wheeling. Pain ripped across his forehead as he plowed face-first into a wall of prickly pine boughs. When he shoved free, his fingers probed a fresh wound above his brow. It was tender and bleeding but didn't seem too deep.

Wiping more rain from his eyes, he considered turning on the Maglite so he could see where the hell he was going, but he didn't dare. He was too close to the cabin. Anyone watching it might spot the light and know someone was afoot.

Rex bumped into a large solid structure. At first he thought it was the outhouse before realizing it was the little lean-to where his father had kept a stockpile of split firewood.

On the far side of it, the ground sloped downward, and he descended carefully. Somewhere nearby, where the soil had eroded along the declivity, was an exposed slab of rock that stretched for fifteen or so feet. Rex and Logan had spent countless hours sliding down it atop a patina of leaves and pine needles and moss, challenging each other to see who could go the farthest, or who could climb back to the top the quickest.

There had always been something forbidding about visiting the rock—

Poison ivy, he thought. Both he and his brother had been severely allergic to the plant's oil. It had never seemed to matter how carefully they crept through the poison ivy patch, or what precautions they took to avoid their skin touching the sea of almond-shaped leaves (such as wearing gum boots that went to their knees or tucking their pants into their socks), they developed an itchy, painful rash each consecutive summer.

During one afternoon visit to the rock, they brought a bucket of water, in the hopes of making the rock's surface especially slippery. They got in a fight about one thing or another, and Rex ended up dumping what remained of the water over Logan's head. In retaliation, Logan plucked some poison ivy plants by the stems, pinned Rex on his back, and rubbed the leaves all over his face.

Rex ran back to the cabin screaming bloody murder. Getting poison ivy on his arms and legs, or between his toes and fingers where the skin blistered and oozed fluid, was bad enough. But on his face!

His mom slathered his skin with Calamine lotion and made him wear a pair of winter mittens she found in the cupboard so he didn't scratch where he would soon begin to itch. Nevertheless, when he woke the next morning, half his face was puffy and inflamed, while one eye was swollen shut. The rash must have lasted three weeks, ruining a good chunk of his summer, and the only silver lining was that he had been allowed as much ice cream as he wanted, which he always made sure to savor in front of his brother.

"Bastard," Rex mumbled quietly to himself, a sad smile ghosting his lips.

He trudged onward, already exhausted from pioneering a path through the dense, wet forest. The terrain flattened out again at the bottom of the small glen. The trees thinned and opened up around him. Yet this slight reprieve lasted for only one hundred feet or so before he found himself climbing the far side of the concavity, struggling with each step to gain reliable footholds in the mud. For every few feet of progress he made, he slipped half that backward. Frustrated but determined, he grasped recklessly at saplings and branches and whatever else he could use to help pull himself up until finally he reached the plateau.

A few paces later gravel crunched beneath his feet, indicating he had reached the neighbor's driveway. Leech had been their surname if he wasn't mistaken. They had a big Alaskan Malamute that barked constantly most days. Rex was amazed he remembered so many of the lake's summer residents given that as a child he had barely met any of them more than once or twice. But he supposed when you're five or six, and your world is not much larger than the size of your residence, everything in it holds extra significance.

Rex took a moment to orientate himself in the dark. Unless he'd gotten completely turned around, the lake—and the Leech's cabin that sat on a small peninsula visible from Rex's dock—was to his left. Which meant the road was to his right.

When Rex reached the juncture where the driveway met the dirt road, he looked both ways. He saw no flashlight beam bobbing through the dark. If the killer was coming after him, he would be as blind as a mole.

Ducking his head against the storm, Rex hurried north along the road toward the Mazda.

ΔΔΔ

Bobby slipped out of bed, clicked on his keychain flashlight, and padded softly to the collection of old furniture stacked in the corner of the attic. The rain was falling on the roof fast now, and the thunder was loud enough to probably knock down trees.

"What are you doing?" Ellie demanded from her bed.

Bobby didn't answer her. Instead, he silently examined the furniture—a low table with sewing machine legs, a white cabinet, a yellow dresser, three wooden shelves attached with metal pipes, a turquoise desk on which sat a clunky black typewriter—before selecting a chair with a plastic seat and black legs, not unlike the one at his desk at school. It rested upside-down atop the white cabinet. He dragged it free and carried it back to his bed.

"What are you doing?" Ellie asked again. She was still in her bed but sitting up now. She was staring at him in challenge like she did when she thought he might be cheating at a game they were playing (he usually wasn't, but it was hard to convince her of that once she made up her mind on the matter). "If you don't tell me," she added, "I'm going to tell my mom."

Bobby set the chair down on the ground to give his arms a break. "You're a tattletale," he said.

"You're going to get in big trouble."

"*Tattleteller.*"

"I'm going to tell right now."

"You'll get in trouble too!"

Ellie seemed to contemplate this, and when Bobby decided she wasn't going to say anything more, he stripped back his bedcover, lifted the chair again, and plunked it down in the middle of his mattress. Then he pulled the heavy cover over the top of the chair.

"You're making a fort!" Ellie exclaimed.

Nodding, Bobby climbed onto the bed and slipped under the

cover. He sat crossed-legged and bent forward so his head didn't brush against the ceiling. He propped the flashlight in his lap and looked around the interior of his fort, pleased with how bright and comfortable it was.

"Can I come in?" Ellie asked, and Bobby heard her hop out of her bed.

"Only boys are allowed," he replied.

"There's no sign that says that."

"I don't need a sign."

Thunder boomed in the sky so loudly and unexpectedly that Bobby flinched and Ellie yelped.

"Let me in!" she said, sounding scared.

"What's the password?"

"I don't know it!"

"What's my favorite TV show?"

"*PJ Masks*?"

"That's *your* favorite show."

"What's your favorite one?"

"*Noddy*."

"Is that the password?"

Bobby hadn't thought of the exact password yet, but "Noddy" would do.

"Yeah…" he said.

"Okay, let me in."

Bobby lifted the bedcover. Ellie's head appeared a moment later. Her wide eyes sparkled as she looked around, and she was smiling. "Neat!" She climbed inside.

"Don't hit the chair!" he said.

"It's small in here," she said, pulling her knees up against her chest and ducking her head like he was. "You should build a second floor."

"How?"

"With more furniture."

"You can't have a second floor in forts."

"Yes, you can," she replied knowingly. Then, suddenly: "Miss Chippy!" She tugged the chipmunk out of her pocket and held the little animal in front of her face. "Were you biting me Miss Chippy? Naughty chippymunk! Are you all better now?"

Bobby stared at her. "You're not allowed to have that up here!"

"Am too!"

"Your mom said you're not allowed to touch it!"

"No, she didn't."

"You shouldn't lie."

"I don't."

"Yes, you do. You always lie. You're lying right now. You lie more than the devil."

Ellie stuffed the chipmunk back in her pocket. "No, I don't. The devil lies the most in the world. And if you tell on me, I'm going to tell on you."

Bobby frowned. "For what?"

"I'll tell my mom you played with Miss Chippy too."

"But I didn't!"

"My mom will believe me. She always believes me."

But Bobby had stopped listening to her. He was looking at his stomach. "Did you hear that?" he asked. "My tummy is making funny sounds."

"That means you're hungry."

"I *am* hungry."

"I wish we could have popcorn."

"We've already had dinner," he reminded her.

"I know. But sometimes my mom lets me have cockporn at nighttime if I've been a good girl all day."

"You said cockporn!"

"No, I didn't, stupid head. I said *pop*corn."

Bobby shrugged. Popcorn sounded pretty good to him right then. It was one of his favorite foods along with chocolate bars, potato chips, and ice cream. He was never allowed to have any of these except on special occasions, like when his dad came home from being away in a different country. "Can you ask your mom to make us some?" he said.

"I don't think your dad bought any at the store."

"He might have."

"He didn't."

"Just ask your mom."

Ellie hesitated. "She's not feeling very well."

Bobby frowned. "Your mom?"

Ellie nodded. "She's scared of the monster."

With all the talk of popcorn, Bobby had almost forgotten about the monster, despite it being the reason he built the fort in the first place. "I think my dad's scared of it too."

"I'm not scared," Ellie proclaimed.

"I'm a little bit," Bobby admitted.

"I'm not," she said defiantly.

"What if it catches us?"

"It can't. It can't get in the fort."

Bobby wanted to believe Ellie that the monster couldn't get in, but he was pretty sure it could if it tried.

Thunder exploded, seeming to shake the entire cabin.

"That was *loud*," Ellie whispered.

Bobby nodded and tried not to think of a tree falling on top of them. "What do you want to do?" he asked her. "Do you want to play a game?"

Ellie held up her hands, her palms facing outward. "Paddy cakes?"

"I'm not a girl! And it's too noisy. Your mom will hear."

Ellie made her thinking face. "Dares?"

Bobby brightened. Dares were always fun if you could think of a good one.

"When I played with my mom," Ellie went on, "she dared me to crack an egg over my head."

"Did you do it?"

She nodded. "You have to. Or else."

"Or else what?"

"You get punished. My mom made me eat a raw carrot once."

"Yuck," he said, glad they didn't have any carrots around.

Ellie sat straight, her head touching the bedcover above her. "Okay, me first. I dare you..." She put on her thinking face again. "I dare you..."

"What?"

"I dare you to…do a chicken dance!"

Bobby couldn't picture what this might look like. "I don't know a chicken dance."

"You have to! I dared you!"

"But I don't know it! I can't do it if I don't know it!"

"Act like a monkey."

Bobby shrugged. He could probably do that.

"I have to go outside the fort."

He slipped under the cover, then hopped off the bed. Ellie stuck her head out to watch him.

Bobby didn't know how he was supposed to act like a monkey without being loud, but he did his best, jumping from foot to foot, holding his arms funny, like he had a coat hanger in the back of his shirt, trying not to make any sound. Ellie giggled wildly.

"Shhh!" he said.

She clamped her hands over her mouth.

"Okay, my turn now," Bobby said. "I dare you…" He looked around the dark attic. The game would be a lot easier if they were playing during the day and didn't have to be so quiet. He could have made Ellie eat a spoonful of mustard from the kitchen or walk backward everywhere with a lampshade on her head, or sing a song in a funny voice. Now he couldn't make her do any of that.

Bobby's eyes paused on the window near the pile of old furniture. When he had his first sleepover after George Papadopoulos's fifth birthday party earlier this year, George's parents let all the kids sleeping over stay up late watching movies and playing video games. After this, when they were lying in sleeping bags on the floor of George's bedroom, Jamie Stevenson—who had an older brother who knew all sorts of cool stuff—explained that if you looked in a mirror after midnight and said "Bloody Mary" three times, you would see the face of a witch covered in blood. Only George and Jamie were brave enough to try it, and they both said they saw Bloody Mary.

Still looking at the window, Bobby thought it would work as a mirror because when it was nighttime, you could never see out a window, only your reflection.

"I dare you," he said, unable to hold back a smile, knowing Ellie was going to be too scaredy-cat to do it, "to go to the window and say Bloody—" He changed his mind. "And say the monster's name three times."

Ellie frowned. "That's a stupid dare."

"No, it's not." Bobby explained what happened at George's sleepover.

Ellie said, "So if we say the monster's name instead, the monster will appear?"

Bobby nodded. "If you don't do it," he said, "you lose and I win."

She looked frightened. "I don't want the monster to appear."

"You have to! I dared you!"

"I don't want to!"

"Then you have to do the punishment."

"What is it?"

Bobby didn't know and didn't bother to think of one. He was having too much fun seeing Ellie scared. "You're a baby," he said, knowing this always got her angry.

"I'm not a baby!" she said.

"Then go look in the window and say the monster's name three times."

They both stuck their heads out of the fort and looked at the window. It was a grave-black square in the wall.

Ellie slipped out head-first, planting her hands on the floor and somersaulting, before standing up beside Bobby.

"You're going to do it?" he said, surprised.

"We don't know the monster's name," she said.

"We can make one up." Bobby shrugged. "Mike?"

"You stole that from *Monster University*."

"So?"

"That's not scary."

"You think of one then."

"Mike's okay. But you have to come with me."

She took his hand in hers and walked slowly to the window. Bobby couldn't believe they were really going to do this. He wanted to run back to the fort, but he knew Ellie would make fun of him if he did.

I just won't look, he thought. *Like at George's, I'll just close my eyes.*

They stopped before the window. Raindrops streaked the glass, creating zigzaggy patterns. Bobby kept the tiny flashlight aimed at the floor. Ellie stood on her tiptoes so she could look out the window.

"I can only see me," she said.

"I told you," he said, "you have to say the monster's name three times. Then you can see it."

After a moment's hesitation, Ellie spoke, and Bobby squeezed his eyes shut as tightly as possible.

"Mike...Mike...Mike..."

△△△

The rain, blown diagonally by the wind, shredded the rainforest's canopy and understory and churned the road into a bubbling stew. Rex's chest heaved and his lungs burned as he kept up a brisk run, even as the road ascended what seemed like a never-ending slope. He was only a few minutes away from the Mazda now. He'd gotten his second wind. He didn't care that his legs were mush. He wouldn't slow down until he reached the car.

Rex still believed fetching the Mazda was the best plan of action, and he hoped Tabitha was holding up okay in his absence. She must be terrified waiting alone for his return. Well, she wasn't alone, of course. She had the kids with her. But their presence most likely only added to her trepidation. She was their sole protector, the one person standing between the killer and them. If he decided to attack before Rex returned—

No, Rex wouldn't think of this. Tabitha was fine. The kids

were fine.

The killer was—

Where? Where *was* the bastard?

He'd been dragging the cop across the road when Rex almost ran him over. Why? To bury him in the woods? Where did he flee to? Rex hadn't gotten much of a look at him, but he figured the guy must be fit and strong. After all, Tony had been muscular, no pushover, and he'd locked himself in a goddamned bedroom, apparently fearful for his safety.

Which brought Rex back to the question of what exactly happened to Tony and Daisy earlier in the evening.

They're sitting at the table in the living room, enjoying some cheese and wine, playing cards, when, what—they hear a noise outside? Tony goes to the door and sees the killer. And locks himself and Daisy in the bedroom without bothering to lock the front door first? That didn't make sense. So perhaps the killer strolled boldly into the cabin. Daisy and Tony, seeing that he is armed, run to the bedroom, lock the door. Then what? The killer scales the partition wall, drops down on top of Tony, and delivers the fatal wound across his gut? And Daisy? She escapes out the window while this is happening. The killer catches up to her somewhere along the road and cuts her too. Yet she has spirit, wants to live. She fights back and gets away and makes it to Rex's cabin with the last of her strength before succumbing to her injury...

It's possible, Rex thought. *It all fits.*

But the big question is, Who the hell is this guy?

Not Rex's father, as Rex had previously speculated. His mother, he now recalled, had said she'd heard their father scream, indicating he was not the attacker but the attacked. And Logan had been attacked too, which meant he would have seen the killer. If it had been their father, he would surely have admitted as much.

Far above in the night sky a yellow bolt of lightning splintered into a constellation of frenetic offshoots. A blast of thunder as loud as cannon fire obediently followed. The rain fell harder.

Rex stepped into a deep pothole filled with rainwater and lost his balance. He toppled forward, his knees and palms slamming into the ground. A piece of gravel the size of a walnut tore into his left kneecap. Crying out in pain, he rolled onto his side, his hands cupping his knee. One of his fingers slipped through the hole where his khakis had torn and touched the pulpy wound beneath.

"Christ!" he hissed.

With effort he managed to straighten his leg. He bent it at the knee and straightened it again. It felt as though someone had taken a sledgehammer to his kneecap, but he would be able to walk.

Carefully he stood. Drenched and shivering, cold rain pelting his face, he took a cautious step forward. His injured leg buckled, but he kept his balance. After a few more tentative steps he attempted a quicker, albeit lurching, pace.

Looking up from the ground, he came to an abrupt halt.

Ahead, in the middle of the road, was a lone dark shape.

CHAPTER 15

T abitha peeled back the pillow from the police officer's abdomen. His bleeding, she was relieved to note, had all but stopped, which likely meant the killer's knife hadn't perforated his liver, kidneys, spleen, or other vital organs. It might have spared his bowels as well. Despite the vicious sweep of the slash, it was made horizontally, not vertically, meaning the knife could have slid between the police officer's intestines, perhaps only nicking them, or even missing them altogether. And if this was the case, his injury was superficial, a flesh wound, and not fatal.

Tabitha replaced the pillow and positioned the police officer's hands atop it, so she didn't have to continue holding it in place.

She got up and padded through the cabin to the bathroom. She used the toilet, then poured water into the bowl so it would flush. The mundane action made her pause. Her life was potentially in danger. She might not survive until morning. Yet still she made sure her urine didn't sit in the toilet bowl for others to see.

Back in the front room, she went to the bookcase she and Rex had moved in front of one of the windows. She studied the family photographs on the top shelf. She'd never seen a photo of Rex from his childhood, and in this one he looked unsurprisingly like a younger, miniaturized version of himself— minus the white hair, of course. She really saw the resemblance to Bobby now. Blonde, blue-eyed, thin-lipped.

On the middle shelf sat several leather-bound photo albums,

their spines facing outward. Tabitha lifted one free. It turned out not to be a photo album but a baby scrapbook. Taped to the first few pages was a photocopy of Rex's birth certificate, a photograph of Rex's mother in a hospital bed holding Rex, recently born into this world. The next page contained a makeshift paper pouch that contained two of Rex's baby teeth. On the page after that, a lock of golden hair. The rest of the book was filled with more cards celebrating his subsequent birthdays: ribbons presumably kept from birthday gifts; a letter Rex had written to Santa Claus, in which he stated he had been a good boy and deserved a lot of presents; a self-portrait done in crayons; and other childhood keepsakes. Amongst all of this were faded photographs annotated in neat handwriting.

Tabitha studied one photo labeled "Happy Fifth Birthday!" In it, Rex sat at the center of a table, attempting to blow out five candles atop a chocolate cake. His friends sat to either side of him, some smiling shyly for the camera, others making funny faces.

Who would have ever thought that little kid would end up flying airplanes through the sky? she thought sentimentally.

Rex had once told Tabitha that he'd always known, for as long as he could remember, that he wanted to be a pilot. So perhaps he had known this even when this picture had been taken. Perhaps when his mother, or his teacher, had asked him that age-old question, "What do you want to be when you grow up?" he had confidently answered, "A pilot!"

She smiled at this, proud of him for seeking out his dreams, even as a shadow of displeasure spread within herself.

Because becoming a flight attendant had not been her dream.

Tabitha liked that her job allowed her to travel, see different places, and meet new people. But the work itself was hardly glamorous.

Tabitha supposed she became a flight attendant the same way a recent college graduate with an Arts degree becomes a human resources administrator or a fast-food restaurant manager: the position was available, any previous experience wasn't necessary, and it paid all right.

So what *had* been her dream? she wondered.

The scary yet truthful answer was that she never really had one. She had never been inspired or impassioned to do any one thing with her life particularly well. She had always been content with mediocrity. Which wasn't necessarily a bad thing. The products of this mediocrity were two beautiful daughters, a loving family, great friends, and a fantastic boyfriend.

She should have been very happy.

Only she wasn't.

Because mediocrity was no longer enough.

She had started feeling this way during the divorce proceedings with Jacob. That was when it dawned on her that she was getting old. When the divorce was finalized in a few weeks, she would be a single mom with no house she could call her own, a ten-year-old car, and zero savings. This was not the life she had envisioned for herself. And she no longer had limitless time for the pieces of the life she *had* envisioned for herself to fall into place. She was almost forty. In another ten years or so she would be fifty.

Yes, she loved Ellie and Vanessa with all her heart and couldn't wait to watch them grow up, and, yes, she was over the moon with Rex and couldn't wait to see how their future unfolded together.

But something was missing from her life that had never been missing before.

Personal fulfillment.

She needed to know she was not simply waking up each morning to pay the bills and to get through the day.

She needed a dream.

Swallowing hard, Tabitha closed the scrapbook and set it back on the shelf.

Her eyes fell on the policeman, and her breath hitched in her throat.

His eyes were open, and he was looking at her.

She crouched next to him. "Oh God, hi," she stammered. "Are

you okay?"

He worked his mouth but didn't answer.

"Water?" she asked, but he shook his head.

He worked his mouth again. "Rex...?" he said.

"Rex is my boyfriend. But he's not here. He went to get the car. We parked way down the road and—"

"Need...t'leave."

"Yes, we know that, we're trying," she said, still rambling. "But why? Who's out there? Who attacked you?"

"Need...t'leave." He licked his dry lips. "Now."

△△△

Paul Harris knew he was cut up in a bad way. A fire burned in his stomach. He could feel copious amounts of blood drying on his skin and clothing. But his injury wasn't what frightened him. It was what was out there in the night.

It exists, he thought, cold with horror, while at the same time a part of his mind admonished himself for not accepting this conclusion years earlier, given the abundance of evidence that had piled up right in front of his nose.

In the fall of 1989, eight years after the Chapman family went missing without a trace, and two after the Peterson family followed suit, Maddy Greene, a sixty-three-year-old widowed pensioner who lived on Highway 99 five kilometers from Pavilion Lake, called the police station in a panic late one evening, saying somebody was lurking around outside her house. She changed her story when Paul arrived to investigate, saying the interloper wasn't someone but some*thing*. She came to this epiphany, she said, when she saw it pass by her kitchen window not two feet away from her glass-pressed nose. She described it to Paul as having gray or black skin, and long, skinny limbs covered with coarse hair that, in her words, "was nicely combed, like with a brush." Its height, she guessed, was roughly seven feet ("tall enough I was looking way up at it, Paul"), and although it walked on two legs like a human, its movement was jerky, its arms raised like the raptorial forearms of a praying mantis. Most surprising was her description of its face. "Hideous eyes, Paul, big like softballs, and a needle-like nose like some of those fish have, those swordfish."

Paul searched outside the house for footprints, but he found none. This wasn't necessarily saying much, as the ground had been hard and dry, and he was no expert at identifying tracks of any sort. He told Maddy that some kids from town had probably been playing a prank on her, and to lock the doors and windows and get some sleep.

Paul didn't give the incident much more thought until the following summer when Jenna and William Jannot, who lived about ten minutes down the highway from Maddy, reported that a half-dozen of their chickens had been slaughtered during the night. Chickens fall prey to foxes, bobcats, and cougars in these parts all the time. After such attacks, however, nothing usually remained of the bird except a few feathers. Yet on this occasion the carcasses of the Jannot's chickens were scattered all around the roofless coop, each one emptied of blood and featuring a well-defined puncture wound in either the neck or the hindquarters.

"Looks like you got yourself a vampire problem," Paul had told William lightheartedly.

"Ayuh, a vampire with one goddamn tooth," William had replied.

"So what do you want me to do, Will?"

"I want you to find out whoever done this, Paul. What the hell were they using, a giant syringe?"

"It's weird, I'll admit that."

"Weird ain't the half of it, Paul. Their blood's clean gone! Jenna's scared shitless. Someone with enough screws loose to do this, who knows what they might try next? I bet ya it's that Jameson girl. She's a bit retarded, ain't she? Always walking up and down the roads at night time by herself, sometimes half-dressed and talking to the moon."

"She's got schizophrenia, Will."

"Exactly! Reason enough to do something like this."

"You're a good twenty kilometers from town. She's never come this far before."

"Maybe last night she did?"

"I'll have a word with her."

Paul never did speak to Penny Jameson. He was pretty sure the culprits were the same kids who had dressed up in the Halloween mask to scare Maddy Greene. In a small town like Lillooet, where the only things the kids had in plentitude were a lot of time and little to do, they could get very creative with the mischief they got into. Throw alcohol and drugs into the mix, along with someone who had their driver's license and access to a beat-up runaround, and nothing was off limits.

Life in the Lillooet Country continued as usual for the next while. The days were quiet and uneventful until the latest local scandal spiced things up every few months or so. Like when Alexis Dempsey, a twenty-five-year-old bank teller, was busted for moonlighting as a prostitute in Whistler Village on weekends. Or when an out-of-towner opened a sex shop on Main Street across from the supermarket (it shut down one month later largely due to the righteous efforts of crossing guard Marjorie Cooper, who sat out in front of it on a folding chair every single day it was in operation, shaming any man who dared to enter). Or when Pastor Joe at the Anglican Church had a heart attack during a Sunday morning mass, croaking in front of the fifty-person congregation that included a dozen children who were told the pastor was such a good man that God had wanted to take him before his time. Or when sycophantic Lewis Edevane, the high school biology/human anatomy teacher, broke into the house of the school's vice principal to steal her supply of anti-depressants.

But nothing else *unexplainable* happened in the remote mountain community again. Not until the spring of 1992, at any rate. It was late April, and the region had just experienced an unseasonal cold snap, along with a foot of snow. On a morning

Paul had planned to spend sitting in front of the police station's fireplace with a pot of hot coffee and copies of *The Toronto Star* and *Vancouver Courier*, Billy Nubian rang up, asking Paul to come out to his property but not saying much more than that. When Paul arrived at Billy's forty-acre farm located equidistant between Lillooet and Pavilion Lake, Billy met him at the front door, where he lit up a cigarette and said, "Come around back, Paul. I want to show you something." He led Paul to the pen where he kept his goats, only now there was only a single goat in it, and it was lying on its side in the snow. "I moved the others in with the sheep so I could put this one down."

They stopped before the animal's lifeless body, and Paul frowned at the grotesque wound that disfigured its belly.

"What the hell happened to it?" he asked.

Billy flicked away his cigarette and immediately lit another. "Something spooked them in the night. Me and the wife could hear them bleating all the way up in the bedroom. I threw on a jacket and came out..." He shook his head. "I swear, Paul, I'm not making this up...but there was...something...in the pen with them."

"Something?"

Billy shrugged. "Some sort of bug thing. I know how that sounds, but..." He shrugged again. "I mean, it had these big, buggy eyes."

Paul thought of Maddy Greene's alleged trespasser and said, "Tall and thin?"

"Yeah, I guess it was. It was crouching froglike over this goat. Like maybe it was getting ready to pick it up and carry it off or something. But yeah, I'd say it was tall and thin." Billy raised his eyebrows. "You've seen this thing before, Paul?"

"Not me. But Maddy Greene claimed to have seen it last year."

"Claimed? I ain't making this up, Paul. I ain't *claiming* anything. I saw what I saw."

"I'm not doubting that, Billy. Wrong choice of words. I believe Maddy saw it too—only, I don't think we're talking about an 'it.' What she saw were probably some kids playing a prank on her.

Maybe you did too? One of them wearing some kind of mask or —?"

"Look at that goat's belly, Paul," he said, jabbing a calloused finger at it. "Torn clean open. No kids did that. Besides, I *saw* the thing, goddammit. It might've been dark out, but I saw it."

When Paul wrote up the incident report, he paraphrased what Billy had told him, mentioning only that an "unknown animal" had attacked one of his goats, along with the rest of the admittedly sparse and inconclusive facts of what happened that night.

And that was that. The world kept turning, and Lillooet went right along with it.

Eighteen-year-old Hunt Fischer was drafted by the Edmonton Oilers and, in recognition, had his mural painted on the wall of the local McDonald's PlayPlace. Lewis Edevane got into trouble again when he hosted a student party at his house that involved a copious amount of pot and alcohol. Lewis's friend and coworker in the high school's math department, Michael Finnegan, resigned after he slept with a female student a week after she graduated (they ended up marrying a few months later and divorcing a few months after that). Notoriously cranky Clyde Johnson had his tractor stolen from one of his fields (it was found two days later in a culvert without its tires and painted purple). And when Pat Florio's namesake son, Pat Jr., came out as gay in the first week of school in the fall of 1996, Father Dempsey excommunicated him from the Catholic Church (public backlash forced the priest to welcome him back into the flock in time for the following Sunday's morning mass).

On July 1, 1998, Paul had been celebrating Canada Day out at Hangman's Tree Park, named so because it was the resting place for William Armitage, who had been convicted and hanged for the murder of a fellow gold seeker in 1863. Standing amongst the revelers next to Hangman's Tree (which had long ago died and was now nothing but a six-foot-tall dead stump), Paul was eating a hot dog and listening to the cover band play CCR's "Bad

Moon Rising" when his cell phone rang. It was his wife, Nancy. Eve Holleman who had a summer cabin on Pavilion Lake had called the station to report screams and gunshots coming from next door.

Paul pulled into the Ryerson's driveway half an hour later. Their potato-brown station wagon was parked in the driveway. Eve Holleman was not there to greet him. More than likely she was hiding inside her cabin with the window blinds drawn and the doors locked.

Paul put the cruiser in Park, got out, and withdrew his Glock from the holster. He had never met Rick Ryerson, or his wife, Sue, though he knew of them, as he knew of every local and summer resident in and around Lillooet. Rick was a dentist from Vancouver. He bought this property five years ago, tore down the shabby hunter's cabin that had stood on it unoccupied for years, and put up the tidy, four-bedroom cottage that Paul was approaching now. The couple had one teenage daughter.

The front door to the cabin was closed. Ignoring it, Paul moved down the side of the building. He came to a large deck that offered unobstructed views of the lake, which dazzled blue in the afternoon sunlight. He crept up the three steps, passed a gas barbecue with marble bench tops, and quietly slid open the glass patio door.

He stepped inside, holding the gun in front of him with both hands to keep it steady.

The large room featured cathedral ceilings, pastoral artwork, and expensive French country furniture—the latter in complete disarray. A floor lamp with a mauve-colored shade lay on its side, next to an overturned ottoman and smashed vintage desk. A heavy oak dining table was shoved pell-mell to one side, toppling some of the chairs that had surrounded it. A mirror lay facedown on the floor on a bed of jagged pieces of loose glass.

Blood was everywhere.

There were two main stains, one on the floor near the dining table, the other in front of and on a three-seater sofa. Both had been stepped in. Crimson footprints created anarchic patterns across the floor, alluding to the bedlam that had taken place here earlier.

Trying not to gag on the sweet, metallic stench permeating the air, Paul stepped over the floor lamp and rounded a Provencal two-drawer dresser that stood incongruously in the middle of the room, as if it had been dragged there to serve as a buffer against an attacker.

"Police!" he called out in an authoritative voice, not expecting an answer and not getting one.

He spent the next ten minutes poking around each room, not touching anything. Then he returned to the back porch and called the Whistler detachment of the Royal Canadian Mounted Police. He remained outside while the forensic guys documented the crime scene before beginning the laborious task of collecting fingerprints, blood samples, and other physical evidence. By the time they wrapped up it was after dark. Most of the other lake residents had gathered out in front of the cabin to rubberneck, looking scared and worried and maybe even a little excited by all the commotion.

Naturally the next day Lillooet's rumor mill went into overdrive, and it wasn't long before the townsfolk were connecting the disappearance of Rick Ryerson and his wife and daughter to the fates of the Chapmans and Petersons. Top-secret government experiments and alien abductions were favorite topics of speculation. So too were legends from the gold mining days involving vengeful spirits and black curses and all that hocus-pocus.

One tale in particular captured everyone's imagination.

In 1904 a man named Dumb John Dagys fatally shot a Chinese miner named Ah Shing on the shores of Pavilion Lake. Six months later, after bragging about the murder during a game of poker, Dagys was arrested. According to court documents, the prosecution described Dagys as a mountain man who would show up now and then in Lillooet with a pocketful of gold nuggets, spending all of them on booze and whores before heading back into the wilds. The consensus at the time, and the eventual conclusion of the court, was that Dagys had discovered a goldmine amidst the mists, thick woods, and rugged terrain near Pavilion Lake—and had murdered the Chinaman, who had discovered the mine's location, to keep it secret. Dagys was hanged in March 1905, and his final words (garbled on account that he had no tongue) before the gallows trap door sprung open were: "Anybody goes looking for my mine will wish they didn't, God have mercy on their soul."

Which begged several questions: Did Troy Chapman find Dagys' mine in '81? Did Marty Peterson find it in '87? Did Rick Ryerson find it most recently?

And did they, and their families, fall victim to Dagys' curse?

Most people Paul talked to seemed to believe this, even if they didn't come right out and say so. And with the RCMP's forensic lab report failing to unmask any terrestrial suspects, the ghost of Dumb John Dagys became the go-to natter whenever talk of the missing families came up

Until the summer of 2009.

While the rest of the world was dealing with the fallout from the US subprime mortgage crisis, the residents of the Lillooet Country were being terrorized by an unknown creature. It was first spotted in the sky out east over Cariboo Road by Tom Eddlemon, who later described it to the local paper as something "about the size of an ape but with large transparent wings." That same week Steve Krugman snapped a photograph of what he believed to be the same creature perched on the roof of his barn (though it had been dark out, and the shape in the photo had been far from conclusive). The final encounter of that eventful summer came on August 1. Before going to bed, George Long found his wife, Heather, passed out in their backyard in her pajamas and housecoat. When she came round, she claimed to have come face to face with a "half-man half-bug." The last thing she remembered was it scooping Sadie, her Jack Russell terrier, into its arms and flying off into the night (the dog has never been seen since).

And while Maddy Greene had been telling anyone who would

listen of her close encounter of the fourth kind for years, and most residents of Lillooet had heard through the grapevine about Jenna and William Jannot's exsanguinated chickens and Billy Nubian's eviscerated goat, it was only now that people were sitting up and listening. Because Tom Eddlemon wasn't a nutty spinster or oddball farmer. He owned and operated the busiest coffee shop in town, knew all of his customers by name, and had once dived into the Fraser River to save twelve-year-old Davy Theodossiou, who had capsized his canoe and nearly drowned.

Not to be outdone, Steve Krugman was the wealthiest man in Lillooet, thanks to his road freight transport business that operated a fleet of vehicles and employed two dozen locals. And Heather Long was a star witness as well, if only because she was considered by many—which included friends and family—to be too much of a bore to make up such a fantastical encounter.

Mr. Wang, who ran the mom-and-pop convenience store on Main Street, was the first to refer to the creature as "Mosquito Man," a sensational moniker that quickly stuck with the populace. He hired local artist, Mary Catherine Jackson, to paint a picture of the creature hovering above the moonlit town, which he hung in the shop's front window between posters advertising Coca-Cola and Lotto 649. A group of hunters led by Hank Crary put a bounty on the creature's head, and they spent countless weekends scouring the woods for it. By the time real estate agent Claude Bumiller announced that he had shot the creature—taping a tuft of its fur (which looked suspiciously like fur from a beaver pelt) in Mr. Wang's shop window—the town's anxiety had hit a fevered pitch.

Nevertheless, as summer faded into fall with no more sightings of the creature, so too did the town's enthusiasm toward it, and by winter the Mosquito Man had lost its cult status, fading back into a thing of legend, or becoming little more than a bogeyman that parents threatened their children with if they came home late for dinner or didn't go to bed on time.

Whenever talk of the Chapmans or Petersons or Ryersons

came up—usually over beers at one of the town's pubs when those imbibing grew tired of bitching about their neighbors or coworkers—people were equally inclined to bring up the ghost of Dumb John Dagys as they were the Mosquito Man or Troy Chapman.

Troy had been the RCMP's original person of interest back in '81. Their thinking had been conventional. Troy got into a fight with his wife Sally and murdered her, either intentionally or unintentionally. He buried her body somewhere in the woods and went on the lam with his two boys. Rex at some point fled in fear, making his way back to town.

When the Petersons disappeared six years later, and there were no clear suspects, Troy Chapman once again became a person of interest. The RCMP speculated that Troy, and possibly his son Logan, had managed to survive the last eight years in the wilderness by living off the land, fishing, hunting, trapping. But that January and February had been the coldest on record in more than two decades, forcing Troy and Logan back to civilization. They took up residence in the Peterson's cabin— and were surprised by the family's unexpected early arrival on March 1 (most residents didn't visit the lake before the May long weekend).

This same thinking applied again in 1998. The Ryersons were the first family to the lake that year, arriving on April 3, and their atypically early arrival surprised a squatting Troy and Logan, who murdered them and once again disposed of the bodies in the woods to muddy the waters of any subsequent investigation.

Being in law enforcement, Paul knew from firsthand experience that a rational explanation existed behind every crime, no matter how well that explanation might be hidden. This was why despite having some questions—namely why Troy and Logan never left behind any evidence of their trespassing, despite allegedly residing in both the Anderson's and Ryerson's houses for some time—Paul had always been on the same page as the Mounties when it came to the missing families.

Stupid, he thought now as he lay half-dead on the floor of Rex

Chapman's cabin. Because in striving for a rational explanation, he had blinded himself to the truth. *Something had been preying on the animals and people of the area, something that didn't give a rat's ass about the difference between beast and human.* His people had seen it for centuries. Maddy Greene had seen it much more recently. Billy Nubian had seen it too. And Tom Eddlemon and Steve Krugman and Heather Long.

And tonight Paul had seen it too.

The woman by the bookcase looked over at him. Her face broke into surprise at finding him alert. "Oh God, hi!" she said, hurrying to his side. "Are you okay? Water?"

He shook his head and tried to generate some saliva. "Rex...?" he said, his voice brittle and cracked.

"Rex is my boyfriend," she said. "But he's not here. He went to get the car. We parked way down the road and—"

"Need...t'leave."

"Yes, we know that. But why? Who's out there? Who attacked you?"

"Need...t'leave." He licked his lips. "Now."

ΔΔΔ

Tabitha stared at the police officer, but he seemed to have used up what little strength he'd mustered. His eyes were once again closed, and he was either resting or comatose.

Leave, he'd told her.

Now, he'd told her.

Roger that, Officer, she thought. *We're out of here just as soon as my boyfriend gets back with the car, don't you worry.*

By the way, do you mind telling me what happened to you? Who cut you? And why? Because I'm pretty much in the dark right now, and it's not a nice place to be.

In fact, it's goddamn terrifying.

Tabitha checked her gold wristwatch. It was 12.53 a.m. Rex had been gone now for more than twenty minutes. He would be back shortly.

Taking a jar candle from the coffee table, she got to her feet and went to the next room. She climbed the steep staircase. The solid planks of timber that formed the steps didn't creak. The interior of the cabin was entirely quiet. Outside was a different matter. The rain continued its unabated assault on the roof, while thunder alternated between mild rumblings and cataclysmic detonations.

When she reached the top of the staircase, her eyes went immediately to Bobby's bed. For a split second she couldn't make out what she was seeing projecting from the mattress in the thick shadows before she realized it must be some kind of fort.

Were the kids inside it? Because Ellie's bed was empty—

In that same instant she noticed a small circle of light at the far end of the attic. Bobby and Ellie stood before the window, looking out.

Tabitha's stomach flipped. "Who's there?" she blurted, dashing across the attic.

Both Bobby and Ellie snapped about, looking both surprised and guilty.

"Who's out there?" Tabitha repeated, crouching before them. She set the candle on the floor and cupped Ellie's face in her hands. "Who did you see, sweetie? Who's out there?"

"No one!"

"No one? Then what are you doing? Why are you looking out the window? Did you hear something?" She looked up at the window. Without waiting for her daughter to answer, she sprang to her feet and pressed her nose to the glass. Little was visible save the black night and the slanting rain. "I can't see anything," she said.

"We were just playing a game," Ellie said.

"A game?" Tabitha said, turning from the window, all her muscles seeming to unknot simultaneously. "What game?"

"Dares," Ellie said. "Bobby dared me to look out the window. He said if I said the monster's name three times, I would see it."

"Oh, baby, why would you want to see—" She cut herself off.

With a last glance at the window—now she could see her glass-caught reflection, as ethereal as that of a ghost's—she picked up the candle and said, "It's time to go. Rex went to get the Mazda. He will be back here any minute. We have to be ready."

"We're going home?" Ellie asked hopefully.

"You bet."

"What about the monster?" Bobby asked.

"There's no such thing as monsters, Bobby, remember?"

"But we almost runned it over."

"That wasn't a monster. It was just an ordinary person. And don't worry about him. Everything's going to be okay."

Tabitha led the two children back downstairs. In the front room, she helped them put on their shoes and tie their laces. The sight of their tiny shoes and their equally tiny feet caused tears to warm her eyes. *Please don't let anything happen to them. They're just children.*

"Okay, all done," she said to Bobby, lowering his foot from her lap to the floor.

He was looking at the supine police officer. "Can he come with us?" he asked.

Even amid this surreal situation, Tabitha found it strange for Bobby to be talking to her without reservation, for his questions to be directed at her and not Rex.

Strange but nice.

And it was an apt question he'd asked. Were they going to take the police officer? It seemed unconscionable not to. If they left him here he would surely die from his injury, or the murderer would finish him off. Yet what if the murderer began shooting at the car as soon as Rex pulled up? There wouldn't be time to help him even if they wanted to. The safety of the kids came first and foremost above all else.

"We'll do our best," she told Bobby.

"Where's he going to fit?" Ellie asked.

"On the back seat," she said. "You two can squeeze up in the front with me."

"But we won't have seatbelts. And we might crash again."

"We won't crash again."

Lightning flashed outside, visible between the edges of the window frames and the drawn blinds. Thunder followed, a deep-bellied reverberation that climaxed in a deafening whack-boom.

"God must be really angry," Ellie said reverently.

"At us?" Bobby asked.

"At you," she said.

"But I've been good."

"He might hit you with lightning."

"Stop that, Ellie," Tabitha said.

"I want my daddy," Bobby said.

"Soon, Bobby," Tabitha said. "Soon. Just stay brave a little longer."

Which was easier said than done. One minute stretched to two. The indeterminable wait became nearly unbearable.

Rex shouldn't be taking this long. Something must have happened to him. The killer—

No.

Tabitha paced. She checked her wristwatch again. She stroked Ellie's hair. She squeezed Bobby's shoulder. She paced some more.

She paused.

Was that a car? Could she hear an engine approaching? Or was it just the storm?

She listened.

All she could hear was the machine-gun rain on the roof.

Screw it.

She went to the door, flicked the deadbolt.

"Where are you going, Mommy? Ellie asked, frightened.

"Just having a quick look outside."

She opened the door and stuck her head out. Rain thrashed her face and the wind whipped her hair in front of her eyes. She couldn't see anything in the dark. Certainly no headlights.

Before she pulled her head back inside, however, she made a startling discovery.

The woman's body was gone.

ΔΔΔ

Tabitha slammed the door, her heart pounding. Then she bolted the deadlock. He had been right outside! The murderer! He had taken the body!

"What's wrong, Mommy?" Ellie asked.

Tabitha realized she was trembling, and her face must have been alabaster white in the candlelight. "It's just really cold out there, sweetie," she said inanely.

"Did you see my dad?" Bobby asked.

"He's not back yet."

Her heart continued to triphammer as her mind reeled, trying to make sense of the events that seemed increasingly to be spinning out of control.

Why did the killer take Daisy's body? Was he taunting them like when he stuffed the truck keys in Tony's gut? Then again, he had been dragging the police officer into the forest before they almost hit him on the road. So he wanted the bodies of his victims. Why? To dispose of them so nobody would find them? Or was he a cannibal? Some freak straight out of *The Hills Have Eyes*?

What the hell was going on?

"He's awake!" Ellie said.

Tabitha blinked, and the room snapped back into focus. She looked at her daughter and saw that she and Bobby were both staring at the police officer.

He was conscious again!

Tabitha knelt next to him. "Are you...?" She was going to ask, *Are you okay?* But that was a moot question when your guts were visible. "Do you want some water? Ellie, sweetie, can you go grab the water bottle? It should be on the kitchen table."

Ellie hurried off without a word.

Tabitha looked back at the police officer. His face was pasty, hollowed, his forehead and upper lip damp with perspiration.

His breath came in shallow, susurrate rasps. He licked his lips and spoke a word. It was garbled, unintelligible.

"Do you have a radio?" she asked him. "We found your gun outside, but there was no radio."

He shook his head slightly.

She didn't understand why he wouldn't need a radio. Perhaps he was the only cop in town after all. "Does anyone know you're out here?" she asked.

He nodded, and her heart lifted.

"Are they coming now?"

He shook his head. "Wife..."

"Only your wife knows?"

He nodded.

"She'll get worried when you don't come back, won't she? It's late. Shouldn't she be already worried?"

He nodded again.

"So do you think someone is coming now?"

"May'b."

"Do you have a phone?"

"Dropped..."

"Rex didn't find it."

The police officer—Paul Harris—cleared his throat. "Rex? Where's Rex?"

"I told you, he went to get his car—"

Ellie came running back into the room. "Here's the water, Mommy," she said.

Tabitha took the bottle, unscrewed the cap. She poured a little bit into the police officer's open mouth. Some spilled out and over his lips. He swallowed and opened his mouth again. She poured more in. This time a little less dribbled out.

He licked his lips. "Thank you."

"More?"

He shook his head and his eyes slid shut.

Tabitha decided to let him rest when he mumbled something she couldn't discern.

"What?" she said, leaning closer.

"Mos...quito."

"Mosquito?" she said, baffled.

"Mosquito... Man."

"Mosquita Man!" Ellie squealed. "Is that the monster's name?"

"Ellie, shush," Tabitha said.

"But that's what the museum woman said! Remember? She said a big mosquita was killing everybody a long time ago! Maybe it's the same monster!"

"That was just a story."

"But the monster had a big nose just like a mosquita!"

"Bar'bra," the cop said, his eyelids fluttering open.

Tabitha nodded. "We stopped by the tourist center on the way here. A tall woman with glasses—yes, Barbara—told us... this story. But what do *you* mean? Are you talking about an exterminator? Is that who attacked you?"

Paul Harris' eyelids continued to flutter as if he were having trouble keeping them open.

"Do you know who it was?" she pressed.

He nodded.

"*Who?*" she demanded. "*Who was it?*"

"Mosquito...Man."

"But does he have a *name*?"

"Story..." He turned his head so he was looking at Ellie. His lips quivered with the effort to speak. "*It's true...*"

"It's true!" Ellie parroted. "The story's true, Mommy!"

Tabitha was shaking her head, but before she said anything, the police officer mumbled incoherently.

"Mommy!" Ellie went on. "*Mommy!*"

"He's not making sense," she said numbly. "I don't know what he's saying."

Only Tabitha did know what he was saying...or trying to say.

And she hated the deep down part of herself that wondered whether it might be true.

CHAPTER 16

Rex stared at the shape in the middle of the road. It was low and small, certainly nowhere near the size of a man. It hadn't been there earlier in the afternoon. Had the killer placed a rock in the middle of the road to prevent Rex from driving the Mazda back to the cabin? That didn't make sense. It would mean the killer was ahead of him on the road. And if that were so, why not just attack him before he reached the car?

A trap then? While Rex was busy moving the object, would the killer sneak out from the trees and stab him in the back?

This scenario seemed a little more plausible, and suddenly Rex felt watched. He wiped the rain from his eyes and looked to the margins of the road. He could see little in the dark. Should he turn on the Maglite? He had traveled much too far for anybody lurking back at the cabin to see the light. They would have to be closer, say within a hundred feet, and if that were the case, then they were likely following Rex and knew of his location anyway.

Rex flicked on the flashlight and shone the beam at the shape in the road—and found himself staring at some sort of alien life form. Its black face was small in comparison to its body, and its piggish eyes appeared to be scowling evilly at him.

"*Oh, Jesus*," he said, even as he realized the creature was not something from the stars but a common North American porcupine.

Its quills, all standing on end, fanned out from its body, creating the illusion of a small face, while at the same time making the rodent seem larger and more threatening than it was.

Rex's muscles unwound with relief.

Just a porcupine.

He continued forward, giving the animal as much space as he could. It turned cumbersomely to follow his progress, clattering its teeth, or perhaps its erect quills, in a warning.

"Take it easy," Rex told it, surprised to see it had a white stripe down the middle of its back, most likely to mimic the look of a skunk to help deter predators.

Less than a minute later the trees lining the road thinned, then retreated completely. Without the canopy to shelter him, the rain struck Rex's face with stinging force. Even with one hand shielding his eyes, he could barely see a few feet in front of him.

He ran the final stretch to the Mazda with his head down. The dirt road boiled around his feet. An earsplitting peal of thunder exploded above him, causing him to instinctively duck. He leaped over a pothole overflowing with water, sidestepped a long furrow, then he was at the car.

He already had his free hand in his pocket, thumb jabbing the unlock button on the remote key. The coupe's headlights and taillights winked. He yanked open the driver's side door and dropped in behind the steering wheel, slamming the door shut behind him.

Grabbing his cell phone from the glove compartment, Rex dialed 9-1-1, pressed Speaker, and set the device on his lap. He jammed the key into the ignition, turned it. The engine revved to life.

"Nine-one-one operator," a curt female voice said. "What's your emergency?"

"I'm on Pavilion Lake," he said. "There've been two murders out here. We need help."

"Pavilion Lake?" He could hear the clicks of a keyboard.

"Did you hear me? There've been two murders."

"I heard you. Now don't hang up. Is the perpetrator still around?"

"Yes!" He shifted into Drive and hit the gas. The car lurched forward.

"Can you describe the person to me?"

"I didn't see him. But two people are dead, and a cop has been injured, badly."

"A police officer?"

He banged over a pothole, flicked on the headlights and windshield wipers, which thumped back and forth at full speed yet were unable to clear the rain faster than it fell.

"Yes! A cop! Send someone!"

"I already got a call started and help on the way. What's your name?"

"Rex."

"Rex, what's your last name?"

"Chapman."

"Chapman. And you said Pavilion Lake—"

"Forty minutes past Lillooet on Highway 99. We're at 5 Lake Road."

"I've got an officer on the way—"

"What?"

"I've got an officer coming, sir. If anything changes before we get there, just give us a call right back—"

Rex hung up.

CHAPTER 17

Bobby kept his mouth shut while Ellie's mom spoke to the policeman. He was too scared to speak. Part of this was due to seeing how beaten up the policeman was. Blood was even coming from his mouth! Bobby had never seen that before. He'd seen a bloody nose—like when a girl a year older than him jumped from the top of the castle in his school's playground, instead of using the slide like you're supposed to, and smashed her knee into her nose—but he's never seen a bloody mouth, and he knew that must mean the policeman was badly hurt because the blood wouldn't be coming from his teeth but from way down inside him.

The other thing scaring Bobby was seeing how frightened Ellie's mom was. He could hear the fear in her voice, in the way she was asking questions, and she was an adult, so if she was this frightened of the monster, then it had to be super dangerous.

Which meant he could no longer pretend the monster wasn't going to get him. It probably was. And it might not just kill him, it might eat him too. He couldn't imagine what it would feel like to be eaten alive, but he knew it would hurt a lot.

And if that happened, and he was eaten alive and went to heaven, what would happen here on earth? Would everything continue as usual? Would his friends keep going to school? Miss Damond might say a prayer for him in the morning before class began. And Tom Harrity would probably miss him because they always played Superheroes at recess (and Bobby had promised to trade his Silver Surfer action figure for Tom's Ant-Man if it came with the helmet and all the other pieces). But what about everybody else? Would they even notice or care if Bobby didn't come to school again? Would someone else get to sit at his desk? Would they get rid of his nametag taped to the top of it that had taken him an entire afternoon to design? It seemed weird *not being there*. And what would happen to all of his toys? Not just his Silver Surfer, but his Nerf N-Strike blaster and his remote control car and all of his Legos, and most important of all, his Nintendo Switch? He wouldn't need them in heaven if he could just wish for new ones. So who would get them all?

Nevertheless, what bothered Bobby the most about dying was that his mom would keep on living wherever she was without him. He wouldn't even be able to say goodbye.

Then again, maybe he could tell her from heaven that he was okay? Maybe he could send her a sign through the TV, or peek over the clouds and smile at her?

The bottom line, he decided, was that he didn't want to die yet. He liked his house and his room and Brett Huggins who lived next door and all his other friends at school. He liked having Cap'n Crunch for breakfast on Saturday mornings (he was only allowed to have plain old Shreddies or Corn Flakes the rest of the week). He liked when his dad took him to McDonald's or KFC or Burger King for a special treat. He liked Christmas and Halloween and his birthday parties. He liked eating cake and opening presents. He liked a whole lot of things he didn't want to change—

Suddenly the cabin door burst open and cold air and rain swept inside.

Along with his dad!

"Daddy!" Bobby cried, springing to his feet. He ran to his dad, who hiked him up into his arms and gave him a big hug and a whisker kiss before setting him back down on the floor.

Ellie's mom was also on her feet. "Rex! I didn't hear the car!"

His dad hugged her next. "Driveway's thick with mud. Didn't want to get stuck."

"Nothing's out there?"

He frowned. "No. Nothing, nobody. But let's not dally. Help me with the cop." He was already moving toward the police officer. "Take his arms."

"What about Ellie and me, Dad?" Bobby asked, already forgetting about death and the afterlife and all that stuff.

"You guys stick right next to us—"

"*Where is she?*" Ellie cried suddenly. She was patting her pockets frantically.

Bobby looked at her. "Who?"

"Miss Chippy!"

Ellie's mom looked in the wooden box where the chipmunk was supposed to be. "Did you take it from there?"

"Yes!"

"I told you—"

"I didn't want her to sleep by herself!"

"She's probably upstairs," Bobby said.

"Can I borrow your flashlight? *Please?*"

Bobby handed her his keychain with the flashlight even as Ellie's mom was shaking her head. "You're not going anywhere, Ellie. There's no time—"

"But I don't want Miss Chippy to die, Mommy! I haven't even played with her yet!"

"I'm not arguing about this—"

Ellie sped from the room.

"Ellie!" her mom shouted. "Ellie, *dammit*, come back here!"

She didn't come back. Bobby heard her feet running up the stairs to the attic.

"That girl!" her mom said, scowling. "Doesn't she know we need to—"

"Forget it," Bobby's dad said. "We'll be back in a minute. Bobby, you wait here for Ellie. Make sure she's ready to go as soon as Tabs and I return. Got it, bud?"

"Okay!" he said, happy at being treated like a big kid for once.

His dad took the policeman's legs, Ellie's mom took his arms, and together they carried him awkwardly into the night.

ΔΔΔ

Ellie scrambled up the staircase so quickly that she bent to all fours so she didn't lose her balance and fall backward. When Rex said they were leaving, she touched her pocket, to make sure Miss Chippy was still there—and she wasn't! The zipper on the pocket was open. She had forgotten to close it earlier. Which meant Miss Chippy had fallen out. Ellie was betting it happened when she somersaulted out of the fort.

Ellie knew she was probably going to get grounded when they got home for running off to look for the chipmunk. Her mom hated it when Ellie "dawdled," especially when her mom was late or rushed. But Ellie couldn't leave Miss Chippy here by herself. They were best friends now, and best friends helped each other.

"Miss Chippy?" Ellie said, hurrying toward the two beds, sweeping Bobby's flashlight back and forth across the dusty floor. Rain pounded the roof. Thunder went off like firecrackers. Outside the window, lightning flashed, momentarily blinding her. When the dancing stars cleared from her vision, the dark seemed even darker than it had moments before.

Ellie slowed, suddenly hesitant about being up here alone. She stopped at the first bed and was about to look under it when a cold breeze blew past her face, smelling damp and earthy.

She shone the flashlight at the window.

It was open.

The tattered curtains on either side of it fluttered as if disturbed by unseen hands. Rain soaked the window ledge and the floor before it, creating a shadowy stain on the wood.

Neither she nor Bobby had opened the window.

So who did?

The wind, she thought. *The wind blew it open.*

Only it wasn't a window that opened sideways. You had to push the windowpane up.

The wind couldn't do that.

Could it?

Go back downstairs!

A squeak.

Miss Chippy!

Ellie peeked under the bed—

(*the monster lives there*)

(*I don't care!*)

—and staring right back at her was the chipmunk.

"Miss Chippy!"

She reached her arm under the bed and grabbed Miss Chippy in her hand, careful not to squeeze too tightly. The chipmunk didn't run. Miss Chippy was a good girl. Or maybe she was just too injured. Either way, Ellie had her now.

Withdrawing her arm and sitting up, she lifted the chipmunk to her face, touched their noses, and said, "Silly little chippymunk! We almost left you behind!"

Ellie stuck the chipmunk in her pocket—and secured the zipper tight.

All of a sudden she heard a buzzing sound from somewhere in the attic. It reminded her of the whirling her mom's electric toothbrush made, only it was much, much louder, and angrier.

Ellie peeked up over the bed—and screamed.

△△△

Tabitha and Rex had just laid the police officer's limp body across the Mazda's back seat and were returning to the cabin when Ellie's scream cut through the night.

No! was Tabitha's first and only thought.

Anesthetized with terror, she burst past Rex and entered the cabin. Snatching the Maglite and Glock from the coffee table, holding one in each hand, she plowed through the afghan and took the steps to the attic two at a time.

She had no plan of action. When she reached the top of the staircase, she was simply going to charge straight into the killer, fighting tooth and nail to drive him away from her daughter.

Only it wasn't the killer who awaited her.

At least, not the killer she had expected.

It was a creature whose improbable reality caused her to come to an abrupt halt.

Tabitha's eyes took in the monstrous abomination all at once. Then, as if unable to accept what they were seeing, they played over it a second time in slow-motion horror.

Two compound eyes, alien and emotionless, protruded from the creature's small, round head like grotesque tumors. A pair of feathery antennae sprouted between them, probing the air. Where the mandible should have been located was a tube-like proboscis, as long and deadly looking as a rapier.

The ghastly thing—*Mosquito Man*, her mind whispered, a moniker that could have graced the neon marquee of a 1980s movie theater showing a midnight creature-feature special— stood upright on two absurdly long, thick legs. Filling the space between them was a plump, insectoid abdomen that bypassed a pelvic region to connect directly to a barrel-chested, black-furred thorax. It was from this truncated middle section that the legs originated, along with four arms that tapered into slender pinchers.

Two of those pinchers held Ellie in a secure grip.

"*Mommy!*" her daughter screamed, kicking and squirming futilely.

"Ellie...?" she said, her voice faltering in the face of the abomination that stood before her.

"*Mommy! Help me!*"

Tabitha found she could not move. The creature's eyes held her in place as securely as a tractor beam. They exhibited no evil, no gleeful malevolence. Yet it was this stone-cold indifference to her presence that made them so utterly horrifying, that stirred within her not only revulsion and fear but ineffable despair.

She was nothing but food to it.

"*Mommeeee!*"

"Baby...?" she murmured.

The creature took a herky-jerky step forward, a bassy,

strumming sound emanating from somewhere deep inside its body. It raised its two free pincers before it in the prayer-like manner of a praying mantis.

"*Mom-meeeeee!*" Ellie wailed, the word disintegrating into a keening shriek.

Tabitha's paralysis shattered. She raised the pistol, aimed high for the creature's head so she didn't hit Ellie, and squeezed the trigger. The muzzle flash briefly illuminated the darkness, but the bullet missed its mark because the creature didn't even flinch.

Tabitha squeezed the trigger a second time but realized belatedly the gun was no longer in her hand. One of the creature's pincers had knocked it free. At the same time she realized this, a jolt of pain shot through her head.

Pincer again.

So fast.

Tabitha collapsed to her knees, dazed. The creature loomed above her—

Something smashed into it, and she grasped groggily that Rex was beside her, swinging the wooden golf club. He struck the monstrous thing again, but this time it slashed back.

Rex grunted in pain.

Then the creature—*Mosquito Man*, Tabitha reminded herself deliriously—turned and scuttled across the attic to the open window, great transparent wings unfolding from its back.

Tabitha struggled to her feet and stumbled after it, still holding the flashlight, the yellow beam painting the attic in hysterical patterns.

The creature flitted through the window into the storming night, wings buzzing, whining.

"No!" Tabitha cried, slamming into the window ledge. A burst of sheet lightning backlit the thunderheads, and in the purple light she watched helplessly as the creature touched down gracefully on the ground.

Tabitha couldn't fully comprehend what had just happened. *Did the Mosquito Man, the goddamn Mosquito Man, just steal her daughter? Where was it taking her? What did it want with her?*

During a subsequent flash of lightning, she saw the creature moving into the forest and heard Ellie's screams fading beneath the roar of the rain.

Rex gripped her shoulders, spoke to her, though she couldn't make out what he was saying.

"Tabs!" he said, shaking harder. "Tabs!"

The bubble she'd been in suddenly popped. The dumbed-down sounds and sensations she'd been experiencing snapped into crystalline clarity. The underwater viscosity of time fast-forwarded to its normal speed. Blood pounded in her temples while fear the likes of which she had never known iced every fiber of her being.

Ellie's gone. It took her.

"You're cut!" Rex told her, brushing hair from her forehead.

"I need to find Ellie!" she cried.

"I'll go! I'll get her!"

"No—"

"Stay here! Watch Bobby! Fix that cut!"

Bobby. Bobby was still downstairs, she thought. And Rex was right. She couldn't help Ellie in the condition she was in.

"Go!" she sobbed, tears flooding her eyes. "Go get my baby."

CHAPTER 18

Rex charged through the dark, wet forest. The Maglite illuminated glimpses of the vegetation he was trampling, but he was moving so quickly and recklessly, his visibility was so impeded by the rain, he was nevertheless getting flayed alive by branches, twigs, and other woody hindrances.

He barely noticed.

He was moving on auto-pilot, his mind on fire.

It's real! he thought wildly. *Jesus Christ, it's real!*

And not only this, he *remembered* it.

He remembered everything now.

"Take your brother, Rex, and go hide right now. You boys are good at that."

She went to the door.

"Mom!" Rex cried. "Don't leave us!"

"I have to lead him away." She pushed her dark hair from her dark eyes, which were looking at Rex but didn't seem to be seeing him.

"Hide with us," he pleaded.

Attempting a smile that trembled and became a frown, she left the cabin, closing the door behind her.

Rex turned to Logan, whose mouth was twisted in pain. "Did he have a knife?" he asked.

"It wasn't a person," Logan mumbled, and then he began sobbing.

"What?"

"I'm scared, Rex."

"What was it, Loge?"

"I don't know!"

Although Rex was the little brother, he knew he was going to have to make the decision of where to hide. Logan was acting way too weird.

Upstairs under their beds was the first spot that came to his mind. But he quickly dismissed this possibility. That was the first place where people looked when they wanted to find where you were hiding.

In the chimney?

Rex grabbed Logan's hand and all but dragged him into the connecting room. He stuck his head into the fireplace's firebox and looked up. The flue was too narrow. Neither of them would fit. When he pulled his head back out, Logan had already thrown the little rug back to reveal the trap door to the root cellar. Rex and Logan had used to play down there. But then at the beginning of the summer, their dad found that a family of raccoons had moved in and told them it was off limits, and they hadn't been down there since.

Logan jumped into the hole. "Come on!" he said, his head poking up above the floor.

Rex hesitated. If he went down too, who would put the rug back in place? Someone needed to, or the man who attacked their dad would easily find them (Rex couldn't believe that the person coming after them wasn't a person).

He started swinging the hatch back into place.

Logan stopped it with one of his hands. "What are you doing?"

"I need to put the rug back."

"Where are you going to hide?"

"I'll find a better spot."

Logan held his red-stained hands in front of him. "Am I losing too much blood, Rex?"

Rex shook his head. "I don't think so."

"I don't feel good."

"Just hide. Mom will be back soon."

Rex closed the hatch and pulled the rug back in place. With his heart beating so fast and loud in his chest he could hear it in his ears, he tried to think of a place to hide. In the stove? He was too big. Under the sofa? That was as bad as under the bed. In the closet? No room with the shelves. The bathroom? He could lock the door. No, the attacker would just break it down.

Outside, he decided. There were way more places to hide outside than inside.

Rex left the cabin. It was late afternoon, the sky dull and gray. The forest seemed especially quiet and still. His mind raced through all the places where he had hidden before when he and Logan played Hide and Seek—

His mom screamed.

She sounded like she was near the Sanders' place, which was next door but still far away. Maybe she was going there for help? No, it was late summer, and Rex and his family were the last people remaining on the lake. She understood that. She was just leading the attacker away—

(and he caught her)

Rex grimaced. His first instinct was to go and help her, but he knew he would be too late and too small to help. His second instinct was not to hide but to run. He could try to get to the highway, and then to town. Even though nobody was on the lake, there were always cars on the highway. If he could reach it, someone would drive by and pick him up and—

His mom screamed again. It sounded like she was in great pain. This terrified Rex because he had never heard his mother in pain before. Adults, he had thought up until that point in his young life, didn't feel pain, at least not the way kids did, which was why they never cried.

But was his mom crying right then? It sounded like maybe she was, crying and screaming at the same time.

Rex ran down the driveway toward the road. The air was warm, laced with the scent of pine needles and earth and wildflowers. This felt out of place. Nobody should be screaming when the smell of wildflowers was in the air. Especially not his mom. She should be down at the dock with him and Loge, wearing her straw hat, reading one of her books and sipping a glass of lemonade.

When Rex reached the road, he did not turn down it toward town. He continued straight across it, crashing into the woods, in the direction he'd heard his mom screaming.

He bashed through branches and trampled saplings and small brush, barely slowing, and then he saw her in the distance, his mom, and the thing dragging her by one arm.

It was a bug.

A huge human-sized bug. But not like the ones in the old black-and-white monster movies. It was the same size as a man in a suit, but everything else about it was wrong. Its legs and arms were too long to be human. Its waist was too skinny. Its upper body was too compact. Its head was too small. And it moved in an unnatural yet effortless and precise way. Not how a human moved. More like how a man on stilts might look if captured on film and fast-forwarded.

"Mom!" he shouted in fright.

"Rex?"

Rex kept running toward her, closing the distance. His mom's face, he could now see, was ghostly white and slack, her eyes closed. Her beige shirt was torn open and her tummy was covered in blood.

The bug-thing either didn't hear him approaching or didn't care. It kept moving without looking back.

"Mom!"

"Rex?" Her eyes opened. They appeared dead. Eyes of the living dead, or of the living who knew they were going to be dead any moment. "Rex? Baby, no..."

"Stop!" he cried, coming to a stop a dozen feet behind the bug. "Leave my mom alone!" He scavenged a pinecone from the ground and threw it. It whizzed past the bug's head, but it got its attention. Its head turned independently of its body, just enough so one buggy eye could look back at him.

The eye was so devoid of emotion, so utterly alien, that everything inside of Rex turned into a mushy soup of uncontrollable fear.

"Mom...?" he rasped, stumbling backward.

"Rex," she said, "go, get away, go..."

The bug released her arm. She fell limply onto her back.

It came for him, fast.

Rex turned and ran, careening through the trees as quickly as his legs would take him, no looking back, no slowing down. He was blind with terror. Even when he reached the road he didn't look back or slow down. He just ran and kept running to the highway. He didn't remember when he finally slowed to a walk, but he did at some point because when a white pickup truck pulled up beside him he was limping on scorched feet. The window was rolled down, and a man was asking him where he was going.

Rex no longer knew. He didn't even know what he was doing on the highway. The man told him to get in, he would give him a lift to town. Rex knew not to accept rides from strangers, but that didn't seem important right then. There was a coldness inside him, a steady throbbing of terror and loss and unfamiliarity, and nothing and nobody seemed important right then, and so he got in the truck and stared silently out the window, watching the world pass by in a film of darkening despair.

△△△

Ellie screamed from somewhere ahead of Rex, tugging him back to the present. He wiped the rain from his eyes, shouted back, told her he was coming.

He couldn't risk falling any further behind. If he did, Ellie was a goner. The forest stretched for millions of hectares. It could swallow an army without a trace.

He ran faster.

△△△

He'd been giving chase for what must have been ten minutes now, and Ellie's plaintive screams were becoming faint and far in between. Rex tried to keep his thoughts positive, but he knew he wasn't going to be able to catch up to her. The beast was too fast. He was falling too far behind.

This understanding enraged him. He was the only person in the world that could save Ellie, her young life depended on his perseverance, and he wasn't up to the task.

Rex sagged next to a giant tree trunk, his breath coming in heaving rasps, his stomach so nauseated he thought he might throw up.

As the rain tore through the canopy and beat down upon him, he realized he could no longer hear Ellie's cries for help.

"Ellie!" he shouted, shoving himself away from the trunk in pursuit once more.

"*Help!*" came a faint cry.

"Ellie," he said to himself, and it was almost a moan. "Ellie!" he repeated, louder.

"*Help!*" Distant, evanescent. "*Help!*"

It was a haunting and surreal experience to be running through a primeval forest in a raging thunderstorm, trying to locate a child only by her terrified screams. It was so outside the norm of daily existence that Rex could scarcely believe it was happening, and for perhaps the first time in his life he understood why people who experienced something horribly uncanny often believed themselves to be sleeping and having a bad dream.

"Ellie!" he shouted.

Her reply was a distant shriek, yet different than all the others, for it also held the glassy urgency and intensity of pain.

What had the beast done to her? Rex thought frantically, at the same time wondering if beast was the right word to describe the ungodly thing. Because although "beast" usually referred to a large, scary animal, it was an animal with a backbone. And the thing that had taken his mother thirty-eight years ago, and Ellie now, was by all appearances an invertebrate, an insect.

A mosquito.

A six-foot-tall mosquito that stands like a man.

Rex came to a halt at the base of a crag where the ground rose steeply and abruptly, and where an abundance of talus had collected from a long-ago rockslide. He turned in a circle until he was facing the scree once more.

A dead-end.

He was not about to turn back, which meant his only option was to climb the debris and see where it led him. Before he could do this, however, Ellie cried out—and it seemed her voice originated from beneath the ground.

Stymied, Rex tore through the vegetation clinging to the rocks and boulders before him...and discovered rotting slabs of timber framing the entrance to a mine.

In his excitement, Rex nearly called to Ellie again, to tell her he was coming, but he didn't, deciding it was best not to let the creature know he had discovered its lair.

ΔΔΔ

Inside the mine the air was cool, moist, and stale. The blackness was stuffy and suffocating.

Rex ran his hand through his wet hair, mustered his nerves, and started into the depths of the mine, sweeping the flashlight beam ahead of him.

The passageway was roughly hewn, circular in shape, the floor strewn with loose stones. A little way in, it angled downward, leading to a new horizontal shaft that conformed to a more rectangular shape. Here, a set of flat-bottom steel rails resting on timber ties disappeared deeper into the darkness.

Rex followed them, passing a table on which sat an ancient Edison alkaline primary battery, and a marking on the wall, made by the smoke of a carbine lamp, that read Dec. 18, 1902. Roughly fifty feet along, he came to a metal hand winch that stood at the top of a steep thirty-degree rocky stope.

He skidded down the stope, stones shifting beneath his feet. Twice he nearly fell over but managed to keep his balance. At the bottom, he hurried forward—and didn't notice the false floor until he was halfway across it.

He came to an abrupt halt. The series of timber boards

beneath his feet creaked precariously. What lay below them? A hundred-foot vertical shaft? One of those booby-trapped spiked pits from an *Indiana Jones* or *Tomb Raider* film?

He took a cautious step forward, testing the strength of the boards with his foot before exerting his full weight. They flexed and creaked more but held. He took another step, then another, then he was back on solid ground.

Rex picked up his pace once again, wondering how deep the tunnels snaked. It would depend on the length of the ore vein they pursued, but they could easily meander for miles. Thankfully, there had so far only been a single, albeit zigzagging, path. Which meant he was not lost. He was on Ellie's trail. He would be able to find his way back to the surface.

He was still telling himself this when the passageway branched in two.

Of course, he thought mordantly.

Rex shone the Maglite down each passage. Both appeared nearly identical. There was no reason to choose one over the other.

"Shit," he mumbled, randomly going right.

The passageway's walls and ceiling closed quickly around him, the rock becoming increasingly jagged and cave-like. Then the tunnel came to an abrupt end. Evidently it had been an exploratory shaft that had struck out.

Rex had only taken a dozen steps back the way he had come when Ellie cried out, her voice small and distant. He resisted the impulse to call back and broke into a reckless trot to make up for the lost time. Soon his lungs were heaving and his heart was pounding so quickly and painfully he wouldn't be surprised if it seized up in cardiac arrest. Nevertheless, his only concern right then was finding the poor girl. He could scarcely imagine the terror she must be experiencing. Not only had she been kidnapped by something from the mind of H.R. Giger, but she was also being whisked away deep into the bowels of the earth—

He tripped over a loose pile of rocks, landing hard on his hands and knees. Grunting in surprise and pain, he glanced back over his shoulder. What appeared to be a small cairn, the size of an ottoman, rose in the center of the tunnel. He'd scattered several of the stacked rocks when he'd driven his foot through it, but the pyramidal shape remained intact. His first thought, ludicrous as it might be, was that the creature had laid a trap for him. But then the flashlight beam revealed a portal in the ceiling directly above the cairn: an ore chute from a higher-level stope. The pile of rocks was not a conscience creation but the result of gravity.

Rex got back to his feet—and hesitated. The creature had wings. It would likely have no problem flying up the ore chute, even burdened as it was with Ellie's weight.

Was that where it had gone?

No, he decided. Ellie's cry had come from somewhere below him, not above.

Hadn't it?

He didn't know for certain. The enclosure of rock and earth dampened sound, making it difficult to judge the distance and direction of the source.

Besides, whether the creature went up the chute or not was a moot point. Rex didn't have wings and couldn't follow it that way even if he wanted to. There was only one direction he could go, and that was forward.

Fifty yards onward the rail tracks ended at a sharp corner where an ore cart, empty of any cargo, lay toppled on its side. Another fifty yards after this, a wall of debris blocked the passageway.

Rex experienced a moment of gut-churning defeat until he got close enough to determine there was just enough space along the left wall for him to pass. Carefully, he shimmied sideways between wall and debris, trying not to think about a cave-in and failing miserably. In fact, as his shoulders scraped the unyielding rock, and clumps of dirt fell from the ceiling to break apart over his head and shoulders, a cave-in was suddenly the *only* thing he could think about. The experience of being buried alive beneath tons of dirt, unable to move anything except your fingers and toes, and maybe not even those, taking your last few tortured breaths as the world faded around you into oblivion…

Rex stumbled free of the narrow space, doubling over, gasping for breath. He closed his eyes and felt as though he might be swaying. Yet with each passing second he felt a little bit better, and when he opened his eyes again the symptoms had passed.

He continued down the passageway, now all too aware of the shortness of his breath and the tightness in his chest and the trembling in his muscles, though he did his best to ignore these discomforts. The one sure way to have another panic attack was to think about having another panic attack.

He was so preoccupied with these thoughts, he once again didn't realize the false floor beneath him before it was too late—only this time it really was too late.

There was a loud crack-splinter, and then he was falling through the air. His feet struck the ground hard, and he fell backward onto his butt. Pain shot through his tailbone and up his spine. The Maglite launched from his hand and clicked off upon colliding with something.

Blackness reigned.

Rex scrambled around on all fours until his hand curled around the cylindrical barrel of the flashlight. Switching it back on—*still worked, thank God!*—he aimed the beam at the hole he'd fallen through.

He didn't think he could monkey his way back up there, which meant he would have to continue the way he had been going and hope this new shaft mirrored the direction of the one above.

Back on his feet, ignoring the dull pain pulsing in his bones, he went straight for fifty feet or so before veering left and downward. Twenty feet later he did a double take, snapping the flashlight beam back to what it had flitted over.

A skeleton.

It was small, yellowed, most likely avian. Yet a skeleton was still a skeleton, a representation and reminder of death, and his stomach soured.

Rex pressed on, though his mind remained on the bird. What had it been? A canary that had escaped a miner's cage? A crow or sparrow that had flown into the tunnel system and had gotten lost and died? He didn't know, and he told himself the bird didn't matter, shouldn't matter...but it did. There was something about its remains, something sinister, something he was missing...

Wildlife, he thought in an epiphany.

Where was all the wildlife?

Thus far, the mine had been completely barren of any such life. This was wrong, unnatural. An abandoned mine was the perfect habitat for bats, owls, rattlesnakes, rats, mice. Maybe even a mountain lion or a black bear. So why had he not yet come across a single living animal?

The tunnels might have been filled with lethal concentrations of dangerous gases—methane or carbon monoxide perhaps, or hydrogen sulfide—killing trespassers not long after they entered.

Yet the more probable explanation, he believed, was that wildlife simply knew not to come down here, knew, or sensed, that it was home to an apex predator that outclassed anything else on the food chain.

ΔΔΔ

The tunnel led to a dead end. At least Rex thought it did, for a moment. Then he saw the square hole cut into the rock floor. He knelt at the lip of it. A wooden ladder descended into its inky depth.

He frowned. The creature didn't climb down a ladder. Its physiology would make this unlikely, comical even. *Ladders are for humans, stupid.*

Nevertheless, what option did Rex have but to descend?

Turning around would lead him nowhere.

Maneuvering to his butt, his legs dangling into the hole, he tucked the Maglite beneath his left armpit and latched onto the ladder. It was bolted into the rock. He descended, keeping his left arm pressed tightly to his side so as not to drop the flashlight. It was a long way to the bottom, made more so by how slowly he seemed to be progressing. He couldn't help but think he was entering the depths of hell, a clichéd metaphor, but apt for the circumstances.

He counted forty-one rungs—perhaps the height of a three-story building—before the rock opened around him, and another ten rungs before he stepped off the last one onto solid ground.

Transferring the flashlight to his hand, he turned around, sweeping the beam through the dark—and found himself in a passageway similar to all the others. He wasn't sure what he'd been expecting, but more of the same depressed him. He was wandering blindly, irrationally hoping that the passageway he'd departed when he'd crashed through the floor would eventually meet up with wherever this one led him.

In truth, he was getting lost.

Rex was tempted to finally call Ellie's name, but he didn't. The reason for remaining silent was not only to keep his presence secret, as it had been when he'd first entered the mine, but because he now feared Ellie might not call back.

And a lack of response would be the worst possible reply.

The time for wishful thinking had long passed, and he had to be brutally honest with himself. There was no sugarcoating Ellie's predicament. This was not a movie in which the creature was going to keep her alive only for Rex to ingenuously rescue her at the last moment. It had brought her down here for one reason and one reason alone: to devour her. So if he called to her, and she didn't call back, that meant she was likely already dead, and he didn't know if he could deal with that reality right then —sometimes you're better off not knowing, isn't that what they say?—and so he kept quiet as he forged resolutely, and perhaps pointlessly, ahead.

Twenty feet on, the tunnel split.

He chose left.

Twenty more feet and it split again.

He chose right.

He came to several more crossroads and selected his path equally recklessly and randomly as he zigzagged ever deeper into the underground labyrinth.

He was no longer even pretending to keep track of the way he'd come. The lack of natural light was not only disheartening but disorientating. He was not getting lost; he *was* lost. He knew that—and in a moment of self-loathing he realized he almost secretly hoped he was lost because then he could turn around and leave this dank tomb. He would not have to face off against the abysmal creature, an encounter no bookie worth their salt would back him to win, even armed with a pistol as he was. He would not find and rescue Ellie

(she was already dead)

but she wasn't even his kid anyway. If it were Bobby down here, he would spend his dying breaths tracking him down. But Ellie...wasn't his kid. He loved her, he thought she was a great girl, but she wasn't his. So why was he risking his life to find her? It was madness. She was gone, and Bobby was still alive. That's what mattered. *Bobby was alive.* He needed his father. So it was time Rex stopped playing hero and got the hell out of there. That was the

(cowardly)

right thing to do. Get back to the cabin, protect Bobby until the police arrived. This nightmare could all be over in a few hours. He and Bobby and Tabitha would be safe. Ellie would be gone, but the rest of them would be safe...

Rex realized he was mumbling unintelligibly and viciously to himself. He was losing it. He really was.

Stop being such a fucking pussy. You're not a coward. You never have been. Ellie's down here, and you're going to find her, and you're going to kill the abomination that's taken her.

You're going to do all of that, or you're going to die trying.

ΔΔΔ

Later.

Rex was deep in the earth. Very deep. The section of mine he had recently descended to was not solid rock, nor was it shored up with timber supports. It was simply compressed dirt, the walls lined with backfill. A smaller tunnel veered left. He ignored it, continuing straight on his chosen path.

Soon he came to yet another false floor. Most of the timber boards were missing. Looking down, he could see a lower, irregularly shaped stope.

He dropped onto the rubble pile. The stope led to a new subterranean corridor that was nearly twice as wide and tall as all the others he had passed through. It was also the most precarious looking, with a patchwork of stulls bracing up platforms that would have once supported miners, the series of wooden props held in place with nothing more than rusty nails and baling wire.

The ground was strewn with relics from the past. Another Edison battery, like the one he'd first seen upon entering the mine. Bits of rusted machinery of which he could make neither heads nor tails. A tobacco tin. What appeared to be a utilitarian lunchbox. A dynamite box labeled "Hercules I.C.C.C 14." A repurposed can turned into a sieve. Blasting caps, wooden ties, a pickaxe.

Further along, Rex entered another stope, different than the last, as this one was so large the flashlight beam didn't reach the far side, revealing instead only impenetrable darkness.

In fact, it wasn't a stope at all. It was a natural cavern. Swaths of the walls and ceiling were stained aqua blue by dripping water. Translucent calcite crystals as large as his fingers sprouted from the rock, alongside deposits of brilliant shiny gray galena, and buttery-hued fool's gold.

Rex entered the vast space cautiously. The ground was littered with more junk the miners had left behind, including a faded newspaper from the turn of the last century with the headline proclaiming "Russia at War with Japan," and a denim jacket missing one sleeve and covered in white drops that might have been candle wax.

The flashlight beam played over another skeleton.

Not a small bird this time. The animal had once been a mature stag. A set of tined antlers were still attached to the skull, though something had happened to its legs, as only an elongated vertebra and a partial ribcage remained of the body.

The sight, morose as it was, buoyed Rex's spirit. It meant there must be another way to get down here other than via the ladder shaft.

Which meant there was another, and likely closer, way out as well.

Two dozen paces onward the ground disappeared into a great black hole at least fifty feet wide and who knew how many across.

A subterranean sinkhole?

Struck by an idea, Rex retrieved a stone from the ground and threw it into the hole. Only it wasn't a hole. It was, as he'd suspected upon second analysis, a subterranean lake. The water, which had been as smooth as a black mirror moments before, now rippled around the spot where the stone had plopped and sunk.

He started along the lake's perimeter—and came to four more skeletons. They had once been animals the size of cougars or wolves, and they were within touching distance of one another.

Rex frowned.

Animals did not die together like that.

Not naturally, at least.

△△△

Sensing he was no longer on a wild goose chase, Rex continued along the shore of the subterranean lake—discovering more and more piles of bones. Two here, six there. They were all largish animals, with one skeleton appearing to be the remains of a bear.

The creature had not only killed a bear, but it had also carried it down here.

A bear for God's sake.

How the hell did it do that?

While Rex worried about this, the piles of bones multiplied rapidly, becoming so numerous they were no longer individual islands but a connected sea of white, flooding the ground as far as the flashlight beam allowed him to see.

Rex's head spun, even as an odd numbness anesthetized his terror, allowing him to think relatively calmly and clearly.

It would take decades, perhaps tens of decades, for the creature to devour this many animals. So how long had it inhabited the cavern? Had others before it called it home as well? Did those ancestors discover the cavern once the mine was abandoned? Or were they here *before* the mine? Did the miners inadvertently blast into this cavern, stirring up the proverbial hornet's nest? Was this why the mine shut down?

Were some of these bones human?

Banishing these questions from his mind—the pitch black was not the place you wanted to ask such things—Rex longed to return to the surface more than ever. He should never have come down here. He was in way over his head. Ellie was dead, and he was going to be dead very shortly too. He was going to become a meal to a prehistoric insect that had no right existing in the modern world. This was his sad fate.

Unless he turned around.

Rex's pulse quickened at the prospect. He would have to climb up and out the hole through which he had fallen earlier. He had not thought this possible before, but it had not been a matter of life and death then. Now, he sensed, it was, and if he could find his way back to the hole, he was sure he could climb out of it. He could scavenge some timber, build a rudimentary ladder. Tricky, no question, but doable. And once he was back on that upper level, it was easy sailing. Twenty minutes to the surface. Less than that. Because he would be running this time, hazards be damned, running for all he was worth to get away from this crypt and the evil it harbored.

All he had to do was turn around.

△△△

He couldn't, he thought with angry despair. He simply couldn't.

He couldn't abandon Ellie if there was even the slightest chance she was still alive.

He forced himself to continue forward, toward his all too likely doom.

△△△

Ellie didn't believe that any of what was happening to her was real.

On one level she did. She knew the monster had kidnapped her. It had brought her to its underground home, and it was going to eat her, using her bones as toothpicks to clean its teeth when it was full. She knew all of this as she sat where the monster had left her, with her back against a rock wall in the perfect black, too terrified to move, listening for it to return.

But *knowing* this didn't mean she had to *believe* it. Believing was a choice. It was like pretending. You could know something was true but just pretend it wasn't. She did this all the time. Like if she was playing a game with Bobby, and she was losing, she would pretend she didn't know the score so he couldn't win. Or if she wanted to use a certain toy in the classroom at school during free time, and it was someone else's turn with it, she would pretend she forgot the rules so she could still use it and not get in trouble.

She was doing the same kind of pretending now—pretending that none of this was real, that it wasn't happening, that she would wake up and it would be one of her bad dreams.

The problem with pretending, however, was that she always *knew* when she was pretending. It was like lying. When she lied to her mom or her teacher, she knew she was lying, but just pretended she didn't know what they wanted to know.

So maybe pretending wasn't *like* lying, she decided. Maybe it *was* lying. And if that was the case, she was lying to herself right now.

The monster was real.

It was going to eat her.

Ellie felt tears spill down her cheeks. She squeezed her eyes shut tighter than they already were and pressed the balls of her hands against them, so she didn't accidentally peek and see something in the dark she didn't want to see. *I promise, God, that I'll never pretend or lie again if you send me back to my mommy right now. I'll even be nice to Bobby and stop cheating when we play games. I'll wash the dishes when my mom asks me to and I'll do all my work at school and try my hardest at everything. Please, God? Is that good enough? Just send me back to my mommy with your magic. Please, God? God? Are you listening? I'm still here. It's still dark. It's so dark. I hate the dark. I'm really scared, God. Please send me back to my mommy.*

And then just as Ellie was giving up hope that God was listening, He appeared.

△△△

Brittle femurs and cracked tibias and splintered jawbones snapped beneath each step that Rex took as he continued along the edge of the subterranean lake.

Time was playing tricks with his mind. He had only been underground for fifteen or twenty minutes, yet it felt like days; he had only been in this large chamber for a couple of minutes, yet it too felt like much longer. It was akin to those last sixty-seconds in a hockey game when your team was winning by a one-goal margin and the other team had their goalie out and an extra attacker on the ice. Those sixty seconds could feel like an eternity.

How's this match going to play out, Rex? he asked himself. *You going to win or lose? There won't be a draw. That's not happening, so hope you don't lose, really hope you don't, because there'll be no rematch either. That'll be it. You'll be dead. Ellie will be dead. Nobody will ever know what happened to both of you. Nobody will believe Tabitha that the Mosquito Man got you. They'll have a good laugh over that, no doubt. You'll become a joke, a punch line at summer barbecues while people are swatting mosquitos. And after that, when you're no longer even relevant enough to be a punch line, you and Ellie will simply be gone, numbers added to the sad statistic of people who go missing and are never found. Like Mom and Dad. Like Logan. Only Loge's body did turn up, that was true, but Mom's and Dad's didn't. They didn't bleed to death beneath the cabin. They just vanished into thin air—*

Rex froze as suddenly as if he had just stepped on top of his own grave. His heart reared in his chest. The flashlight beam did not move an inch from the grisly remains directly before him.

The skeleton was different from all the others he had already become desensitized to. It was human and fully clothed. A beige cowl-neck shirt draped pointy shoulders and a flattened ribcage. A pair of flared yellow shorts outlined a butterfly-shaped pelvis and sticklike legs. Silver bangles encircled a bony wrist. Platform shoes held no feet inside them. Dark shoulder-length hair sat atop the skull like a wig. The two crusty orbits stared at him blankly if not facetiously, as if amused he wasn't in on the morbid joke that death was.

"Mom..." he said, barely aware he had spoken.

Look at you, Rexy, all grown up, she said inside his head, the tender, smiling sound of her voice forgotten to him until that moment. *My little boy, all grown up.* Her tone changed, hardened. *But you shouldn't be down here, Rexy. It's not safe.*

"Mom…" he said again, the strength leaving his body in a rush. He sank to his knees, stretching a trembling hand toward her.

I told you to go, didn't I, Rexy? Yes, I did. My little boy, my October pumpkin, I told you to run, and you did, you ran and you ran and you ran…

"Mom…" he mumbled for a third time, the backs of his fingers brushing the smooth coolness of her cheekbone. "I'm sorry, I'm so sorry. I should have stayed. I should have tried to help. But I was so young, so afraid…"

Whatever else he had to say was drowned out in a choke of sobs.

△△△

Ellie mistook Rex's voice for that of God's, and when she opened her eyes in innocent relief and saw the bright beam of the flashlight, she cried at the top of her small lungs: "God! I'm right here! I'm right here!"

△△△

Rex's head snapped toward the cries of alarm emanating from somewhere in the dark directly ahead of him.

"Ellie!" he said, arcing the flashlight from side to side.

"I'm right here!"

Rex leaped to his feet and stumbled forward, careful to give his mother's remains a wide berth. Yet in his haste to reach Ellie he tripped over other bones and fell to his knees, tripped and fell and scrambled. Then he saw Ellie standing against a looming wall. She was squinting at the light blinding her eyes and waving her hands over her head like a castaway lost at sea trying to catch the attention of a passing boat.

"Ellie!" he said when he reached her, scooping her into his arms and holding her tightly against his chest. "You're alive," he whispered into her hair. "Thank God, oh thank God."

"T-Rex?" she said, her voice muffled against his chest. It was shaky and uncertain like it got when she was all cried out after a big blow-up with her mom. "I thought *you* were God."

"*Shhh, shhh, shhh,*" he said. "We have to get out of here, okay?" He set her down and aimed the light at a patch of the floor with no bones so they could see each other in the backsplash. "Where's the creature?" he asked quietly.

"I don't know! It just left me here."

Rex didn't like the sound of that. *Just left her here?* Did it understand that, as a young child, she would be too frightened to attempt to escape on her own? This seemed improbable, which meant it likely had a way to track its prey in the dark.

Was it watching them, or monitoring them, right now?

"This way." He nudged Ellie along the wall. The direction they chose didn't matter. Both would lead them back to the entrance to the chamber. It might take them a little longer than following the shore of the lake, but they would not be so exposed. They would have the rock wall at their backs if the creature attacked them.

When they were halfway or so back to the entrance of the cavern, Ellie yelped and pointed.

Twenty feet away Daisy lay on her back, just as dead as she'd been on the cabin porch, the difference being her arms and legs were now stiff with rigor mortis, and three creatures sat around her body. They were just babies, Ellie's size. Their bodies appeared to be soft and fleshy, their appendages glued down with a slimy substance. Each had a proboscis plugged deep into Daisy's chest.

Ellie had begun making a sound Rex had never heard anyone make before: a mewling whine that was equal parts loathing, pity, and terror.

And then before he knew what he was doing, he was moving, closing the distance to the abominations quickly. They did not look at him, did not react in any way to his approach.

Were they too stupid to register him as a threat, just as

mosquitos were too stupid to realize they were going to get swatted if they landed on your skin? Or were they simply too busy sucking up blood?

These thoughts came and went in the time it took Rex to withdraw the pistol from the waistband of his pants. He aimed three times and squeezed the trigger three times: *pop, pop, pop.*

The head of each creature—pupae?—exploded in blood and pus and goo, and their obscene bodies slumped forward onto poor Daisy's corpse.

△△△

Everything was coming together inside Rex's head at an almost nauseating pace, everything was ticking, clicking, and making sense. *It's why it guts you. No major veins or arteries in your stomach. That means no hemorrhage, no wasted blood. It guts you to incapacitate you, so it can carry you down here. At least large prey like humans. Smaller stuff—birds, rodents, chickens maybe—it just slaughters on the spot. But for something big—a human has one and a half gallons of blood inside it, a deer or bear much more—it brings it down here so it can suck away at its leisure. Not to mention offer up a blood buffet to its greedy little offspring.*

That's what happened to his mom. Probably his dad too.

And the Petersons? And the Ryersons? Were their skeletons—their leftovers—down here somewhere? The Ryersons had two girls. Were they down here? Had they been exsanguinated? Perhaps while they were still alive? Because that's another reason it gutted its prey, wasn't it? It takes a long time to die from a stomach wound, days sometimes, and as long as your heart's pumping, your blood's getting oxygen, staying fresh.

Oh, Jesus—was that why Ellie wasn't gutted? So she could be served fresh?

These thoughts filled Rex with not only disgust but insensate rage, and right then in the heat of the moment, he almost wanted the adult creature to show its hideous face.

He wanted revenge, hot, hot revenge.

CHAPTER 19

Tabitha was worried sick. She couldn't concentrate, couldn't sit still. Her thoughts were racing, her stomach twisted inside out. She'd spent the last forty minutes pacing, crying, talking to herself, bemoaning ever letting Ellie out of her sight, acting like a certifiable crazy person.

The behavior wasn't helping Bobby's temperament any. When she cried, he cried. When he asked her a question, she either ignored him or snapped at him. She couldn't help herself.

Her daughter was taken. Gone. Maybe dead. Yes, maybe dead, because Rex should have been back by now. He should have been back with Ellie in his arms. Her Ellie. Her spunky little girl. Her baby.

I'm never going to see her again, am I?

It was a reasonable question, asked matter-of-factly, and it fueled her despair, and right then she hated herself. Hated herself for letting events come to this. She was Ellie's mother. She was her protector. She failed her little girl.

Tabitha sank to the sofa, curled up, and rocked and cried.

Bobby was speaking to her. She looked at him through itchy, bleary eyes. She didn't know how long she'd been crying, only that it had been a while. She wiped her eyes and nose with the backs of her hands. She needed to pull herself together for his sake.

She tried a smile that felt like the saddest facial gesture she had ever made. "Come here, Bobby, I'm sorry, come here." She opened her arms.

Bobby seemed hesitant, but he came to her, and she drew him into her embrace.

They had never hugged before. He had always been too standoffish. His small body against hers felt so much like Ellie's, so soft and fragile and young, and she thought, *Why couldn't the creature have taken you instead?*

The thought startled her, and she shoved it promptly aside, ashamed of herself.

Why couldn't it have been me? That's what I should be asking. Why not me? It should have been me.

She began to cry again, silently this time, with tears only. Bobby didn't say anything. He just held on to her. She bit her bottom lip. It continued to tremble. She tried thinking about anything but her daughter.

It was impossible. She couldn't do it.

The darkness inside her became overwhelming.

She eased Bobby aside. She tried another phony smile. "You're such a brave boy, you know that?" she said, the words coming out of her mouth before she was fully cognizant of what she was planning on saying and doing. She thought she knew. The plan was there, in her head, vague, yet taking shape quickly. "You're so brave, Bobby, and when your dad comes back, you're going to be brave for him too, okay?"

What are you doing? she thought, a niggle of panic cutting through the despair. *Don't set this in motion. Don't set this up. You might go through with it.*

She kept talking. "I want you to go upstairs and hide under the bed and stay there until your daddy returns. Can you do that for me, Bobby?"

He looked terrified at the idea. "I want to stay here with you."

"It's best you go upstairs."

"But that's where the monster got Ellie!"

Hearing her daughter's name spoken aloud broke Tabitha's heart all over again. "The monster's not coming back," she said tightly. "You'll be safe up there. Just until your daddy comes back."

"But I don't want to go!"

His refusal strengthened Tabitha's resolve to commit to her plan. She sat up straight. "We're not going to argue about this, Bobby. You do as I say."

Bobby frowned, then slid off the sofa.

She nodded. "Go on now."

He departed to the other room, and the last of her reservations went with him. She gasped as if she had been holding her breath for the last minute or so. She covered her mouth with her fingers. She was going to do this, wasn't she? Yes, she was. She couldn't live without Ellie. She couldn't live not knowing what happened to her, or, perhaps more accurately, knowing what happened to her, because there was only one reason the creature took her.

So how are you going to do it?

The easiest method would be to hang herself. She had spent enough time since Katy Pignette's murder in morbid contemplation of just such an act, and she knew she could use the sash from her bathrobe as the ligature. Tie one end around the horizontal metal pole in the closet. Stick her head in a noose, kneel, and lean forward. The pressure on her carotid artery would cause her to black out in seconds, even if the lack of blood reaching her brain wouldn't kill her for another half hour.

Yet that was the problem.

Rex might return before she could die properly, or Bobby might come downstairs. Either one of them could "save" her—which would probably leave her with serious brain damage, or in a vegetative state. More than that, she simply didn't want Bobby to be the one to find her. He was five years old. After tonight, he was going to have enough issues to last him a lifetime; she wasn't going to dump anything more on him.

She'd need to do it outside, she decided. She would have to get far away from the cabin, not to mention find a branch that was the right height and would not snap under her weight. Doing this would be uncomfortable in the storm. She would get cold and wet—

You're killing yourself! she thought indignantly. *It's the last thing you'll ever do. And you're worried about getting cold and wet?*

Tabitha stood on suddenly shaky legs. Adrenaline coursed through her veins. Every object in the room came into angelic focus. And despite being terrified right then, she found herself decidedly excited. She would finally be free.

Yes, Tabs, you damn sicko, you definitely have a bad gene inside you. More than likely, you have a whole handful of them inside you.

Moving robotically, Tabitha went to her suitcase, withdrew her bathrobe, snaked the sash free from the loops. She had bought the bathrobe at a shopping mall last June while visiting her younger sister, Ivy, in Olympia. They'd spent the morning browsing the shops for a present for Ivy's husband's upcoming birthday. They'd had coffee in a pleasant little café, and lunch at an Italian eatery, where the waiter had hit on both of them. It had been a fun weekend.

You'll never get to see Ivy again. Or Beth. Or Vanessa or Rex, for that matter...

Yes, all of that was true, but she would never see her little girl again either, and that was the harshest reality, the one she could not live with.

Tabitha left the cabin as quietly as she could. As soon as she stepped outside into the night, the storm iced her skin and chilled her to the bone. She set off in an arbitrary direction, her hands shielding her eyes from the slanting rain.

A blast of lightning stabbed the sky purple. And in that brief moment, through the silhouetted, swaying trees, she saw the vast, dark expanse of the lake, its previous calm surface now boiling with whitecaps.

She made her way toward it.

CHAPTER 20

Moments after Rex returned to Ellie's side, a high-pitched whine filled the air.

"It's coming!" Ellie cried.

Heart thumping, Rex aimed both Maglite and pistol into the void above them.

He caught a glimpse of the creature.

It strafed right. He tracked it. Squeezed the trigger in panic.

Did he hit it?

The whining receded but didn't fade completely.

"Where is it?" Ellie cried.

"Run!" he said, barely getting the word out of his fear-shrunken lungs.

She took off ahead of him. He followed, scanning the darkness. He could still hear the whine of the creature's wings. It was either on the other side of the chamber or very high above them.

Had the bullet struck it? Was it injured? Or had the shot merely scared it off?

He shouldn't have slaughtered the pupae, he realized. They hadn't been a threat. And now there were only three rounds left in the pistol's magazine.

Ellie tripped and fell. Said "Ouch!" when her hands and knees slapped the ground. Before Rex could help her she was up and running again.

The whining increased in volume and intensity from somewhere directly in front of them.

He shouted, "Ellie! Stop!"

She skidded to a stop and whipped her head around to look at him, her loose black hair falling across her childish face. He moved in front of her and aimed the flashlight and gun straight ahead. The whining changed in pitch and direction. Confused, he aimed up, straight, right, left, up again.

Where the hell was it?

The whining stopped.

"Stay behind me," he whispered harshly.

Blinking perspiration from his eyes, Rex crept forward, keeping his back to the rock, his arms outstretched in a shooter's position, his trigger finger slick with sweat.

Don't get spooked. Don't fire again until you have a sure shot.

He heard a noise at two o'clock, a shifting of rubble, or bones.

He aimed the flashlight beam accordingly.

The man-sized insect was thirty feet away from him, standing perfectly still, its compound eyes unreadable, its antennae twitching as if smelling or tasting the air, its proboscis jutting from its face phallically. It stood erect on its two long legs. Its pinchers were raised before it, the concave jaws snipping silently at the air.

"Eat lead," he said quietly, aware of the absurdity of the comment as he squeezed the trigger.

The shot—both deafening and gratifyingly powerful—struck the thing square in the thorax. It squealed and twisted its body sideways. Its translucent wings sprang open from where they had been folded closed behind its back and buzzed frantically.

Rex fired again and again. The last two bullets both hit their mark.

Nevertheless, the creature was gaining lift fast, disappearing into the void above them once more.

Rex's ears rang hollowly. His pulse galloped. His eyes stung with sweat.

Ellie was screaming.

He spun toward her, crouching at the same time.

"I hit it!" he said. "Now's our chance! Run!"

She clamped her mouth shut and ran.

Rex stuck right behind her.

They reached the exit to the chamber quickly. Rex's spirit soared, and he experienced the closest thing to hope since entering the mine.

They could do this. They could escape alive.

Tossing aside the now useless pistol, he scooped Ellie into his arms so they could move faster. A strange calmness fell over him as he selected without hesitation or error each tunnel leading them back the way he had come. When they reached the spot where he had fallen through the timber boards to this Dantean lower level, he hiked Ellie onto his shoulders.

"Stand up," he instructed her, transferring his hands to her ankles to support her. "Can you reach the boards?"

She was standing at full height. "Yes!"

"Okay, hold on tight. I'm going to push you up higher."

He slipped his hands beneath her sneakered feet and pressed upward like he was using the shoulder press machine at the gym. Almost immediately Ellie's weight lightened as she wormed up onto the jutting planks, her feet kicking.

Then her head peeked back over the hole. "Come too!"

"I'm coming. I just need to find—"

The words died in his mouth. Killed by the whining of wings.

Everything inside Rex wilted. He had run out of time. He was trapped and unarmed.

I don't want to die, he thought. And a split second later: *Everybody dies eventually.*

He looked up at Ellie. "You have to go without me." Standing on his tiptoes, he passed the flashlight to her. "Just keep choosing whatever tunnel leads up."

"No!" she whispered breathlessly, and at that moment he saw the beautiful woman she was going to become. "No! T-Rex! Please!"

The whining was drawing closer, shrill, like an angry dentist's drill.

"There's no time for this, Ellie!

"But—"

"Go! Get away! Go!" he said, realizing sickly that he was repeating verbatim what his mother had told him thirty-eight years earlier. "Get back to the cabin! Your mom's worried sick about you! Go!"

The mention of Tabitha clearly struck a note within her, because the fear on her face hardened into resolve. "See you later, alligator," she said, grinning expectantly.

"In a while, crocodile," he replied, swallowing hard.

Her head vanished. The light receded. Blackness cocooned him.

Exhaling deeply, resignedly—*I did my best, let it be enough*—Rex turned to face the hellish abomination approaching him in the uncompromising dark.

CHAPTER 21

Teeth chattering and body shivering, arms folded across her chest, Tabitha stood at the start of the dock, staring out at the frothing lake.

She no longer noticed the rain slapping her face or the wind tearing at her clothing and hair. She wasn't even really seeing the lake. She was staring inward, asking questions that had eluded philosophers since the beginning of recorded history.

What's the point of it all? Why are we here? Why give us the awareness that life is fleeting, that we're going to die? Why make us love others when it's so easy to lose them?

She didn't have answers to these queries, of course. But suddenly existence seemed absurdly comical. One big joke that a higher being was having at humankind's expense.

No, not a joke, she amended, an experiment. We were nothing but curious bacteria under a God-like scientist's microscope. We were insignificant in the big picture of things and thus our individual lives were not deserving of meaning.

Because if God the Joker cared about us, if God the Scientist cared, He wouldn't make life so cruel. He wouldn't give Tabitha a husband who was a lying cheat, or a teenage daughter who hated her guts. He most certainly wouldn't have allowed a giant insect to steal away her innocent baby.

It used to make sense. Life. It used to make perfect sense. Wake up, make the girls their lunch, drop off Ellie at school, fly the short-haul route to Olympia and back to Seattle again, smile at the passengers, serve them their snacks, pick up Ellie from the daycare, make dinner, try to engage Vanessa in talk, speak to Rex on the phone, watch some TV, go to sleep, do it all over again the next day.

Mundane, maybe, but it made *sense*. There was a purpose to it all. Being a good mother. A productive citizen. A compatible partner. All small steps, agreed, but steps that felt like they were going in the right direction.

Yet it was all bullshit, wasn't it? All a charade. A façade we imposed on life to give purpose where there was no purpose, meaning where there was no meaning.

Without Ellie, without her baby, this all became strikingly clear to her.

Thunder growled. Lightning flashed. Rain fell. Wind blew. The lake roiled.

Tabitha picked up the large stone at her feet. She had found it on the way down to the lake. It weighed at least ten pounds or more.

She carried it to the end of the dock. She stopped. Stared down at the choppy water.

Vanessa would be okay. Tabitha had life insurance and a modest nest egg. Vanessa would get that. And she would finally get to live with her father. She would...graduate high school, graduate university, get a job, get married, have kids...and die too.

Jesus Christ, what a joke.

Tabitha inched forward so her toes cantilevered over the water.

She thought about the end of *Romeo and Juliet*. Romeo thinking Juliet was dead and killing himself only for Juliet to wake moments later.

What if Ellie was okay?

What if she returned and found her mother dead?

This was only wishful thinking, of course. Rex had been gone for more than an hour now. If he'd somehow caught the creature and rescued Ellie, he would have been back long ago. The fact he hadn't returned meant only two things. He was either still searching the forest for Ellie (and if this were the case, Ellie was as good as dead), or he had fallen victim to the creature himself.

Tabitha scuffed another inch forward. The weight of the stone was already causing her arms and shoulders to ache. It was either now or never.

Another inch. Only her heels remained planted on the dock.

She felt herself tipping forward, falling.

The water smashed her face. Her lungs shucked up at the coldness of it. The stone threatened to slip free from her grasp, and she gripped it more tightly.

She sank.

CHAPTER 22

The whining stopped.

The creature had landed. Probably no more than ten feet away from Rex. He could smell a repugnant oily scent.

He didn't feel fear. He had expended all his fear.

He felt only rage. Rage that this creature had invaded his life twice now. Rage that it had killed his family and ruined his childhood. Rage that it had killed Daisy and Tony and maybe the cop back in the cabin. Rage that it had taken Ellie. Rage that it had led him to this inevitable sacrifice.

Rex heard the thing moving toward him. It didn't make much noise, but without sight, his ears, like his smell, were fine-tuned.

Come on, you fucking bug.

It came. Slowly. It knew he was there, surely. It knew it out-powered him too. So it was probably unsure why he wasn't running away.

Come on.

The savage fury building inside him turned into bloodlust.

Oh, he wanted it dead. He so wanted it dead.

Before entering the bone chamber, Rex had scavenged a stick of dynamite from one of the several wooden Hercules boxes he had come across. He now held the stick in his left hand. The absorbents and stabilizers were long past their expiry date. The stick was damp with sweated nitroglycerin. Small crystals had formed on its surface.

The dynamite was unstable as hell.

He had been crazy to be carrying it around with him. But when he'd picked it up he'd largely conceded he'd been heading to his death, and when he'd miraculously found Ellie, he'd completely forgotten about it.

He sparked the flint of his Bic lighter. A bluish flame appeared.

The creature, he saw in the anemic light, was only a few feet away from him now.

Sneaky bastard.

Rex touched the flame to the short fuse. It caught with a hiss and burned hungrily toward the blasting cap.

The creature attacked. One of its pincers arced toward his neck.

Rex's last thought was, *Figured you'd go for my gut.*

The stick of dynamite dropped from his grip and landed on the earthy ground.

His decapitated head thumped next to it a moment later.

ΔΔΔ

Two shafts higher Ellie came to a fork in the tunnels. T-Rex had told her to pick tunnels that went up, so she picked the left one. She was only a few steps into it when an enormous blast shook the mine system. She stumbled forward and landed on all fours. Dirt from the ceiling fell onto her head and shoulders and back.

She couldn't fathom what had caused the blast—she had a half-formed thought of a waking dragon bellowing fire from its mouth—but she knew it wasn't a gunshot.

Maybe T-Rex had found a cannon somewhere to shoot the monster with?

She was tempted to turn around and go find him, but he'd told her that her mom was worried sick, and she most likely was. She got worried sick when Ellie went to the cereal aisle in the supermarket without telling her.

Ellie scrambled back to her feet, shook the dirt from her hair, and hurried on.

CHAPTER 23

Constables Stephen Garlund and Karl Dunn had been thirty kilometers north of Whistler Blackcomb in the town of Pemberton, investigating a report of domestic violence (iced-up junkie who hadn't slept in days smacking around his subservient girlfriend), and thus they were the northernmost officers on night shift when the call came over the Motorola two-way radio of multiple homicides on Pavilion Lake.

That had been ninety minutes ago. Now Garlund was navigating the big Chevy Suburban carefully down the shitty road that served the lake, trying to avoid the worst of the bumpy craters. The storm wasn't making the going any easier.

Garlund had always preferred working a one-man car. He enjoyed the freedom of driving around by himself, eating whatever he wanted, listening to whatever music he wanted, pretty much doing whatever he liked. If performing some community relations so fancied him, he could talk to business owners or say hi to the folks at the community center without a partner getting impatient with him. If he saw a traffic violation, he could use his discretion to pursue it or not without having to justify his decision. Nevertheless, the winter season at Whistler Blackcomb was kicking off soon. The influx of skiers and snowboarders turned the small mountain community into a den of revelry and boozing, and the powers that be were experimenting with pairing up patrol officers, despite the fact this meant halving the patrol coverage.

Anyway, Garlund couldn't complain too much. Constable

Karl Dunn was a good guy. Bit of a straight arrow, but easy enough to get along with. Curly blond hair, lively blue eyes, and he always seemed to be smiling, even when he was talking about nothing funny.

"So what are these rumors I'm hearing about?" Dunn asked out of the blue.

Garlund glanced at him to see if he was smiling. Sure was. Smiling on the way to the scene of multiple homicides. "What rumors?" he asked, swerving hard to avoid a flooded pothole he saw at the last moment. The windshield wipers beat back and forth hypnotically.

"Heard you bought a house in North Vancouver," Dunn said.

"Yup," Garlund said.

"You never told me."

"Never told anyone. Maybe one or two people."

"It's just that I've been your partner these past couple weeks, eight hours a day we're together, and you're going to be relocating, and you don't tell me?"

"I never told anyone anything about leaving. Maybe I won't."

"Won't leave? Why'd you buy a house then?"

Garlund shrugged. "I don't know what I'm going to do with it yet. Maybe rent it out. Maybe move. I don't know."

"Hey, you don't like me that much, that you gotta move away, just ask for a new partner."

"You are a bit nosey, Hoops." Hoops was Dunn's nickname, on account he was decent at playing basketball, especially hitting three-pointers.

"So what is it, Steve? Tired of Whistler? Bored out here?"

"I told you, I haven't decided if I'm going anywhere."

"But you're thinking about it."

Garlund shrugged again. "I like Whistler. I like my job here. It's Clara."

"What about Clara?"

"We're separating."

He frowned. "Shit! I didn't know that."

"Because I never told you. I haven't told anyone. So don't go yapping."

"Is it…a mutual thing?"

"I suppose so. You got to be young to have a one-sided breakup. When you're both fifty-two and have kids, you're too tired to get passionate about it. We just sat down and discussed it. Made sense for both of us. Decided we'd do it when the youngest, Joey, graduates high school in the spring."

"Oh man, Steve. I didn't know—I just mean, I'm surprised. You and Clara always seemed fine when I saw you together, you know?"

"We are fine. We're just not great anymore. We get on each other's nerves. We annoy each other. Being around someone for long enough, that just happens. You'll find out."

The smile returned, proud. "Jenny and me are all good."

"You've been married for how long?"

"Three years."

"Nothing bugs you about her?"

Dunn thought about it for a few seconds. "Sure, some things."

"Take all those things and multiply them by ten. And then think about how much they annoy you and multiply that by ten too. Then you'll probably know what it's like to live with her in thirty years."

"Jeez, you're a fun guy sometimes, Steve. What does Clara do that bugs you so much?"

"Lotta things."

"Name one."

"She's stopped brushing her teeth."

Dunn laughed, a rapid-fire burst of merriment. "What?"

"Not all the time, Hoops. But she doesn't do it two or three times a day like she used to. Some days she'll brush them in the morning, or before bed. Some days she won't. It's annoying. How hard is it to brush your teeth?"

"How do you know she doesn't brush them?"

"I can smell her breath."

"Maybe she just has bad breath?"

"Halitosis? No, she doesn't have that. Anyway, I can tell when her toothbrush hasn't been used."

"How?"

"It's dry."

Dunn sounded surprised. "You check her toothbrush?"

"Sometimes. I think sometimes she doesn't brush her teeth just to piss me off."

"Jesus, Steve," Dunn said. "Yeah, maybe you should be getting a divorce, after all, if this is where you guys are at. Shit—lookout!"

Garlund saw the child in the middle of the road too. She was lit up ghost-like in the headlights. He hit the brakes. The SUV slammed to a stop.

The little girl remained standing shock-still, her jet-black hair plastered to her head like a helmet, her eyes wide and unblinking. She wore pink jeans and a soaked-through white tee shirt with the blue Care Bear on it.

Garlund grunted, "Where the fuck did she come from?" He threw open his door and was about to climb out when the girl ran to him instead.

"Are you a policeman?" she asked, looking at his uniform. He was dressed in his open-collar patrol jacket and dark blue trousers with gold strapping. His peaked cap was on the laptop next to him.

"I am," he said. "What are you doing out in this weather? Never mind that, get in, quickly, you're going to catch your death." He opened the back door for her, helped her up onto the plastic seat, and gave her his jacket to drape around her shoulders like a cape. When he returned behind the wheel, he cranked up the heat in the cab, then turned to study her through the wire mesh. She held the jacket closed at her neck. Her lips were blue, and she appeared to be shivering.

"What's your name?" Dunn asked her in a friendly voice.

"Ellie," she said.

"Did you get lost somehow, Ellie?"

"Sort of," she said.

"Sort of?" Garlund said, a bit too roughly.

The girl, Ellie, looked like she might cry. "I just want to find my mom. I want to go home."

Garlund couldn't imagine there being many families on the lake in October, and he made the logical connection. "Are you Rex Chapman's kid?"

Her face brightened. "You know T-Rex?"

"No. But we got a call from him."

"He's not my dad. He's my mom's boyfriend."

"He said there's been some trouble out here?"

The girl nodded but didn't say anything more.

"There been trouble?" Garlund pressed.

"Yes," she said, looking at her lap.

"Some people been hurt?"

She nodded. "A policeman. He got cut in the stomach." She pointed to her belly.

The Chief of Police of Lillooet, Paul Harris, Garlund presumed. The man had been policing when Garlund was still a boy. They'd met on a few occasions, and Garlund had nothing bad to say about him.

"Who cut him?" Garlund asked.

"The Mosquito Man," the girl said.

He blinked. "Who?"

"He's a monster. He took me to his cave. He wanted to eat me."

Garlund and Dunn exchanged glances.

"What did he look like?" Dunn asked, still using his friendly kid voice.

"Like a mosquito!"

"He was wearing a mask?"

"No! He was a real mosquito. But big, like you."

Garlund and Dunn swapped another glance.

"I think we better get to this cabin," Dunn said.

Garlund nodded, faced forward, and put the Chevy Suburban in Drive.

Dunn continued questioning the girl. "So who's at your cabin right now, Ellie?"

"It's not mine," she said. "It's T-Rex's."

"Is he at the cabin?"

"No, he was in the cave with me." Her voice faltered. "He stayed back to fight the Mosquito Man. But he said he was going to meet up again."

"Your mom is there then?"

"Yes, and she's worried sick I'm gone."

"Because you ran away?"

"No! I told you! The Mosquita Man took me. I was looking under my bed for my chippymunk, and the monster kidnapped me. It jumped through the window and ran into the woods."

"This is serious business, Ellie," Dunn said, adopting a slightly stricter tone. "It's not time for make-believe."

"I'm not lying or pretending! I'm telling the truth! I promise!"

"Is the policeman at the cabin?" Garlund asked, glancing in the rearview mirror, but unable to see the girl.

"Yes, my mom's taking care of him."

"Is anyone else there?" Dunn asked.

"Just Bobby."

"Who's Bobby?"

"His dad is T-Rex. We're the same age but we're not friends. Why are these seats so hard?"

"So we can clean them if anybody gets sick back there."

"I'm not going to be sick."

"That's good."

"Are we almost there?"

"There's a light ahead," Garlund said. "Must be it."

He turned up a gravel driveway and parked at the end of it behind a Mazda sedan.

"Ellie," he said, "you're going to have to sit here for a minute while we go see who's inside."

"But I want to see my mommy!"

"You stay here with her, Hoops. I'll go have a quick look."

Dunn nodded.

Clapping his cap on his head, Garlund got out of the SUV and went to the Mazda. He aimed the flashlight into the cab—and saw a person stretched out in the backseat. He opened the back door and recognized the man to be Paul Harris, his craggy face gaunt and pale. He clasped a pillow to his bloodied gut.

Garlund said, "Chief? You with me?"

Harris opened his eyes but didn't say anything.

"Who did this?"

No answer.

"Paramedics will be here soon," he told Harris. "I'll be back." Outside, he unholstered his Smith and Wesson and went to the cabin. He eased open the door and peeked inside. The place was bathed in soft candlelight.

"Hello?" he called.

"Hello?" a young voice called back from somewhere else in the cabin.

"That you, Bobby?" Garlund asked.

A pause. "Who are you?"

"I'm a police officer. You just stay up there for the time being, okay?"

"Okay."

Garlund closed the door and was about to return to the SUV when he spotted a light down by the lake.

Frowning, he waved Dunn over.

The Chevy's door opened, slammed shut. Dunn dashed through the rain.

"The boy's inside," Garlund told him. "Paul Harris too. He looks bad. No other bodies I saw. Bring the girl inside and wait there until backup gets here."

"What about you?" Dunn asked.

Garlund nodded at the lake—and did a double take. The light was gone.

"I saw a light down there a second ago. A flashlight beam. I'm guessing the mom."

"Or whoever cut the cop."

Without replying, Garlund took his flashlight from his duty belt, turned it on, and picked his way down the slope through the trees. The rocky ground was mossy and slippery. At the bottom the wind blowing in off the lake reached gale-like force, sweeping his cap off his head and howling in his ears. A dock jutted over the rough water. Nobody was on it. Nobody along the shore either.

"Hello?" he called, the storm shredding his voice.

There was no reply.

He started along the dock, playing his flashlight over the weathered boards, the dark water—

Ten feet to his right. An arm. Riding the peaks and troughs of the waves.

A head too, black hair fanning around it like a lily pad.

Garlund leaped off the side of the dock. The ice-cold water came to his chest. He splashed toward the body. Reached it, flipped it over. A woman, attractive, her skin fish-belly white.

Garlund dragged her up onto the shore, felt for a pulse.

She wasn't breathing.

He commenced CPR.

CHAPTER 24

Tabitha was in a gigantic forest surrounded by towering flowers and trees the size of skyscrapers. Both rose dizzyingly into the otherworldly sky, making her feel as tiny as a bug.

No, scratch that, she thought. *I* am *a bug.*

She held out her arms to reveal strange black appendages tapering to points. She brushed her face with them, discovering she had globular eyes and a coiled proboscis.

Frantic, she glanced over her shoulder and found a pair of cerulean wings sprouting from her back—and her fear abated with the understanding she was not a mosquito but a butterfly, the latter metamorphosis somehow acceptable.

She didn't attempt to fly. She didn't know how. And so she walked on legs identical to her arms. She knew butterflies didn't walk erect on two legs, and she likely looked ridiculous, but she was moving, and that was all that mattered. She had to find her way out of this forest and get back to the log cabin. She wasn't sure why exactly, but it seemed very important she accomplish this.

Tabitha came to a huge tented maple leaf the size of a car. Something was beneath it. She could hear a *crunch-crunch-crunch*. She lifted one side of the leaf and peeked beneath.

A ladybug was sitting on her rear in a very un-ladybug-like way, munching on a stalk of grass. Black dots spotted glossy red wing covers. A cute black face with white patches on both cheeks looked up and smiled.

"Ellie!" Tabitha exclaimed happily.

"Mommy!"

Tabitha wanted to hug her daughter, but she didn't think she would be able to get her arms around her dome-shaped body. "What are you doing here?" she asked.

"I don't know. What are *you* doing here?"

"I don't know either," she admitted.

"Are we dead?" Ellie asked.

Tabitha had not thought of this possibility. "I don't think so."

"How do you know?"

"Why would we be dead?"

"Because you killed yourself. You jumped off the dock. Remember?"

Tabitha did remember now, and a coldness stole over her. She recalled the all-encompassing darkness. Not knowing up from down. Water entering her mouth and nose. Her throat contracting. Her eyes straining. Her lungs begging for air. Everything turning yellow, then sharp black, then pungent white, the purest color she had ever seen. Then her body going limp as a drowsy acceptance settled over her.

And Ellie speaking calmly and omnisciently to her: *Mommy, I'm safe. I'm okay. Don't die, okay? I'm coming home now. I want to see you. Don't die. Please come back, please open your eyes, please be there for me—*

Tabitha opened her eyes. Choking. Vomiting brackish water. A man pushing on her chest, then rolling her onto her side, patting her back, talking to her.

She tried to speak but only made a strangled noise.

On her second attempt she managed, "Ellie?"

"She's okay," the man said.

CHAPTER 25

"Yuck!" Bobby said, pinching his nose closed with his fingers.

"I told you," Ellie said. "It smells like a toilet."

Bobby leaned forward hesitantly again to smell the monster stench on Ellie's tee shirt. He scrunched up his face. "Like a *wet* toilet. Why didn't the monster eat you?"

"I don't know. Maybe it was full? There were bones everywhere."

"Human bones?"

"Maybe."

"Were you scared?"

"A little bit. You would be too."

"Maybe."

"You would be. I promise. It was really dark too."

"When's my dad coming back?"

"He said he'd meet me here."

"Are you sure he killed the monster?"

"Pretty sure. There was a big boom. It was so loud it made me fall over."

"Sound can't make you fall over. It's invisible."

"Well, it did."

"Can I try on the policeman's jacket?"

Ellie clutched it tightly around her neck. "No. He said only I could wear it."

"Just for a second."

"He'll get mad."

"Please?"

"It's too big for you."

"It's too big for you too!" Bobby reached for it.

Ellie shrieked. "Stop it! You're not allowed!"

Bobby gave up. He didn't want the policeman to get mad and lock him up in jail. "Do you think we're allowed downstairs now?"

"I don't know." She raised her voice. "Mr. Policeman?"

"Yeah?" a voice came back.

"Can we come down now?"

"You're better off up there."

"But we're bored!"

"Stay there!"

The policeman kept talking, and it took Bobby a moment to realize it was no longer to them. "I think my dad's back!" he said.

They both hopped off the bed and ran to the top of the stairs.

"*Ellie?*" a woman called. Her voice was so high-pitched and hyper that Bobby didn't immediately recognize it as belonging to Ellie's mom.

"Mommy!" Ellie cried out. She raced down the stairs.

Bobby hesitated a moment, then followed.

When he reached the bottom, Ellie's mom was on her knees and had Ellie in a big hug, kissing her about a thousand times all over her face.

"Baby baby baby baby," she kept saying over and over again between kisses.

Ellie was giggling madly. "It tickles! Stop! It tickles!"

Bobby noticed the two policemen. They had just pushed past the afghan and entered the room. The older one was soaking wet.

Ellie's mom said, "Where's Rex, baby?"

Ellie shrugged. "He stayed back in the cave to fight the monster."

"*What?*" She looked at the policemen. "Where's Rex? Rex Chapman? He's my boyfriend. He saved my daughter." She looked back at Ellie, confused. "How did you get back here without Rex? Where is he? Where's Rex? *Where is he?*"

△△△

Tabitha listened in stunned silence to Ellie describe what occurred in the cave, myriad questions immediately demanding answers. Had Rex defeated the Mosquito Man? What was the bang that knocked Ellie to the ground? Why wasn't Rex back already? Was he injured? Lost? Dead?

Tabitha turned to the policemen. "We need to find Rex. We need to help him. He could be injured or lost or… I don't know! But we need to help him."

The older officer with the short black buzz cut and grizzled jawline said, "We don't know where this cave is. It will be light shortly. When the rain dies down—"

"There were train tracks in the cave," Ellie said. "But I didn't see a train anywhere."

Train tracks? Tabitha thought. Then, "A mine! She must mean Rex is in an old mine."

The cop nodded. "There are plenty of abandoned mines around these parts. That certainly helps. But without a map—"

"I know you don't believe her," Tabitha said, cutting him off. "But she's telling the truth about this creature. I saw it with my own eyes. It's real. It took her. And she says there's more than one. So Rex is in real danger—" The older policeman began to say something, but she spoke over him. "You don't have to believe whether the creature is real or not. It doesn't matter. But Rex is in danger. You can believe that, can't you? He's out there and he's in danger, so we can't just sit around here and do nothing until morning comes."

The younger cop—her age, maybe, and smiling sympathetically—cocked his head, as if he could hear something no one else could.

But then Tabitha heard the ambulance siren too.

The older cop said, "Excuse us for a moment."

They left the room.

△△△

The paramedics—Rahul Garcia and Andy Macmillan—loaded Paul Harris onto a portable stretcher and carried him to the ambulance parked at the end of the driveway.

Andy, who was as skinny as Rahul was stocky, said to Constable Stephen Garlund, "Watch yourself, Steve. Whoever made that cut has got something big and sharp. Sick sonofabitch."

Garlund asked, "How far behind you is backup?"

"Shouldn't be too much longer."

"Better get going then."

Rahul lugged his ample weight up into the ambulance's cargo hold so he could monitor Paul Harris on the drive to Whistler Blackcomb, while Andy got behind the wheel. A few moments later the vehicle was reversing down the driveway, gumballs flashing.

Garlund turned to Dunn. "Wish I hadn't quit smoking. Could use a cigarette right now."

"You need to get inside and get dry," Dunn said.

The rain had lessened to a hard drizzle, but Garlund was already so wet he hardly noticed. "What the hell's going on here, Hoops? Cabin's all barricaded up like it's *Night of the Living Dead* or something. Girlfriend nearly drowned in the lake. Boyfriend's nowhere to be found. Little girl's running around the woods and spinning stories about a giant insect."

"I don't know what's gone down here, Steve," Dunn said, "but we're not going to find any answers standing around out here in the rain. Now c'mon—" He frowned.

Garlund heard it too.

A strange whining sound, getting louder.

CHAPTER 26

When Tabitha finished drying off Ellie with a fluffy white towel, she draped it around her daughter's shoulders and said, "Baby? A little while ago, did you have…a feeling…that maybe something bad was going to happen to me? Like…I don't know…like maybe I was going to fall in the lake?"

Ellie frowned. "But I was in the monster's cave, remember?"

"Yes, I remember."

"So how could I know?"

She couldn't, of course. Nevertheless, Tabitha couldn't stop thinking about those eternal moments while she'd been drowning, and Ellie's voice had been in her head, telling her that she was safe, that she was coming home, that she needed Tabitha to open her eyes, to be there for her when she returned.

Had those words been the hallucinations of a dying mind? Or had Ellie really communicated with her? Had they shared some sort of mother-daughter supernatural bond?

Tabitha sighed to herself, knowing these were questions to which she would likely never find answers. "It doesn't matter, I guess, honey," she said, kissing her daughter on her ruddy cheek. "All that matters is that you're safe. And it's all over now."

"But T-Rex isn't home yet."

"We're going to find Rex, honey. First thing in the morning—"

Something crashed upstairs.

Wings whined, stopped, whined.

Ellie and Bobby cried out in unison.

Another crash.

No, God, please, no! Why? Tabitha thought in instant hysterics. Without wasting another moment, she grabbed the kids' hands and ran. She threw open the cabin's front door and all but tossed Ellie and Bobby outside ahead of her. She had no idea where they were going, only that they had to get far away—

The kids screamed.

Tabitha saw it too.

A dozen yards away one of the hellish creatures was perched on top of the young officer, its proboscis plugged deep into the man's chest, right where his heart would be, no doubt slurping up blood. The older officer was fleeing from this ghastly scene when suddenly, seemingly from nowhere, a different creature swooped down from the darkness. Its pincers snatched the cop by the shoulders and lifted him, kicking and shouting, a few feet into the air.

Someone was moaning, a sound of utter despair, and Tabitha realized belatedly it was coming from her throat.

We're not getting out of this alive, are we?

From behind her came another crash. She spun around and found one of the creatures standing in the doorway a scant two yards away.

The kids' screams jumped several octaves higher.

"Run!" Tabitha shouted to them. "Hide! Don't wait for me!"

"Mommy, no!" Ellie shrieked.

"Go! Now!"

Tabitha had never in her life placed an aggressive hand on a child, but right then she did just that, shoving Ellie and Bobby away from her with tremendous force. They lurched forward. Ellie fell flat on her face. She glanced back over her shoulder.

"Go!" Tabitha shouted. "Hide!" Without waiting to see whether they obeyed her instructions, she whirled about to face the creature once more.

It was staring straight ahead, and she couldn't tell if it was looking at her or the kids.

Probably both, she thought frenziedly. *Probably can see*

everywhere at once with those goddamn buggy eyes.

"Hey!" she said, waving her hands over her head while angling slowly away from it. "Leave them alone! I'm right here!"

The creature's head swiveled on its pinched neck to look directly at her.

"Yeah, me!" she said, still angling away.

It stepped through the door, walking unashamedly upright on its two thick legs, its abdomen dangling between them like an obscene phallus.

Tabitha glanced behind her.

The farthest creature had given up trying to carry the older police officer away and had instead dropped him to the ground, where it now stood over him, stabbing him repeatedly with its pincers. The closer creature was staring at her, its blood meal forgotten.

A few feet from it, the young officer's pistol lay on the ground.

Tabitha sprinted toward it.

The creature stood.

In one fluid motion she snatched up the gun and aimed the barrel at its hideous face and triple-tapped the trigger, landing three precision shots directly between its antennae.

Before its body hit the ground she was aiming past it, down the sight.

Pop, pop, pop.

The creature atop the older policeman flew backward.

She was already turning, aiming again, finger taking up slack in the trigger.

The final creature that had followed her through the doorway was nearly upon her, coming fast, wings whining at a fever pitch, pincers shearing the air, proboscis erect.

She fired at point-blank range.

The slug blew a large hole through the demonic thing's head. Its momentum propelled it onto its chest, directly at her feet, where its wings ceased beating and its limbs twitched robotically.

Tabitha was about to cry out in triumph when she heard

a distant drone, growing louder by the second. She looked up into the night sky and realized it wasn't a fourth creature approaching.

It was an entire swarm.

△△△

Bobby saw the broken-down car through the trees. It was the one his dad had shown him the day before. He remembered the trunk, wondering if it held any treasure, and he said to Ellie, "We can hide in the trunk!"

They were both huffing and puffing and ready to fall over, and Ellie didn't even try to argue with him.

They stopped when they reached the car. Bobby lifted the trunk lid, and they climbed inside one after the other. Bobby cut his hand on a bit of sharp metal while closing the lid over them, and he bit back a cry.

It was wet and musty in the dark, cramped space. There were holes in the rusted metal too, big enough he could probably stick his arm through one and touch the ground.

Bobby thought about trying this but decided to suck his bleeding finger instead, unbothered by the sour taste of the blood.

Ellie whispered, "Will they find us in here?"

"I don't know," he replied. "There's a lot of them now."

"I want my Mommy—"

"Shhh!" he said.

One of the monsters had landed nearby.

Bobby could hear its wings separate from all the other wings way up in the sky. They stopped beating a moment later, but he knew it was still out there. Coming for them, tiptoeing so they didn't hear it. Any second now it would open the trunk and grin down at them. They would be trapped. Two yummy human children to eat. It would gobble them up—but then maybe it would be too heavy to fly away. It would have to walk back to its cave. Maybe it would be so tired when it got there that it would go to sleep, giving him and Ellie a chance to escape. They could crawl quietly out of its tummy and fill it up with big rocks instead, so when it woke up it still thought they were inside it. And when it went to get a drink, it would fall into the water and drown because it was so heavy. Didn't his dad read him some book in which all this happened? Only the monster in the book was a wolf, and the kids it ate were goats...

"Stop!" Ellie said.

Bobby frowned, not knowing who she was speaking to.

She moved, and then he heard something else moving too, something small and quick. It was running around inside the trunk.

It brushed his hand, which he jerked back in fright.

The thing squeaked, then fell out of the trunk through one of the holes. He heard it thump against the ground. A moment later he heard it scuttling away from them, through the carpet of wet leaves.

It squeaked again—which ended abruptly.

Then Bobby heard a kind of slurping, like when he was trying to get the final few sips of a milkshake with a straw.

This didn't last long, however, and was replaced by the whining of wings.

The monster was taking off!

He listened as it flew higher and higher into the sky—and that was when he realized all the other wings weren't as loud as they were before.

"I think they're going away!" Ellie said.

"I think so too!" Bobby said.

"Should we go look?"

"I don't want to."

"But I need to go check on Miss Chippy. I found her hiding in the bathroom earlier. She got out of my pocket, and I think the monster got her."

"I think it drank her blood."

"Yeah," Ellie said glumly. "I think it did too."

ΔΔΔ

Tabitha had fled into the forest when the sky filled with the sound of wings. She had not called out to either Ellie or Bobby, knowing if they responded they would reveal their location to the creatures. Instead she prayed they had found a spot to hide, and she hid too, dropping down beside a fallen tree trunk and shoving herself as far beneath it as she could. For what seemed like an eternity the only sounds were her heartbeat thudding in her ears, and the drone of wings above her. But eventually the night went quiet again, and when it did, and she was certain the last of the creatures had departed, she got to her feet and called to the kids.

"Mommy!" Ellie's voice came back, from not too far away.

ΔΔΔ

Hunt hunt, eat eat, drink drink, sleep sleep. These were the instincts the creature experienced regularly. But the nest had been attacked. Some in the hive had been killed. And even if the creature did not understand the concept of revenge, or the notion of justice, or experience emotions such as love and loss and hate, it nevertheless understood the new, urgent imperative ticking loudly inside its head: *defend defend.*

Which required seeking out and eliminating the invaders.

So the creature continued its patrol back and forth through the night sky, the dark forest below reflected in a kaleidoscope of images on its fisheye lenses, while it used both its sight and scent to search for the invaders or those related to them.

When it could no longer detect any remaining threats, it changed course, following its brethren north. The old nest was no longer safe. They needed to find a new one. Somewhere dark, somewhere underground.

By the time the fiery reds and oranges of dawn began to light the horizon, the creature was no longer thinking any of these thoughts—it had never really been thinking them in the first place, merely acting upon them—and its primitive mind had once more reverted to its usual refrain:

Hunt hunt, eat eat, drink drink, sleep sleep.

EPILOGUE
A FEW MONTHS LATER

For the third time in seven days, Paul Harris drove out to Pavilion Lake.

He parked the aging Crown Victoria alongside the road a little distance away from the RV-like mobile command center, and the caravan of government-black SUVs used to ferry the NASA scientists and engineers back and forth each day from Lillooet, where they were staying in the scattering of modest motels the town offered.

Paul took the brown paper bag that contained his lunch off the passenger seat and headed into the snow-mantled forest. He made his way to a well-used trail in the snow, which he followed for ten minutes until he reached Dead Man's Mine. He sat down on a log at the top of a knoll, where he liked to eat, as it provided him a clear view of the mine's entrance, as well as the white modular research habitat that looked as though it belonged in deep space rather than the icy Canadian wilderness. Two men in civilian clothes stood guard before the mine. By their posture and discipline Paul had come to the conclusion they were military.

Paul sat on the frosted log for a long while, watching the snow drift silently to the ground around him. His mind wandered. Following the massacre at Rex Chapman's cabin in October, he fell into a week-long coma. When he regained consciousness, his stomach was sewn up, an IV drip was feeding him antibiotics, and according to Nancy, the RCMP had fingered a lone madman for the murders of Rex Chapman, Tony Lyons, Daisy Butterfield, as well as Constables Stephen Garlund and Karl Dunn—the same madman, many people surmised, responsible for all of the disappearances at the lake dating back over the years.

Complete and utter bullshit, of course.

So when two Mounties came by the hospital to get a statement from Paul, he told them he didn't see his attacker, and he didn't remember a thing that happened afterward.

He never let Nancy in on the truth of what he heard and saw. Nor did he go to the press. He had planned to keep silent about the whole incident indefinitely. After all, nobody in their right mind would believe him. But more than this, you never knew to what lengths a government might go to keep matters of national security a secret—and man-sized, deadly insects were most definitely a matter of national security.

Paul wasn't a conspiracy theorist, but hell—what happened to Rex Chapman's flame, Tabitha? He'd tried tracking her down a short time after he'd been released from the hospital, knowing she would be the one person he could speak to about what they'd experienced, but she vanished into thin air. The last any of her coworkers, friends, or neighbors heard from her was a couple of days after she returned to Seattle. Abruptly, phone calls and emails went unanswered. Her house appeared deserted. Nobody knew the whereabouts of the two kids who had been with her either.

As the days stretched into weeks, and then months, Paul became a restless, haunted shadow of his former self. He tossed and turned all night in his sleep. He got headaches, stomach ulcers, joint pain. He couldn't concentrate on work. He was not very good company to be around, and so he kept mostly to himself, in his office, out of sight.

Then, out of the blue, NASA rolled into Lillooet.

Now, NASA personnel can't just show up in some dustbowl town and not arouse suspicion from the locals, hence the story the space agency leaked to the Lillooet *Examiner*. The subterranean lake in the heart of the long-abandoned Dead Man's Mine harbored a species of extremely rare coral-like formations, which were related to life forms that had existed on Earth billions of years previously. NASA wanted to study them in their natural habitat, believing they could aid in the understanding of what life might look like on other planets.

More complete and utter bullshit.

Nevertheless, Paul could no longer sit idly by. Giant insects existed. They had been killing people in his jurisdiction, right under his nose, since his first year as Chief of Police in 1981. Fifteen deaths, by his count. Fifteen deaths he didn't prevent. For his peace of mind and perhaps his sanity, he needed to know more than that these things existed. He needed to know what the hell they were, how they got so big, and whether they were going to be preying on anybody else in these parts again.

And so Paul had driven out to Dead Man's Mine last Tuesday, then again on Friday, and now today, Monday. He had made no mention of the Mosquito Man—correction, Mosquito *Men*—to any of the NASA guys yet. He was simply playing the part of the bored country cop. It was why, he supposed, they put up with him nosing around and asking silly questions.

Paul was halfway through the bologna sandwich Nancy had made for him when the research habitat's airlock opened from the inside, and a man dressed in a heavy winter parka and beige khakis emerged. He lit up a cigarette.

Paul stuffed his sandwich back in the brown paper bag and picked his way through the trees.

"Howdy, Walter," he said, waving pleasantly, his breath frosting in front of his face.

"Back again, are you, Paul?" Walter Williamson said. With his gelled hair, mousy face, and black-rimmed eyeglasses, he looked like a geekish, middle-aged astrobiologist—and that's exactly what he was, or claimed to be.

"Not much to police in a small town," Paul said. "Coming out here breaks up the doldrums. Find any more of those microwhatdoyoucallem?"

"Microbialites," Williamson told him, sticking to the script. "Sure, we found more. Only a few freshwater lakes in the world support this kind of life. It's truly amazing."

"That's good," Paul said. "Real good. Need to know all we can about the Martians before they attack, am I right?"

Williamson chuckled.

"Anyway," Paul went on conversationally, "I'm not here today to talk about coral. My grandson's working on a science project for school. He had a few questions for me last night that I couldn't answer. And then I thought, 'Wait a sec. Walter Williamson out at the habitat is an astrobiologist. He could help!'"

Williamson raised an eyebrow. "What kind of science project is your grandson working on?"

"It's got to do with bugs."

Williamson went poker-faced. "Bugs, huh?"

"Bugs and their evolution," Paul said, rubbing his hands together to stave off the cold in his ungloved fingers.

Williamson took a thoughtful puff of his cigarette, exhaled through his nose. His gray eyes were calculating. "Sounds interesting. What kind of questions was he asking you?"

"Well, he can't figure out why insects were so big back in the time of the dinosaurs, and why they're so small nowadays. Dragonflies had wingspans of three feet! Can you believe that?"

"They were called griffin flies," Williamson said. "But to answer your son's question as to why insects are so small nowadays, it's quite simple really. Millions of years ago, the air surrounding the planet was not only warmer and moister but contained more oxygen. This was important for insects because they don't have lungs like we do. They have an open respiratory system that diffuses oxygen through their bodies. So higher oxygen levels in the atmosphere meant more oxygen could reach their tissues, which in turn meant they could grow to very large sizes. When oxygen levels began to lessen approximately one hundred and fifty million years ago, the largest insects died off. The smaller ones remained unaffected, with many of them surviving to this day."

Paul was nodding agreeably to this line of reasoning. "I read about all that. And you know what else? Some scientists believe birds had a part to play too. Because about the time the large insects were dying off, dinosaurs were taking flight, on their way to becoming birds. As they got better at flying, they became fast and agile hunters, like birds today. Giant insects, on the other hand, remained slow and lumbering. Easy prey."

Williamson frowned. "Seems you know your stuff, Paul. Seems like you just answered your own question." He flicked away his cigarette. "How old did you say your grandson was?"

"I don't think I did say. But he's eight."

"Eight," Williamson repeated as if impressed by the number. "Anyway, I'm freezing my ass off out here, Paul, so if you don't mind—"

"Just a sec, Walter. I have one more question if that's all right?"

"You sure you don't already know the answer to this one too?" he asked shrewdly.

"What I'm wondering," Paul said, ignoring the remark, "is, well...you can get smaller and quicker to outclass your predators. That's one option. But there's another option too." He paused. "You can get bigger and stronger."

Williamson smiled, yet it didn't touch his eyes. If he hadn't known from the get-go that the science project talk was a farce, he certainly did now. "Bigger than griffin flies?" he said. "Those would be some damn big bugs, Paul."

"Maybe even man-sized," Paul said meaningfully. "Could you imagine something like that? A man-sized insect? A man-sized mosquito, say? You know, I have a funny idea of something like that standing on two legs just like us. Standing on two human-like legs. Like some sort of Mosquito Man. Can you picture that?"

Williamson studied Paul, his smile souring to a pucker, as though he'd just bitten into a lemon. "Why don't we cut to the chase here, Paul? What are you getting at?"

"I just…" Paul was a tough man, a proud man, a reserved man, averse to revealing his emotions. But right then he allowed his eyes to reflect the fear and confusion and turmoil that had been eating him up from the inside out these last few months. "I just need to know what in God's name those blasphemous things were, okay?"

Williamson continued to study Paul for a long moment. Paul didn't know what the man was thinking, or what words would come out of his mouth—he half expected the astrophysicist to summon the undercover soldiers to escort him back to the road —but when he spoke his voice was modulated, sympathetic: "If such creatures existed, Paul—and they don't, let's be very clear on that."

"We're clear," Paul said promptly.

"*If* they existed," Williamson continued, "there would be nothing blasphemous about them. Their gigantism would be a matter of evolution, plain and simple."

"But the way they stood—"

Williamson cut him off with a curt wave. "Insects and the rest of arthropods are covered by a more or less hardened exoskeleton. Guys like me call it a cuticle. As you can imagine, it's quite heavy. If an insect grew to be as large as you're suggesting, man-sized, the weight of its cuticle would become a problem. Its legs wouldn't be able to support its mass. It would need much thicker legs. The thing is, all insects have six legs, and if what we're talking about here is a flying insect, it wouldn't be able to get off the ground with six thick legs. You following me, Paul?"

Paul nodded, his attention laser-focused.

Williamson said, "It would probably have to settle for two thick legs."

Paul clamped his jaw tight, visualizing the creature he'd seen. "And if they weren't using the other four legs to stand on, they might evolve into…something else?"

Williamson nodded. "Appendages that could be used to attack or defend. Because while these giant arthropods would have become too large to be hunted by predatory birds, some of the bigger terrestrial animals would likely still pose a threat to them, especially during molting, when they shed their cuticle to grow."

"Pincers," Paul stated flatly.

"Those would do. Especially a lightweight variety."

Paul was silent as he processed this information. Here it was. What he came here for. What he'd so desperately sought. A scientific explanation for the physiology of the nightmare abominations. Did having this new understanding make him feel better about their existence?

Yes, in a way it did.

The creatures were not some alien life form from outer space, or some demonkind arriving on the express elevator up from the depths of hell.

They were, as Walter Williamson put it, a matter of evolution, plain and simple.

Williamson said, "I really am freezing my ass off out here, Paul. I need to get back to work."

"Right," Paul said distractedly as a huge weight seemed to melt from his shoulders. "And...thanks, Walter. I—"

"I won't be seeing you out here anymore, will I, Paul?"

"No, I don't think you will."

"That would be for the best." He turned toward the habitat.

"Walter?"

Williamson glanced back.

"Those microbialites you're studying...after you fellows leave...I'm not going to have to worry about them causing any problems around here, am I?"

"No, you're not. You have my word on that."

Nodding more to himself than to Williamson, Paul tucked his hands into the pockets of his jacket, drew a breath of pine-scented winter air into his lungs, and started back through the snow toward the police cruiser, remembering that Nancy had said she would be preparing an early supper. He was looking forward to that tremendously.

ABOUT THE AUTHOR

Jeremy Bates

 USA TODAY and #1 AMAZON bestselling author Jeremy Bates has published more than twenty novels and novellas. They have sold more than one million copies, been translated into several languages, and been optioned for film and TV by major studios. Midwest Book Review compares his work to "Stephen King, Joe Lansdale, and other masters of the art." He has won both an Australian Shadows Award and a Canadian Arthur Ellis Award. He was also a finalist in the Goodreads Choice Awards, the only major book awards decided by readers.

Made in United States
North Haven, CT
04 January 2024

46991576R00171